# THE INUGAMI CURSE

# THE INUGAMI CURSE

V

PUSHKIN
VERTIGO

## Seishi Yokomizo

Translated from the Japanese by Yumiko Yamazaki

Pushkin Press
71–75 Shelton Street
London WC2H 9JQ

INUGAMIKE NO ICHIZOKU
© Seishi YOKOMIZO 1972

First published in Japan in 1972 by KADOKAWA CORPORATION, Tokyo.

English translation rights arranged with KADOKAWA CORPORATION,
Tokyo through JAPAN UNI AGENCY, INC., Tokyo.

English translation by Yumiko Yamazaki

First published by Pushkin Press in 2020

1 3 5 7 9 8 6 4 2

ISBN 13: 978-1-78227-503-9

Designed and typeset by Tetragon, London
Printed and bound in the United States

www.pushkinpress.com

# CONTENTS

# CHARACTER LIST

| | |
|---|---|
| Sahei Inugami | *Wealthy and eccentric businessman; the head of the Inugami clan* |
| Daini Nonomiya | *The former priest of Nasu Shrine* |
| Haruyo Nonomiya | *Daini's wife* |
| Tamayo Nonomiya | *The granddaughter of Daini and Haruyo Nonomiya* |
| Matsuko Inugami | *Sahei's eldest daughter* |
| Kiyo Inugami | *Matsuko's son* |
| Takeko Inugami | *Sahei's second daughter* |
| Toranosuke Inugami | *Takeko's husband* |
| Také Inugami | *The son of Takeko and Toranosuke* |
| Sayoko Inugami | *The daughter of Takeko and Toranosuke and the younger sister of Také* |
| Umeko Inugami | *Sahei's third daughter* |
| Kokichi Inugami | *Umeko's husband* |
| Tomo Inugami | *The son of Umeko and Kokichi* |
| Kyozo Furudate | *The Inugami clan's attorney* |
| Kosuke Kindaichi | *A private investigator* |
| Toyoichiro Wakabayashi | *A lawyer at the Furudate Law Office* |
| Monkey | *Tamayo's friend and bodyguard* |
| Kikuno Aonuma | *Sahei's former mistress* |
| Shizuma Aonuma | *Kikuno's son* |
| Taisuke Oyama | *The priest of Nasu Shrine* |
| Chief Tachibana | *The chief of the Nasu Police Department* |
| Kokin Miyakawa | *Matsuko's koto teacher* |

# The Tale Begins

In February 194_, Sahei Inugami—one of the leading businessmen of the Shinshu region, the founder of the Inugami Group, and the so-called Silk King of Japan—died at his lakeside villa in Nasu at the venerable age of eighty-one. After his death, the rags-to-riches tale of this self-made man, already related over several decades in various newspaper and magazine articles, was published by the Inugami Foundation in its most detailed version to date.

According to this book, *The Life of Sahei Inugami*, Sahei was orphaned at a young age and drifted to the Lake Nasu region when he was seventeen. He had no idea where he had been born, who his parents were, or even whether his unusual surname, literally "dog god," had been inherited from his ancestors or conferred by someone with a fertile imagination.

Most men embellish their family trees when they become rich or famous, but Sahei Inugami made no attempt to do so. "We're all born without a stitch on our backs" was his constant declaration to those around him. "Until I turned seventeen, I was like a pauper, drifting from place to place," he would say without hesitation. "It was only when I found my way to Nasu, and Mr. Nonomiya took me in, that fortune finally smiled on me."

Daini Nonomiya was the priest of Nasu Shrine, a Shinto complex that graced the shores of Lake Nasu. Sahei felt he owed him a lifelong debt. So etched in his mind was

Daini's generosity that the usually bold and arrogant Sahei would always sit up straight in humble respect whenever Nonomiya's name was mentioned. Yet, while his unchanging gratitude and devotion to the priest's family were certainly commendable, Sahei failed to realize that everything—even gratitude—has a limit that should not be exceeded, and that his excessive gratitude toward the Nonomiya family would embroil his own kin in a series of bloody murders after his death. Let it be a lesson to us all that even good intentions can lead to great tragedy if not executed with the utmost care.

When the two men first met, young Sahei was, as he later recounted, an indigent drifter. One day, he lay exhausted under the raised floor of the worship hall of Nasu Shrine. It was late autumn and impossible to live without heat in this bitterly cold lakeside region, but Sahei was dressed only in the flimsiest rags, tied around him by a rope, and he had eaten hardly anything for three days. Starved and freezing, he knew he was dying. In fact, if Daini had found him any later, Sahei probably would have died there like a dog.

Astounded to discover a young pauper beneath the floorboards of the worship hall, Daini carried him back to his house so his wife, Haruyo, could tend to him. And thus began the unusual relationship between the two men. According to *The Life of Sahei Inugami*, Daini was forty-two at that time, while Haruyo was a young woman of twenty-two. Sahei would later say that she was as kind-hearted as a saint and as lovely as an angel.

Sahei had a naturally sturdy constitution, and thanks to the couple's generous ministrations, he soon recovered completely. Daini, however, did not wish to see him go and, learning of Sahei's wretched circumstances, urged him to stay. Because Sahei, too, was loath to leave the warm nest he had found, he continued to live with the priest of Nasu Shrine and his wife, not quite a freeloader but not quite a servant. Realizing that Sahei had never spent a day of his life in school and that he was totally illiterate, Daini took him under his wing and educated him diligently, as a father would a son.

Why did Daini so lavish his attentions on Sahei? True, he may have perceived the future that Sahei's sharp intelligence promised, but there is said to have been another, darker reason, not mentioned even in *The Life of Sahei Inugami*: Sahei was an extraordinarily handsome young man. He was radiantly handsome and would retain traces of that attractiveness even in his declining years. Because of this youthful radiance, Daini was drawn to Sahei. People whispered of a homosexual relationship between them and pointed out that Haruyo, as soft-hearted and understanding as she was, left Daini a little more than a year after Sahei's arrival and returned to her parents' home for a time. Daini, as rumor had it, was so infatuated with Sahei that he completely ignored her.

After Sahei found other lodgings, however, the rift between husband and wife appeared to be mended, and Haruyo soon returned. Perhaps the couple grew closer, for Haruyo gave birth to a daughter, Noriko, several years later. Noriko eventually married and was blessed with a daughter she named Tamayo—one of the principals of our tale.

After leaving Daini's home, Sahei, with the priest's help, found employment at a small silk mill. Who would have guessed that from this humble beginning he would eventually establish the Inugami Group, one of Japan's leading business enterprises? Smart and quick, Sahei mastered in one year what it took others several to learn. Moreover, although he had left Daini's house, he remained a frequent visitor, and the priest continued to enrich Sahei's mind, gradually transforming him into an educated and cultured man. Even Haruyo, who had left her husband once on account of Sahei, must have come to terms with her feelings, for she is said to have treated him like a brother, busily seeing to his needs whenever he visited.

The Japanese raw silk industry was in its infancy when Sahei was first employed at the silk mill in 1887. He soon understood the organization of the mill and the how-tos of selling raw silk, and when he decided to strike out on his own, it was Daini Nonomiya who provided him with the necessary capital.

Sahei's business grew by leaps and bounds. As Japan became more powerful during the years of the Sino-Japanese War, the Russo-Japanese War, and World War I, raw silk became a major export item, and the Inugami Silk Company was solidly established as a top-ranking business enterprise.

Daini Nonomiya died in 1911 at the age of sixty-eight. Although he had been the first to finance Sahei's business, he had steadfastly refused to accept any share of the Inugami Group's enormous profits. No matter how much Sahei protested, Daini would accept only the amount he had originally invested, plus a bit of interest. The priest led a life of noble poverty to the end. Soon after Daini's death, Sahei found a suitable husband for Noriko, a man who would marry into the Nonomiya family and succeed Daini as priest of Nasu Shrine. For a long time, Noriko and her husband were childless, but in 1924, more than ten years after they wed, they were blessed with a daughter they named Tamayo.

Both Noriko and her husband, however, died before Tamayo reached the age of twenty. And because Tamayo's grandmother Haruyo had died before she was born, the young woman found herself with no one to turn to. Sahei therefore brought her into the Inugami household, seeing to it that this orphaned daughter from the family of his revered master and mentor was treated with the courtesy due a special guest.

Sahei himself, for some unknown reason, never married. He sired three children—three daughters—all with different women, none of whom he made his legal wife. His three daughters married and had children of their own, with each bridegroom marrying into the Inugami clan, taking on the family name, and being appointed manager of one of the company's offices. The husband of the eldest daughter, Matsuko, was placed in charge of the Nasu head office, that of the second daughter, Takeko, the Tokyo branch office, and that of the third and youngest daughter, Umeko, the Kobe branch office. Until the day he died, however, Sahei refused to hand over the all-powerful helm of the Inugami Group to any of his sons-in-law.

On February 18, 194_, the members of the Inugami clan were gathered around the dying Sahei. Matsuko, the eldest daughter, was in her early fifties, and at the time was leading the most solitary life of all the members of the clan. Her husband had died a few years before, and her only son, Kiyo, had not yet returned from the war. He was alive, she knew, for he had written to her from Burma soon after the war's end, but she had no idea when he would be allowed to come home. Kiyo was the only one of Sahei's three grandsons who was not present on this day.

Next to Matsuko sat the second daughter, Takeko, her husband, Toranosuke, and their children, Také and Sayoko. Také was twenty-eight, and his sister, Sayoko, twenty-two. Behind them were Sahei's youngest daughter, Umeko, her husband, Kokichi, and their only son, Tomo, who was a year younger than Také. These nine people—the eight present plus the absent Kiyo—were Sahei's relations, making up the entire Inugami clan.

There was, however, another person—a person whose fate was closely intertwined with Sahei's—who kept watch by his deathbed. This was the Nonomiya family's sole surviving member, Tamayo. She was twenty-six.

Everyone sat silently, listening to the old man's breathing become weaker and weaker. Strangely, they showed no trace of grief at losing a loved one. Not only was there no grief, but impatience—terrible impatience about something—was written on the faces of all except Tamayo, as they sat wondering, guessing, and conniving to find out what the others had in mind. Whenever they looked away from the old man, who was sinking fast, their eyes would invariably dart over the faces of the others.

It was their ignorance of Sahei's intentions that was causing their impatience. Who would take over the huge Inugami Group after the old man's death? How would his enormous fortune be divided? He had never given any indication of his wishes. Then, too, there was a particular reason for their irritation and anxiety: Sahei, for reasons unknown, had never felt any love for his daughters and, what was more, had not an ounce of faith in any of their husbands.

As the doctor took his pulse, Sahei's breathing weakened further still. Unable to restrain herself any longer, Matsuko leaned forward. "Any last words, Father? Any last words for us?"

Sahei must have heard her voice, for his eyes opened slightly.

"Father, if you have any last wishes, please tell us. We all want to hear what you have to say."

He must have understood Matsuko's true meaning, for the old man smiled faintly and pointed his trembling finger at a man seated at the far end of the room. Indicated thus by Sahei, Kyozo Furudate, the Inugami clan's attorney, coughed softly and said, "I have Mr. Inugami's last will and testament in my safekeeping."

Furudate's statement exploded like a bomb in the hushed scene of impending death. Everyone except Tamayo turned in shock toward the lawyer.

"So, there's a will…" Toranosuke gasped softly. Flustered, he took out a handkerchief from his pocket and wiped his brow, wet with perspiration even in the February cold.

"And when is this will to be read? As soon as the chief is dead?" Kokichi, too, could not conceal his impatience.

"No, I'm afraid not. According to Mr. Inugami's wishes, his will is to be read only when Mr. Kiyo has returned."

"When Kiyo has returned…" muttered Také, an uneasy look on his face.

"I hate to say it, but what if Kiyo doesn't make it back?" At Takeko's words, Matsuko shot a menacing glare at her half-sister.

"Takeko's right," chimed in Umeko. "He might be alive, but he's in far-off Burma. Who knows what could happen before he reaches Japan?" There was venom in her voice, as if she cared not at all about Matsuko's feelings.

"Well, should that be the case," the lawyer said, clearing his throat softly, "I am authorized to read the will on the first anniversary of Mr. Inugami's death. Until that time, the Inugami Foundation will be entirely in charge of managing all Inugami businesses and the estate."

An uncomfortable silence fell over the group. On everyone's face—everyone's, that is, except Tamayo's—there was restlessness, apprehension, and a certain hostility. Even Matsuko stared at the old man's face with a mixture of hope, anxiety, expectation, and hate.

Sahei, however, continued to lie with a faint smile on his lips. Opening wide his eyes, which could no longer focus clearly, he looked one by one at the faces of Matsuko and the other members of his clan. Finally, his gaze reached Tamayo and stopped. The doctor, who had been taking Sahei's pulse, solemnly proclaimed him dead.

That was the end of the life of Sahei Inugami—the end of his eighty-one turbulent years. In hindsight, we now know that his death set in motion the blood-soaked series of events that later befell the Inugami clan.

# A Woman of Extraordinary Beauty

On October 18, eight months after Sahei's death, a man checked into the lakeside Nasu Inn. He was, to put it mildly, of less-than-impressive appearance: mid-thirties, slightly built, with an unruly mop of hair, and wearing an unfashionable serge kimono and wide-legged, pleated hakama trousers, both very wrinkled and worn—and he had a slight tendency to stutter. The name he wrote in the guest register was Kosuke Kindaichi.

Those who have read of Kindaichi's exploits in the series of chronicles that begin with *The Honjin Murders* are, of course, already familiar with him. For those readers who have yet to meet him, I will briefly introduce him.

Kosuke Kindaichi is a private investigator. He has what can be described as an inscrutable air, seeming, as he does, to float above worldly cares and desires. Physically, he is a stammering, inconsequential fellow with nothing to recommend him, but his remarkable faculty for reasoning and deduction has been attested to in the cases of *The Honjin Murders*, *Gokumon Island*, and *Yatsuhaka Village*. When he is excited, his stuttering is aggravated, and he tends to scratch his tousle-haired head with frightful vigor. It is not a very pleasant habit.

Shown by the maid into a second-floor tatami-mat room commanding a view of the lake, Kindaichi immediately picked up the phone and asked the operator for an outside line.

"Yes, in an hour, then. That's fine. I'll be waiting for you."
He hung up and glanced back at the maid. "I'm expecting
someone in about an hour. When he comes and asks for me,
please show him to this room. My name? Kindaichi."

After a quick soak in the inn's bath, Kindaichi returned
to his room. Then, with a frown forming on his face, he took
a book and a letter from his suitcase. The book was *The Life
of Sahei Inugami*, which had been published by the Inugami
Foundation the previous month. The letter was from a man
named Toyoichiro Wakabayashi of the Furudate Law Office
in Nasu.

Kindaichi pulled a chair onto the balcony overlooking the
lake and began leafing through the pages of the obviously
much-read book. Soon, laying the book aside, he took the
letter from its envelope and began rereading its extraordinary contents:

Dear Mr. Kindaichi:

It is with tremendous regret that I, who have not yet
had the pleasure of your acquaintance, am disturbing
you with this unexpected correspondence, but there
is something that I absolutely must request of you. My
request involves the surviving family of none other than
Sahei Inugami, whose biography I have taken upon myself
to send to you under separate cover. I am extremely concerned that the Inugami clan will be faced with a grave
situation in the near future. By grave situation, I mean
events soaked in blood, the sort of events which I believe
are your specialty. One family member after another falling victim—when I think of this, I cannot sleep at night.
In fact, it is not a situation that might occur in the future;

18

it is already occurring this very minute. If we ignore it, I have no idea what a terrible catastrophe it could lead to. Therefore, although I realize the impertinence of my request, I am writing to bid you to come to Nasu and to conduct an investigation into this matter, so as to prevent such a tragedy. When you read this letter, you will probably doubt my sanity. But let me assure you, I am not insane. It is not because of insanity, but from the utmost anxiety, dread, and terror, that I am imploring you for help.

If upon your arrival, you will please phone me at the Furudate Law Office number shown on the envelope, I will come to see you immediately. On bended knees, I beseech you not to ignore my request.

Best regards,

TOYOICHIRO WAKABAYASHI

P.S. Please keep the contents of this letter strictly confidential.

The letter was awkwardly written, as if someone used to writing in a formal epistolary style was trying hard to adopt a colloquial tone. When he had first received it, even Kindaichi, who was rarely perturbed, could not help but be stunned. "I am not insane," the correspondent had written, but everything indicated otherwise. Kindaichi had even considered the possibility of a practical joke.

The words "events soaked in blood" and "one family member after another falling victim" meant that the writer was anticipating a series of murders. But if so, how could he know that? Someone planning a murder would not divulge such a secret, and besides, murder is not something that

19

can be carried out so easily, even if one has formed a plan to do so. The writer's strong confidence that the impending murders were certain to occur made him sound a little crazy.

Assume, then, that such a plan did exist and that this Wakabayashi had somehow found out about it. Why not, then, inform the potential victims? Even if he found it difficult to go to the police when no crime had yet been committed, he could surely whisper it confidentially to those unfortunate enough to be the intended victims. If for some reason he could not tell them in person, he could use some other means—an anonymous letter, for instance.

At first, therefore, Kindaichi had considered just laughing off the letter. But a certain sentence had left him vaguely uneasy: "In fact, it is not a situation that might occur in the future; it is already occurring this very minute." Did the writer mean that some sinister event had already transpired? Kindaichi had also been struck by how Wakabayashi seemed to work for a law office, indicating that he was probably an attorney or trainee—a person who might indeed be in a position to uncover a family secret and detect a murder plot.

For these reasons, Kindaichi had studied the letter repeatedly and then read the copy of *The Life of Sahei Inugami* that Wakabayashi had sent. His interest had instantly been aroused by the book's description of the complex family circumstances surrounding the Inugami clan. Kindaichi already knew that old Sahei Inugami had died in early spring, but when he recalled having learned somewhere that the reading of Sahei's will was being postponed until one of his grandsons was repatriated, his curiosity grew even more. So, Kindaichi had scurried to finish the case that had been occupying him at the time, and with suitcase in hand, he had appeared suddenly in Nasu.

With the letter and book in his lap, Kindaichi was abstract-edly mulling over the situation when the maid entered his room, bringing tea.

"Oh, Miss, Miss." Kindaichi hastily stopped her, for she had turned to go as soon as she had placed the cup of tea on the table. "Where is the Inugami estate?"

"You can see it over there." Looking to where the maid pointed, Kindaichi saw, several blocks from the inn, a hand-some, cream-colored European-style villa and a Japanese-style building, topped by a roof with an intricate confusion of angles. The back yard extended all the way to the lake and was connected with its waters by a large sluice.

"I see. A grand mansion indeed. By the way, I read that one of Mr. Inugami's grandsons hasn't returned from the war yet. Has anything happened since? Is there no word yet?"

"Actually, they say that Mr. Kiyo arrived in Hakata the other day. His mother was overjoyed, of course, and she's gone to fetch him. I heard they're staying at their house in Tokyo right now, but that they're coming to Nasu in a few days."

"Ah, so he's back in Japan." The timing of this new turn of events made Kindaichi's heart race.

Just then, the sluice gate of the Inugami estate slid silently upward, and a rowboat glided out onto the lake. In it was a lone figure, a young woman. A man ran onto the berm out-side the gate as if to see her off, and they exchanged a few words, but she waved goodbye and the man shuffled back inside the gate. The woman rowed smoothly, pulling the oars with accomplished strokes. She was clearly enjoying herself.

"Is that woman one of the Inugamis?" asked Kindaichi.

"Oh, that's Miss Tamayo," the maid replied. "No, she's not a family member, but I heard that she's related to someone who used to be like a master to old Mr. Inugami. She's so unbelievably beautiful. Everyone says there couldn't be anyone more beautiful in all of Japan."

"Wow, that attractive? Alright, let's get a good look at her face."

Chuckling at the maid's exaggerated words, Kindaichi fished a pair of binoculars out of his suitcase and focused it on the woman in the boat. As he fixed his eyes on the comely face that appeared through the lens, a thrill ran up his spine. The maid had not exaggerated. Kindaichi, too, had never seen such an extraordinary beauty in all his life. As Tamayo pulled on the oars with her chin slightly lifted, lost in her pleasure, her loveliness was almost ethereal. Her shoulder-length hair curled softly at the ends, and she had full, healthy cheeks, long eyelashes, a well-shaped nose, and irresistible, charming lips. With her sporty outfit clinging tightly to her supple body, the graceful line of her figure was something words could not adequately describe.

When a woman is so exquisite, the effect can be frightening, even terrifying. Kindaichi was watching Tamayo with bated breath, when suddenly her expression changed. Tamayo stopped rowing and glanced quickly around the bottom of the boat. Then, for some reason, she cried out, dropping her oars, causing the boat to list and sway violently. She stood up, eyes wide with terror, and frantically waved her hands above her head. The boat was rapidly sinking beneath her. Kindaichi leaped out of his wicker chair.

# The Viper in the Bedroom

Kindaichi had by no means forgotten about the visitor he was expecting, but he assumed Wakabayashi would not arrive for some time. Besides, he could not ignore someone drowning in front of his eyes. He therefore dashed headlong out of his room and down the stairs. In hindsight, this was the first event that disrupted his investigation of the Inugami case. If Tamayo had not been facing a watery death at that moment, and if Kindaichi had not rushed to her rescue, no doubt he would have been able to solve the case much earlier than he did.

Kindaichi scrambled down to the ground floor, the maid following close behind. Shouting, "This way, sir!" she dashed into the yard in her socks and began running toward the back gate. Kindaichi chased after her. The lake was nearby, and moored to the small pier were several of the inn's boats, provided so guests could enjoy themselves on the lake.

"Can you handle a rowboat, sir?"

"Yes, don't worry." He knew he was a good oarsman. Kindaichi jumped into one of the boats, and the maid swiftly undid the mooring line.

"Be careful, sir."

"Right." Taking hold of the oars, Kindaichi began rowing with all his strength. Looking out toward the middle of the lake, he saw the boat, already half submerged, and Tamayo crying desperately for help.

Lake Nasu was not very deep, but its shallowness made it all the more treacherous. The weeds grew to lengths of several meters from the bottom, and tangled as they were, like a woman's hair, it was not unusual for someone—even an expert swimmer—to drown if accidentally caught in them. What was more, it often took a very long time for the corpse to rise to the surface.

Others must have heard Tamayo's screams, for soon after Kindaichi set off, several boats began pulling away from the pier of the boat rental shop across the way. From the inn, too, the manager and other male employees who had rushed outside at the maid's calls were noisily following in other boats. Ahead of them all, Kindaichi was rowing frantically, when all of a sudden he noticed a man—the one whom he had earlier seen waving at Tamayo—run from the area of the sluice gate onto the berm. Realizing what was happening out on the water, the man swiftly took off his jacket and trousers and, diving with a splash into the lake, started swimming toward the sinking boat.

His speed was amazing. His arms whirled round and round like waterwheels, raising a terrific spray. Leaving a long trail behind him like a silver snake slithering over the water, he made straight for the boat.

In the end, it was he who reached Tamayo first. By the time Kindaichi finally drew near, her boat was already submerged up to the gunwale, and the man was holding her, as she slumped exhausted in the water.

"Are you alright? Come on, climb up quick."

"Thanks, sir. Help Missy here, will you? I'll keep the boat steady."

"Alright, then, let me have her."

Tamayo thanked Kindaichi and, clinging to his arm, just barely managed to pull herself into his boat.

"Now it's your turn," Kindaichi said to the man. "Climb aboard."

"Yeah, thanks. Don't mind if I do. Will you hold on to that side so the boat don't flip over?"

He scrambled aboard with great agility, and in that moment, Kindaichi, observing him square in the face for the first time, was struck by a singular impression: the man looked just like a monkey. With his low brow, deep-set eyes, and abnormally hollow cheeks, his appearance could only be described as simian. Yet though his face was ugly beyond measure, his every action radiated sincerity.

The man spoke sharply to Tamayo as if scolding her. "See now, Missy, I told you so. Didn't I tell you over and over to be careful? I mean, this is the third time."

The third time? The words rang loudly in Kindaichi's ears.

Tamayo looked somewhat startled and, like a child reprimanded for being disobedient, half laughed and half cried, "But, Monkey, there was nothing I could do. I had no idea there was a hole in the boat."

"There was a hole in the boat?" Kindaichi stared at Tamayo in spite of himself, eyes wide in surprise.

"Yes, I think so. It seems there was a hole, and someone had plugged it up with something. Whatever it was, it got dislodged and…"

Just then, the manager of the inn and a crowd of customers from the boat rental shop drew near. Kindaichi sat lost in thought for some time before turning to the manager. "I wonder if you could do something for me. Could you find some way to keep this boat afloat and tow it back to shore? I'd like to take a look at it later on."

The manager agreed to do so, though he had a puzzled expression on his face. Ignoring his look, Kindaichi turned to Tamayo. "Okay, let's take you home. As soon as you get there, I want you to jump into a hot bath and keep warm so you don't catch cold."

"Yes," she replied. "Thank you very much."

Leaving the manager and onlookers still clamoring loudly about this and that, Kindaichi began slowly rowing the boat, Tamayo and Monkey sitting in front of him. With her head resting against Monkey's broad chest, Tamayo seemed completely reassured and content. Monkey had a horribly unattractive face but a powerful, rock-like body, and as Kindaichi watched Tamayo being held securely in Monkey's thick, sturdy arms, he was reminded of a fragile vine clinging to an ancient pine tree.

Seen up close in this way, Tamayo's beauty was all the more remarkable. The loveliness of her features went without saying, but the faint, youthful glow of her wet skin was absolutely radiant. Even Kindaichi, who was rarely affected by feminine allure, felt his heart pounding.

He sat gazing dreamily at Tamayo's face for some time, but realizing that she had noticed his stare and was blushing, he became flustered and gulped. Somewhat abashed, he turned to Monkey. "You said something strange a while ago—that this was the third time. Have things like this happened before?"

Monkey's eyes flashed suspiciously. Searching Kindaichi's face, he said sullenly, "Yeah, a lot of strange things have been happening recently. That's why I'm worried."

"Strange things?"

"Oh, it's nothing, really," Tamayo interjected. "Monkey, you're just being foolish. Are you still dwelling on what happened? Those were just silly accidents."

"Accidents? Missy, you could've been killed. I just think it's all very strange."

"What do you mean? Just what kind of things have happened?"

"One time, a snake was coiled up inside Missy's bedding. Good thing she noticed quick like, 'cause if it'd bit her, well, she may not have died, but she would've been really sick. Then, the second time, somebody messed with the brakes on her car so they wouldn't work. Almost went off a cliff, she did."

"No, no, it wasn't like that. It all happened purely by chance. Monkey, you just worry too much."

"But if these kinds of things keep happening, who knows what might happen next? When I think of that, I get really worried."

"You silly thing. What more could possibly happen? I've got luck on my side. I'm just naturally lucky, so I've always come out alright. Don't worry so much, or you'll end up making me nervous." As Tamayo and Monkey were thus sparring, the boat reached the sluice gate of the Inugami estate.

Kindaichi left them on the berm. They thanked him, and he rowed back toward the inn. On the way, he reflected upon what he had just heard from Monkey. A viper in the bedroom, faulty brakes, and now, a hole in the boat—were they really all chance occurrences, as Tamayo insisted? Or was someone's relentless will at work? If the latter, it meant only one thing: that someone was after Tamayo's life. Couldn't there also be some connection between these so-called accidents and Wakabayashi's ominous premonition? Yes, he would ask Wakabayashi, who should be arriving at the inn soon. Kindaichi began to pull the oars more strongly.

Returning to the inn, he found that Wakabayashi had already arrived. The maid informed him, "Your guest came asking for you, sir, so I showed him up to your room."

Kindaichi hastened to the second floor and went to his room, but Wakabayashi was nowhere in sight. He had definitely been there, however, for a cigarette butt lay still smoldering in the ashtray and an unfamiliar hat had been tossed in a corner of the tatami-mat room. He must have gone to the restroom, Kindaichi thought, and sat down in the wicker chair. But wait as he did, the visitor did not reappear. Too impatient to wait any longer, Kindaichi rang for the maid.

"What happened to my guest? He seems to have disappeared."

"He has? I wonder what happened. Maybe he's gone to the restroom."

"That's possible, but even so, he's been gone too long. Maybe he's waiting in some other room by mistake. Try to find him, will you?"

"How strange. I wonder where he's gone." The maid left with a puzzled expression on her face. She had not been gone long, however, when Kindaichi heard her shrill scream. Leaping to his feet in alarm, he ran in the direction of her voice and found her cowering in front of the restroom, her face pale as if drained of all blood.

"W-w-what's wrong?"

"Sir, sir, your guest, your guest…"

Kindaichi looked where she was pointing. The door of the restroom was ajar, and through the opening he could see a man's legs sprawled across the floor. With a sharp intake of breath, he opened the door and stepped inside the restroom. The sight before him riveted him where he stood.

A man wearing dark sunglasses was lying prone on the white tile floor of the restroom. He must have writhed in horrible agony before he died, for the collar of his overcoat and his muffler were in disarray, and his fingers were contorted, as if he had desperately clawed the floor. The white tiles were spattered with the blood he had coughed up.

Kindaichi stood frozen for a while, but then approached cautiously and lifted the man's arm. Of course, there was no pulse. He removed the man's sunglasses and looked back at the maid. "Do you recognize him?"

The maid peered fearfully into the dead man's face. "Why, it's Mr. Wakabayashi!"

At her words, Kindaichi's heart turned over. Stunned, he was unable to move.

# Mr. Furudate

Kindaichi could not imagine a worse disgrace. He had always believed the relationship between private investigator and client to be like that between priest and confessor. Just as a sinful confessor pours out his soul to his priest and places himself in the priest's hands, a client divulges to a detective secrets he would never tell anyone else and seeks his help. To do this, a client must have the utmost confidence in the detective's character, and so the detective must repay his client's trust. Kindaichi had always believed this and prided himself on never having betrayed a client's trust. With this case, however, no sooner had the client turned to him for help than he had been murdered, and after coming to Kindaichi's own room, no less. For Kindaichi, could there be a worse humiliation?

Examined from a different angle, moreover, it seemed undeniable that the person who had killed Wakabayashi had realized that the victim had intended to reveal at least part of his secret to a detective named Kindaichi, and that the killer had resorted to such a ruthless act so as to prevent this from occurring. That would mean that the murderer already knew of Kindaichi's existence and was presenting him with a challenge. Speculating in this way, Kindaichi felt his blood boil and a fierce desire to fight growing inside him.

At first, Kindaichi had been rather skeptical about this case and had doubted that the events Wakabayashi feared would actually come to pass. Now, however, all his doubts had been cast aside. The case seemed to have roots far deeper than even Wakabayashi's letter had indicated.

Be that as it may, Kindaichi at the outset found himself in a rather awkward position. He was not, after all, Sherlock Holmes: his renown had not reached every far corner of the earth—including this one. It was therefore quite difficult for him to explain his situation to the chief of the Nasu police and the detective in charge, both of whom had rushed to the inn upon hearing the news. Moreover, he had some scruples about making the contents of Wakabayashi's letter public immediately, and for that reason especially, he hesitated to let the police know his real reason for coming to Nasu.

As a result, the detective in charge was vaguely suspicious of Kindaichi. He interrogated him regarding every minor detail of his relationship with Wakabayashi. Kindaichi finally hedged by saying that he had been commissioned to conduct an investigation, but that now, with the client dead, he had no way of finding out what it was about. The detective made it clear, although he took pains to phrase it discreetly, that Kindaichi was to remain in Nasu for the time being—something to which Kindaichi had no objections, for he himself had firmly resolved not to leave town until he had solved the case.

An autopsy was conducted on Wakabayashi's body that very day, and the cause of death was confirmed. He had indeed been poisoned. Oddly, however, the poison had been detected not in gastric tissue but in lung tissue. In short, Wakabayashi had not drunk the poison, but had smoked it.

With this revelation, the cigarette butt the victim had left in the ashtray instantly commanded attention. It was a foreign brand, and tests showed that the poison had been mixed in with the tobacco. Curiously, too, although several cigarettes still remained in Wakabayashi's cigarette case, none of them had been tampered with, and only the one in the ashtray had been lethal. In other words, the murderer had not decided to kill Wakabayashi on a specific day or at a specific time; all that mattered was that he die sooner or later.

This method seemed extremely casual, yet for that reason it was all the more subtle and ingenious. The killer did not need to be in the victim's presence when the death occurred and so would be much less likely to fall under suspicion than with other means of poisoning. Kindaichi could not help but marvel at this devious plan. The person who had thrown this challenge in his face was no easy foe.

On the day after Wakabayashi's death, Kindaichi received a visitor at the Nasu Inn. The card the maid brought up read "Kyozo Furudate."

Recognizing the name with a start, Kindaichi narrowed his eyes. This Furudate must be the head of the Furudate Law Office, the man who was the Inugami clan's family lawyer and who was charged with the safekeeping of Sahei Inugami's will. With some apprehension, Kindaichi told the maid to show him up immediately.

Furudate was a middle-aged gentleman of swarthy complexion and a rather stern countenance. All the time observing Kindaichi cautiously, with a lawyer's sharp, shrewd eyes, he nonetheless used the politest of terms to introduce himself and to apologize for visiting unannounced.

Kindaichi, as was his habit, scratched his head briskly. "I must say, I was quite shocked yesterday. But it must have come as a big blow to you, too."

"Yes, it's so extraordinary, I still can't believe it's true. I came here today because I wanted to ask you about it."

"Yes?"

"The police told me just now that Wakabayashi intended to commission you to investigate some matter."

"Yes, that's right. But he was killed before he had a chance to tell me what it was, so I'm afraid I'll never know what he wanted me to look into."

"Surely you must have some idea. I mean, he must have contacted you by letter or something."

"Well, yes…" Kindaichi fixed his gaze intently on the lawyer. "Mr. Furudate, you're the Inugami clan's attorney, are you not?"

"Yes, I am."

"In that case, you wish to protect the family's honor?"

"Of course."

"To tell the truth, Mr. Furudate," Kindaichi abruptly lowered his voice, "I kept this from the police since I, too, did not want to damage their honor, and I thought it best not to say anything unnecessarily—but I received this letter from Mr. Wakabayashi." Kindaichi took out the letter, passed it to Furudate, and carefully studied his expression as he read it.

Profound surprise swept rapidly over the lawyer's face. Deep furrows lined his dark brow, and he began to perspire freely. His hands trembled as he held the letter.

"Mr. Furudate, do you know anything about what is written in this letter?"

Furudate, who had sat stupefied for some time, started when Kindaichi spoke. "Well, no…"

"I find it quite strange. I mean, even if there were indications that something might happen to the Inugamis, why would Mr. Wakabayashi know about it? From this letter, it seems that he was quite certain. Do you have any idea why he felt so sure?"

An expression of utmost agitation had appeared on Furudate's face. He obviously knew something.

Kindaichi leaned forward. "Mr. Furudate, weren't you aware that Mr. Wakabayashi had sent this letter, that he had asked me to investigate something?"

"Not at all. Thinking back, though, he was acting strange. He seemed jumpy, afraid of something."

"Afraid of something?"

"Yes. Of course, I realized this only after he was killed."

"What could he have been afraid of? Do you have any idea?"

"Well, in regard to that…" Furudate seemed to be debating something with himself. Making up his mind, he went on, "Actually, that's what I came to discuss with you today. It's about Sahei Inugami's will."

"What about the will?"

"I have the will locked inside my office safe. Yesterday, after what happened to Wakabayashi, I felt uneasy, so I looked inside the safe. There are indications that someone has opened and read it."

"Someone's read the will?"

Furudate nodded gravely. Kindaichi asked somewhat breathlessly, "And would there be a problem if someone has read the will?"

"Well, it would have been opened and read sooner or later anyway. Now, of course, since Kiyo has finally returned, it will be read in a few days. But I have always been concerned that it might cause big trouble."

"Is there something unusual about the will?"

"Extremely!" Furudate spoke with emotion. "It is so unusual as to be somewhat irrational. I tried my best to dissuade the old man—I told him it would make the members of his family hate each other—but he was so stubborn."

"Can't you tell me what it says?"

"Oh, no," Furudate refused with a gesture of his hand. "That wouldn't be right. According to the wishes of the deceased, the contents of the will are not to be released, on any account, until Kiyo returns to the family home in Nasu."

"I understand. In that case, I won't press the matter. But the only people interested in its contents would be the members of the Inugami clan, so if the will appears to have been read, that means one of them must have opened…"

"But that's impossible. I can't see how any of the Inugamis could have had a chance to open that safe. No, the way I see it, someone must have bribed Wakabayashi. He would have been able to open the safe, so one of the Inugamis must have asked him to make a copy of the will. Then when strange things started happening in the household, Wakabayashi must have become scared."

"What do you mean by strange things?"

Furudate peered at Kindaichi's face searchingly. "I think you've probably guessed. Yesterday, for instance, I heard that something strange happened out on the lake."

Kindaichi jerked. "The boat…"

"Yes. I heard you examined the boat."

"I did. Someone had bored a hole in the bottom and plugged it with some kind of putty. So, that woman, Tamayo, is mentioned in the will?"

"Oh, yes. The whole will revolves around her. She is in a position of absolute advantage as regards the Inugami inheritance. Unless she dies, she alone will decide who inherits the family fortune."

All at once, memories of the lovely woman of yesterday flooded over Kindaichi. What destiny had Sahei Inugami prepared for that rare beauty, that radiant goddess? In his mind's eye, Kindaichi saw the boat again, sinking rapidly in the afternoon sun, Tamayo inside, desperately waving her arms above her—and a huge, shadowy black hand looming threateningly behind her.

# Kiyo's Return

November 1, 194_. Two weeks had passed since Kindaichi's arrival. From the morning hours, the town of Nasu, nestled on the shores of Lake Nasu in the Shinshu region, buzzed with a portentous air. The news was all over town: Kiyo Inugami, the heir apparent to the Inugami throne, who for reasons unknown had been lingering in Tokyo after his repatriation from Southeast Asia, had finally returned late last night to the family home in Nasu with his mother, Matsuko, who had gone to meet him.

The prosperity of Nasu depended entirely on the fate of the Inugami clan. As the clan prospered, so did the town. Formerly an impoverished lakeside village in mountainous terrain, buffeted by a harsh climate and poorly endowed agriculturally, Nasu had grown to its present population of more than one hundred thousand only because the Inugami Group, with the power of its vast capital, had sown its seeds there. As the seeds had sprouted, grown, and flowered, the surrounding region also had flourished, giving rise to the present-day community of Nasu.

For this reason, there was no one living in Nasu or its environs, whether directly connected with the operations of the Inugami Group or not, who had not benefited to some degree from its presence. In one way or another, they all lived off the crumbs thrown to them by one of the family enterprises, so that the Inugamis were in fact the true lords of Nasu.

No wonder, then, that the good people of Nasu were immensely curious about the Inugamis. It would be no exaggeration to say that after old Sahei's passing the fate of the clan was a matter of concern for each and every resident of the region. Holding the fate of the Inugami clan in his hands was Matsuko's only son, Kiyo, whose homecoming, as everyone knew, would finally allow Sahei's will to be read. Therefore, they had awaited Kiyo's repatriation as eagerly as—no, perhaps even more eagerly than—the family members had.

Finally, the people had heard that Kiyo had returned to Japan. The news that he had landed in Hakata had zipped through the town like an electrical current through wire. They had longed impatiently for the man who would perhaps be their new lord and master, wanting him to rush back to Nasu without delay.

Wait as they had, however, Kiyo had not come home. He and his mother, Matsuko, who had gone to meet him in Hakata, had stopped off at their city house in Tokyo and had shown no signs of leaving it. A delay of a couple of days, the people of Nasu could understand, but as their sojourn had lengthened to a week, then to ten days, the people had become concerned.

Why didn't Kiyo come home? Why didn't he hasten back at top speed and demand that his grandfather's will be read? His mother, Matsuko, would be more aware than anyone how the entire situation depended on him.

Perhaps, someone had proposed, Kiyo was ill and convalescing at the Tokyo house. No, others had countered, how could that be the case? If he were convalescing, the country air of Nasu would be much more suitable than Tokyo's.

Besides, if he had had the strength to make his way back from far-off Hakata to Tokyo, there should be no problem in extending the journey the short distance to Nasu. As wealthy as the Inugamis were, if a train trip was difficult they could always rent a car. As for doctors, too, the family surely had the means to summon the finest from Tokyo to Nasu. Besides, Kiyo had never liked living in the big city, even as a boy. He dearly loved the Lake Nasu area—its nature, climate, and people—and he was intensely attached to the lakeside villa where he had been born. If the long war and subsequent detention had exhausted him and ruined his health, what better place for him to rest and recuperate than the main family home by Lake Nasu? So, the people had said, it was hard to attribute Kiyo's and Matsuko's extended stay in Tokyo to illness.

No one, in the end, was able to explain adequately what could be detaining the mother and son in Tokyo. Why on earth were Kiyo and Matsuko tormenting the other family members and the people of Nasu like this?

If the townspeople had felt this way, imagine the impatience of the other family members. Having gone alone to Hakata to meet her son, Matsuko had wired her two half-sisters through their husbands, telling them to await her and Kiyo in Nasu. Takeko, Umeko, and their families had rushed to Nasu from Tokyo and Kobe, respectively, and had been waiting irritably, day after day, for Matsuko and Kiyo to return.

Strangely, though, having unpacked their bags at their city house in Tokyo, Matsuko and Kiyo had remained there, dropping out of touch, for more than two weeks. When the family had sent messages urging their speedy return, they had wired back saying they would set out that day, then the next, but in fact they had shown no signs of stirring.

Even more oddly, when Takeko and Umeko, no longer able to stand the suspense, secretly arranged for a detective to investigate the comings and goings of mother and son, he had reported being unable to ascertain anything at all. Matsuko and Kiyo had remained secluded in their private quarters and had not shown themselves to anyone. Thus, their stay in Tokyo had drawn increasing suspicion and, together with the murder of Wakabayashi, had cast a dark shadow over the entire town of Nasu.

On the morning of November 1, Kindaichi had overslept, and now, at past eleven, he had just finished brunch. He dragged a chair onto the balcony overlooking the lake and was absentmindedly cleaning his teeth with a toothpick when he was surprised by an unexpected visitor, the Inugami clan's attorney, Kyozo Furudate.

"Well, hello! I'm rather surprised to see you today." Kindaichi greeted him with his characteristic, affable grin. Furudate, as usual, looked troubled and dour.

"Why do you say that?"

"Why? Well, I heard that he has come home. If that's true, I supposed that the Inugamis would arrange to have the will read immediately, so they'd have you in their clutches and be keeping you insanely busy."

"Oh, so you've heard about it already."

"Of course. It's such a small town. Besides, the Inugamis are like lord and master to the people around here. Word of anything that happens to them, big or small, spreads like wildfire through the town. The maid came in this morning, as soon as I awoke, and shouted, 'Extra! Late-breaking news!'"

he explained, laughing heartily. "Oh, where are my manners? Please sit down."

Furudate nodded slightly, but remained standing on the balcony gazing at the Inugami villa. Then, raising his shoulders with a shudder, he noiselessly seated himself across from Kindaichi.

Kindaichi noticed that Furudate was in morning dress and held a large portfolio under his arm. Laying his portfolio down softly on the wicker tea table, the lawyer sat for a while without speaking. Kindaichi studied him silently. But finally, grinning and scratching his head, he asked, "What's wrong? You seem totally lost in thought. Where are you going in those clothes?"

"Well," Furudate cleared his throat as if jerked back to reality, "to tell the truth, I'm about to go to the Inugamis' villa. But I suddenly felt the urge to see you before that."

"Is there something I can do for you?"

"No, I've nothing in particular to ask you, but…" Furudate mumbled. Soon, though, he continued more strongly, as if angry, "Of course, I don't need to tell you why I've been summoned to the Inugamis' villa today. As you yourself just said, it's to read Sahei's will. So my sole duty is to go straight there and read the will in front of the assembled family. My job is over then. I shouldn't have any qualms. So why, then, am I hesitating like this? Why am I vacillating so? And why have I come here to you to say these idiotic things? I don't understand. I don't even understand myself any more."

Kindaichi, who had been staring at the lawyer's face dumbfounded, presently sighed audibly and said, "Mr. Furudate, you're tired. I'm sure it's fatigue. You really ought to be more careful. And," his eyes twinkled impishly, "as for why you're here—I know the reason. This proves that whether you're aware of it or not, you've gradually begun to trust me."

Furudate raised his eyebrows and glared at Kindaichi, but soon contorted his face in a wry smile. "You know, you may be right. Actually, Mr. Kindaichi, I owe you an apology."

"An apology?"

"To tell the truth, I asked a fellow attorney I know in Tokyo to investigate your background."

At this, Kindaichi widened his eyes in surprise. He sat staring open-mouthed for a while, but then exploded in a roar of laughter.

"W-w-well, well! Th-the famous investigator is investigated! No, no, you don't have to apologize, Mr. Furudate. In fact, you've taught me a very good lesson. You know, I might not look it, but I'm actually quite vain, and I was confident that everyone in Japan knew the name of Kosuke Kindaichi. Ha!" he chuckled. "No, no, I'm just kidding, of course. But, anyway, what did your friend tell you?"

"Well, as a matter of fact," Furudate squirmed on his seat as if the chair was uncomfortable, "he gave you his unconditional seal of approval. He said that I could trust you completely, both professionally and personally." Having said that, though, the lawyer still seemed unable to erase the expression of doubt from his face.

"Thank you. I'm honored that you would say that." And, as was his habit when something delighted him, Kindaichi vigorously scratched his head, with its unruly mop of hair. "So that's why you came to me before this family conference that you're not sure how to handle."

"Yes, you could say that. As I told you before, I dislike this will. I shouldn't make any comments, positive or negative, about a client's wishes, but this will is just too outrageous. It will be like hurling the remaining members of the Inugami clan into a maelstrom of conflict, kin against kin. What an uproar there will be when this is announced—I've had that vague, uneasy feeling ever since I was first asked to prepare the will. Then, Wakabayashi is murdered. And now, with the case still unsolved, Kiyo returns—which is not to say that's not a good thing. Whether Kiyo's homecoming turns out to be a cause for celebration for the Inugamis or not, it's certainly a happy occasion that a man who has suffered overseas for so long has finally come home. But why did Kiyo have to return home so surreptitiously, avoiding everyone? Why does he so dislike for people to see his face? That just makes me uncomfortable."

Kindaichi had been listening attentively to Furudate's increasingly emotional words, but at that point, he suddenly lifted his eyebrows. "Kiyo's avoiding being seen?"

"That's right."

"He doesn't want people to see his face?"

"That's right, Mr. Kindaichi. Haven't you heard about it yet?"

With a blank look, Kindaichi shook his head. Furudate leaned forward over the tea table. "Actually, I heard this from one of the Inugamis' servants: Matsuko and Kiyo returned to the estate suddenly last night without any warning. They must have come from Tokyo on the last train. It was quite late when the bell rang, and the houseboy in charge of the front entrance went to open the gate, wondering who on earth could be visiting at that hour. He was astonished to find Matsuko waiting there. Behind her, a man came in through the gate with the collar of his coat turned up around his neck, and this man, the houseboy said, had his head covered completely with something like a black hood."

Kindaichi's eyes widened in astonishment. Listening to the lawyer's story, he felt his blood go cold.

"A hood?"

"Yes, and as the houseboy stood there in surprise, Matsuko said simply, 'It's Kiyo,' and quickly led her son from the foyer back to her own sitting room. Of course, the rest of the family heard from the houseboy what had happened, and they were all in an uproar. After all, Takeko, Umeko, and their families had been standing by at the villa, waiting impatiently for weeks for the two of them to return. They immediately rushed to Matsuko's room, which is in a far annex of the house, but she refused to let them see Kiyo, telling them that both she and Kiyo were tired and would talk to them in the morning. That was last night, but no one has yet seen Kiyo's face. Just one person, a maid, saw someone she assumed to be Kiyo coming out of the bathroom, but he had a black hood over his head even then. Apparently, the hood has two holes where the eyes are, and when she saw his eyes glint from behind them, it was so spooky, she said, she thought she was going to faint."

A feeling of the utmost delight began growing inside Kindaichi. Something was going on: Matsuko's and Kiyo's inexplicable stay in Tokyo, Kiyo hiding his face. He smelled something not right, something abnormal. The more the case reeked of the unnatural, the more strongly Kindaichi's professional appetite was whetted.

Kindaichi enthusiastically scratched his head. "But, Mr. Furudate, Kiyo can't hide his face forever. He has to take off his hood sooner or later to prove that he really is Kiyo Inugami."

"Of course. Take today, for example. I can't read the will until I make certain that the man who has returned is indeed Kiyo. So I intend to insist that he take off his hood. But when I imagine what we might find beneath it, I get a sick feeling in the pit of my stomach."

Kindaichi frowned for a time, pondering the situation, but then said, "Well, it might be nothing to worry about at all. I mean, he's been in battle, so his face might be scarred, or something like that." Abruptly he leaned over the tea table. "But changing the subject to Mr. Wakabayashi, have you found out to whom he leaked the contents of the will?"

"Not yet. The police seem to have studied his diary and so on carefully, but they haven't any leads yet."

"But who among the Inugamis was on the closest terms with him? In other words, who had the best opportunity to bribe him?"

"I really have no idea," Furudate admitted, furrowing his brow. "All the members of the clan stayed in Nasu for some time after old Sahei died, and since then they've gathered numerous times for memorial services. So, anyone who might have wanted to bribe Wakabayashi would have had the chance."

"But even Mr. Wakabayashi wouldn't let himself be bribed by just anyone. Isn't there someone in particular, someone special, he would go out of his way for?"

It was a casual question, but Furudate appeared thunder-struck, catching his breath in surprise. He remained staring off into space for some time, but eventually took out his handkerchief and started to wipe his neck nervously, saying, "No, no. That can't be. After all, she's the one who's been in danger so many times recently."

It was Kindaichi's turn to be surprised. He stared at Furudate's face, transfixed. Presently, he whispered in a hoarse voice, "M-Mr. Furudate, are you talking about that woman Tamayo?"

"Well, yes. It's clear from Wakabayashi's diary that he was secretly in love with her. I'm sure he would have done anything she asked him to do."

"Mr. Wakabayashi is supposed to have stopped by the Inugami house right before coming here to see me. Did he see Tamayo at that time?"

"I don't know anything about that, but even if he did… a beautiful woman like that? Giving him a poisoned cigarette? No, I can't believe it…" Furudate stammered as he wiped his sweaty brow. "Besides, at that time, the entire Inugami clan was gathered in that house—except Matsuko, of course, who was in Tokyo."

"Mr. Furudate, who is that man named Monkey? He seemed terribly devoted to Tamayo."

"Oh, him. He's—" Furudate glanced at his watch hurriedly and said, "That late already? Mr. Kindaichi, I'm sorry but I must be leaving. They're waiting for me at the villa."

"Mr. Furudate," Kindaichi called to the lawyer, running after him as he rushed from the room carrying his portfolio. "You can tell me the contents of the will after you've read it at the Inugami villa, can't you?"

Furudate stopped in his tracks with a start and glanced back at Kindaichi. "Of course. There wouldn't be any problem with that. I'll stop by on my way back and fill you in."

With those parting words, Furudate, portfolio under his arm, swiftly descended the stairs as if running away from something. Little did Kindaichi know then, but he would be given the chance to learn the contents of the will much sooner than he expected.

# The Three Heirlooms

After Furudate left, Kindaichi remained on the balcony for a while, leaning back in his wicker chair with an empty look on his face. The autumn had grown deep in this mountainous region, and a pleasant breeze swept shimmering over the azure-green surface of the lake. It was high noon, and across the way, the autumn sun glittered on the stained glass windows of the Inugamis' European-style villa. Everything was peaceful, a moment caught in a painted landscape. Yet, as he gazed at the enormous building on the lake, Kindaichi could not help but feel a chill run up his spine.

At that very moment, Sahei's will—a will whose contents, according to Furudate, were explosive—was about to be read. What would happen inside that elegant mansion when Sahei's last instructions were made known?

Kindaichi again picked up *The Life of Sahei Inugami*. For an hour or so, he sat leafing here and there through its pages, but looked up in surprise when a voice suddenly called from the direction of the lake. A single boat was docked at the pier of the inn, and inside it, standing and waving, was the man called Monkey. Kindaichi frowned and leaned over the railing, because Monkey seemed to be beckoning to him.

"Are you calling me?"

Monkey nodded in affirmation with an exaggerated gesture. With a strange sense of apprehension, Kindaichi hastened at top speed down the stairs and out to the pier behind the inn.

"What is it?"

"Mr. Furudate told me to come get you," Monkey answered in his usual brusque manner.

"Mr. Furudate? Has something happened at the Inugamis'?"

"Not that I know. He said he's going to read the will now, so he wants you to come if you like."

"Oh, I see. I'll be just a minute. Wait here for me, will you?"

Hurrying back to his room, Kindaichi changed out of the inn's robe into his own kimono and hakama trousers. As soon as he returned to the boat and got in, Monkey started rowing.

"Monkey, do the family members know I'm coming?"

"Yeah, it was the Missus's orders."

"The Missus? You mean, Mrs. Matsuko, who came back last night?"

"That's right."

Furudate must have appealed to Matsuko, citing what had happened to Wakabayashi in her absence as well as his own disturbing premonitions. He must have suggested to her that they invite Kindaichi to be present, to help avert any evil incidents that might arise after the reading of the will.

Kindaichi's heart pounded. In any case, he was happy that he was being presented with the opportunity to meet the Inugami clan so soon.

"Monkey, has Miss Tamayo been alright since the problem with the boat?"

"Yeah, thanks to you."

"That boat, do all the Inugamis go out on the lake in that boat?"

"Nah, that's Missy's boat. She's the only one who uses that one."

Monkey's answer disturbed Kindaichi. If that boat was used exclusively by Tamayo, then without question the person who bored a hole in it was after her life and hers alone. "Monkey, you said something strange the other day, that Miss Tamayo has had peculiar mishaps several times recently."

"Yeah."

"When did these mishaps start occurring?"

"When? Oh, I guess about the end of spring."

"Right after Mr. Inugami died."

"Yeah."

"Who on earth would play such pranks on her? Do you have any ideas, Monkey?"

"If I knew that," Monkey's eyes flashed, "I'd make sure they didn't get away with it."

"What exactly is your relationship with Miss Tamayo?"

"She's my very, very precious Missy. Mr. Inugami told me to protect her with my life," Monkey proclaimed proudly, baring his teeth in a savage grin. Looking at the powerful, rock-like chest and thick arms of this ugly giant, Kindaichi felt queasy. God forbid this colossus should consider him an enemy. No doubt Monkey always guarded Tamayo like a faithful dog would, and if anyone should so much as try to harm a hair on her head, he would immediately pounce on the culprit and break that person's neck.

"By the way, Monkey, I heard Kiyo returned last night."

"Yeah" Monkey grew taciturn again.

"Did you see him?"

"Nah, nobody's seen him yet."

"Did Kiyo—" As Kindaichi began to speak, the boat passed through the sluice gate and glided into the boat-house of the Inugami estate.

Exiting the boathouse, Kindaichi was astounded by the huge number of large-bloomed, potted chrysanthemums placed everywhere throughout the extensive grounds. Even though Kindaichi was not particularly given to botanical appreciation, he could not help but marvel at these magnificent specimens at the height of their glory. In one corner of the grounds there was even a chrysanthemum field covered with a latticed paper screen to protect the flowers from frost.

"How magnificent! Whose work is this?"

"I take care of them. The chrysanthemum's one of the Inugami heirlooms."

"Heirlooms?" Kindaichi repeated, but Monkey began walking rapidly ahead without answering and led him into the foyer.

"Guest's here," called Monkey, and a maid immediately appeared from somewhere inside the house.

"Please come in. They're waiting for you." She led Kindaichi down a long, long corridor that seemed never to end, then on through a maze of other corridors that opened onto countless tatami-mat rooms. Not a soul, however, was to be seen in any of them, and the entire house, in tense expectation of the momentous event, was as hushed as a graveyard.

The maid finally reached the room where the Inugami clan had assembled. "Your guest has arrived," she said, and after dropping to her knees and bowing slightly, hands touching the floor, she slid open the door. At that instant, Kindaichi felt all eyes turn simultaneously to him. Furudate acknowledged him with his eyes and said, "Thank you for coming. Please have a seat over there. I hope you don't mind being seated at the back of the room."

When Kindaichi bowed slightly and sat down, Furudate continued, "Ladies and gentlemen, this is Mr. Kosuke Kindaichi, whom I was just telling you about." Each of the Inugamis acknowledged Kindaichi with a slight nod of the head. Kindaichi waited until everyone's eyes had left him and were focused on the lawyer once again, and then he slowly glanced around the room.

The large room in which they were seated had been made by removing the partitions between two twelve-mat rooms. Placed on the plain wood altar at the head of the room was a photograph of the late Sahei Inugami, adorned with large chrysanthemum blooms. In front of the altar sat three young men wearing formal black kimonos. But the sight of the one sitting in the seat of honor at the farthest end made Kindaichi's heart pound uneasily. The figure wore a black hood over his head, with two holes cut for his eyes. He hung his head and gazed downward, however, so that Kindaichi could not see past the openings. This had to be the recently returned Kiyo.

The faces of the two young men seated next to Kiyo— Také, the son of Sahei's second daughter, Takeko, and Tomo, the only child of the third daughter, Umeko—were familiar to Kindaichi from their photographs in *The Life of Sahei Inugami*. Také was a stocky man, as wide as he was tall, while Tomo was slender and seemed to be of delicate constitution. Také sat with a taciturn, haughty expression that revealed his disdain for all, while Tomo, looking somehow cunning and insincere, shifted his eyes ceaselessly from place to place. Their personalities were in sharp contrast to each other.

Seated by herself somewhat apart from these three men was Tamayo, elegant and correct. Quiet and reserved in this way, her attractiveness was even more remarkable. Unlike the other day, she was wearing a black kimono with a bit of white showing around the neck. She looked older, but her beauty now had an almost spiritual aura.

Furudate sat slightly apart from Tamayo. Facing Tamayo were, in order, Matsuko; Takeko and her husband, Toranosuke; their daughter, Sayoko; and Umeko and her husband, Kokichi.

Sayoko, too, was quite attractive and would have been considered pretty enough if Tamayo were not in the same room. Compared directly with Tamayo's rare beauty, however, her physical attributes paled badly. Sayoko herself seemed aware of this, for the looks she cast at Tamayo were filled with tremendous hostility. Her beauty concealed thorns.

Furudate, with a light cough, took up the thick envelope he had in his lap. "I will now read the last will and testament of Mr. Sahei Inugami. But before that, I would like to make a request of Mrs. Matsuko."

Matsuko looked at Furudate without a word. She was a middle-aged woman of fifty or so who seemed used to getting her own way.

"As you know," Furudate continued, "I am authorized to open and read this will only when Mr. Kiyo has been repatriated and all the family members are gathered together."

"I know. Kiyo is sitting right there, as you see."

"But…"—the lawyer spoke somewhat falteringly—"I cannot tell if this is really… Of course, I am not doubting your word, but if I could just take a look at his face."

Matsuko's eyes blazed intensely. "What? Are you suggesting, Mr. Furudate, that Kiyo is an imposter?" Her voice was deep and husky, and had something malicious about it.

"No, no. That's not what I mean. What about the rest of you? Do you mind if we let the matter drop?"

"Of course we mind," Takeko interjected immediately. In contrast to her elder half-sister, Matsuko, who had a thin frame that looked as strong as bamboo, the double-chinned Takeko was short and heavy, like a small mountain, and looked full of vitality. Yet, she had none of the kind-heartedness often found in buxom matrons. She seemed as mean-spirited as her half-sister. "Umeko, what do you think? Don't you think Kiyo should take off his hood and let us see his face?"

"Of course," Umeko answered without hesitation. Of the three half-sisters, she was the most attractive, but she looked the most venomous of the three as well.

Takeko's husband, Toranosuke, and Umeko's husband, Kokichi, expressed their agreement. Toranosuke was a fifty-ish, heavy-set man with a florid complexion, an arrogant air, and a menacing look in his eyes. It was obvious that Také had inherited his physique and demeanor from his parents. Compared to Toranosuke, Umeko's husband, Kokichi, was much smaller and paler and had what at first looked like a mild-mannered air, but the restless eyes, identical to those of his son, revealed the evil in his mind. A faint smile never left his thin lips.

The room grew hushed for a moment, and then Matsuko suddenly screeched, "Kiyo, take off your hood for them!"

The hooded head jerked. Then, after a long hesitation, Kiyo's trembling right hand rose and gradually began to raise the hood from his face. Kiyo's face—yes, Kindaichi remembered it from the photograph in *The Life of Sahei Inugami*— but what a peculiar face! Its features were frozen, completely immobile. The face was—to use a sinister comparison—like that of a dead man. It was a face that was lifeless, devoid of human warmth.

Sayoko screamed, and the room was hurled into confusion, as Matsuko's hysterical voice, furious with rage, rang over the din. "Kiyo received a horrible wound, so I had that mask made for him. That's why we stayed in Tokyo so long. I had a mask made to look just the way Kiyo's face used to be. Kiyo, raise your mask a little for them!"

Kiyo touched his chin with his trembling hand and began to pull the mask up over his chin as if peeling the skin off his face. Sayoko again screamed sharply. Kindaichi could not keep his knees from shaking. He felt something heavy in the pit of his stomach, as if he'd swallowed lead.

From beneath the precisely made rubber mask appeared a jaw and lips that looked identical to those on the mask. They looked perfectly normal. When Kiyo raised the mask further, however, Sayoko screamed a third time.

Kiyo's nose was gone. In its place was a pulpy, reddish-black mass of flesh that looked as if it had festered and burst.

"Kiyo, that's enough! Put your mask back on!" When Kiyo rearranged his mask as it had been, everyone in the room felt they had seen enough. If they had been shown any more of that disgusting, formless mass of flesh, none of them would have been able to keep their food down for quite some time after.

"So, Mr. Furudate, are you satisfied? There can be no doubt this is Kiyo. His face might be a little changed, but I'm his mother and I guarantee it: this is my son Kiyo. So, please, hurry up and read the will."

Furudate, stunned, had been staring with bated breath, but suddenly pulled back to reality by Matsuko's words, he looked around the room. No one dared object any longer. Overcome by the intense shock, Takeko, Umeko, and their husbands had lost all composure and had forgotten their usual pettiness.

"Then…" Furudate, with trembling fingers, tore open the all-important envelope. With a low but resonant voice, he began to read the will. "I, Sahei Inugami, hereby declare this to be my Last Will and Testament.

"Article One. I give and bequeath the three heirlooms of the Inugami clan—the ax, zither, and chrysanthemum—which signify the right to inherit all my property and any business enterprise owned or controlled by me, to Tamayo Nonomiya, subject to the conditions set forth in the following articles."

The color drained from Tamayo's lovely face. The other faces in the room turned pale as well, and their hate-filled gazes pierced Tamayo like flaming arrows.

Furudate, however, paid them no heed and continued.

"Article Two. Tamayo Nonomiya must marry one of my three grandsons, Kiyo Inugami, Také Inugami, or Tomo Inugami. The choice will be hers to make. However, if she refuses to marry any of them and instead chooses to marry another, she shall forfeit her right to inherit the ax, zither, and chrysanthemum."

In other words, all the Inugami property and businesses would fall to whichever of the three Inugami grandsons—Kiyo, Také, or Tomo—could win Tamayo's love. Kindaichi shuddered with an indefinable excitement, but the will had more strange surprises in store.

# The Blood-Colored Will

With shaking voice, Furudate continued reading the will. "Article Three. Tamayo Nonomiya must choose to marry either Kiyo Inugami, Také Inugami, or Tomo Inugami within three months of the date of the reading of this will. If the one she chooses refuses to marry her, he will forfeit all claims to my estate. Therefore, if Kiyo, Také, and Tomo all refuse to marry Tamayo or if all three predecease her, Tamayo shall be released from the condition set forth in Article Two and shall be free to marry anyone she wishes."

The atmosphere in the room grew even more strained. Tamayo, as white as a sheet, bent her head low, but her quivering shoulders revealed her intense excitement. The hostile looks the Inugamis shot in her direction grew increasingly overt and venomous. If looks could kill, Tamayo would have been dead on the spot.

Within this tense, dangerous atmosphere, Furudate's shaky but resonant voice continued like a chant summoning the evil spirits of revenge from the depths of hell.

"Article Four. If Tamayo Nonomiya forfeits or loses the right to inherit the ax, zither, and chrysanthemum, or if she dies before or within three months of the date of the reading of this will, any business enterprises owned or controlled by me shall pass to Kiyo Inugami. Také Inugami and Tomo Inugami shall assist Kiyo in the management of the businesses from the positions their fathers now occupy. The remainder of my estate shall be divided evenly into five shares by the Inugami Foundation, with one share each to be given to Kiyo, Také, and Tomo, and the remaining two shares to be given to Shizuma Aonuma, the son of Kikuno Aonuma. Each party receiving a share of my estate, however, must donate twenty percent of that share to the Inugami Foundation."

Shizuma Aonuma, the son of Kikuno Aonuma—Kindaichi contorted his face, puzzled at the mention of these two new names. His surprise, however, could not compare with the shock felt by the others in the room, for whom the revelation seemed devastating. They all grew pale the instant Furudate uttered the names, but the blow appeared to be particularly severe for Matsuko, Takeko, and Umeko, who seemed as if felled by a force violent enough to literally knock them to the ground. After a while, however, they exchanged glances with eyes consumed with hatred—a hatred no less intense than that which seethed within them the moment they learned everything would go to Tamayo.

Who was this Shizuma Aonuma? Kindaichi had perused *The Life of Sahei Inugami* repeatedly but had never come across such a name. Shizuma, the son of Kikuno Aonuma—what kind of connection did he have with Sahei that he should be the recipient of such fabulous generosity? Then, too, why did Matsuko, Takeko, and Umeko burn with such hatred when they heard the name? Were they simply angry that someone would rob their sons of a share of the wealth? No, there was, Kindaichi felt sure, a more deep-seated reason.

Kindaichi sat contemplating the faces of the members of the Inugami clan with a mixture of intense interest and curiosity, until Furudate coughed lightly and began reading the will again. "Article Five. The Inugami Foundation shall make every effort to locate Shizuma Aonuma within three months of the date of the reading of this will. If it is unable to locate him during this time or if it confirms his death, the entire share of my estate that he would have received shall be donated to the Inugami Foundation. If Shizuma Aonuma is not found living within Japan, but if the possibility exists of his survival overseas, that amount shall be retained by the Inugami Foundation for three years from the date of the reading of this will. If Shizuma returns to Japan during that time, his share shall pass to him, but if he does not return, his share shall pass to the Inugami Foundation."

The room was hushed; the silence was unnerving. The ineffable evil pervading the frozen stillness made Kindaichi's blood run cold.

After a pause, Furudate continued once again. "Article Six. If Tamayo Nonomiya loses the right to inherit the ax, zither, and chrysanthemum, or if she dies before or within three months of the reading of this will, and if Kiyo, Také, or Tomo also dies, all my property and any business enterprise owned or controlled by me shall be managed in the following way. First, if Kiyo dies, any business enterprise owned or controlled by me shall pass to Také and Tomo, who shall be equal partners. They shall have equal authority and shall continue these business enterprises and make concerted efforts to develop them further. The share of the remainder of my estate that would have passed to Kiyo, however, shall pass to Shizuma Aonuma. Second, if either Také or Tomo dies, his share shall also pass to Shizuma Aonuma. Thus, if any one of my three grandsons dies, the share that the deceased would have received shall pass to Shizuma Aonuma. That share shall be managed as specified in Article Five, depending on Shizuma's survival or death. However, if Kiyo, Také, and Tomo all die, both the remainder of my estate and any business enterprise owned or controlled by me shall pass to Shizuma Aonuma, together with the three heirlooms, i.e., the ax, zither, and chrysanthemum."

Sahei's will actually continued much longer, like a puzzle exploring all possible combinations of the death or survival of the five people named in the will—Tamayo, the three cousins Kiyo, Také, and Tomo, and the man named Shizuma Aonuma. I have omitted further reiteration of the specific conditions, however, because that would become tedious and overly digressive. Let it suffice to say that Tamayo's position of almost absolute advantage was immediately obvious to everyone.

It was unthinkable that Tamayo, young and healthy as she was, would die within the next three months. That being the case, the decision as to who would actually inherit the entire Inugami estate and its businesses would be hers alone to make. In other words, the fates of Kiyo, Také, and Tomo depended on her decision.

Besides the power given to Tamayo, the other remarkable aspect of the will was the name Shizuma Aonuma, for anyone inspecting the will closely would realize that his position was second only to Tamayo's. Kiyo, Také, and Tomo could receive a share of their grandfather's fortune without being affected by Tamayo's opinion of them only if she forfeited her rights or died; but if that happened, then this Shizuma would suddenly come into the picture.

True, he would not be able to participate in the Inugami businesses, but in the division of the estate his share would amount to twice that received by each of the other three.

Moreover, although no benefit would accrue to Kiyo or his two cousins if Shizuma died, if the reverse were to occur, that is, if either Kiyo, Také, or Tomo should die, the dead man's share would go right into Shizuma's pocket. What was more, if Tamayo and all three cousins were to die, then everything—the entire Inugami estate and all the businesses—would pass directly to this mysterious person called Shizuma Aonuma.

In short, according to the terms of the will, all Sahei's fortune and businesses would first be under Tamayo's control and, if it should come to this, would ultimately go to Shizuma. Within this scheme, there was no possible way that Kiyo, Také, or Tomo could monopolize the property and businesses of the Inugami clan. Even if one cousin were to survive and all the rest, including Tamayo and Shizuma, were to die, he still would not receive all the family fortune, because the share that would have gone to Shizuma would then be donated directly to the Inugami Foundation.

What a strange will! What a cursed, malicious will! Kindaichi could now understand why Furudate had feared that it would hurl the members of the clan into conflict, kin against kin.

Was Sahei really of sound mind when he wrote this will? If he was, then why was he so cold to his own blood grandchildren yet so kind to Tamayo, descended from his revered benefactor though she may be, as well as to this unknown named Shizuma Aonuma? No, it was not just Sahei's three grandsons who were slighted by his will: their mothers and fathers had been given even less consideration—completely ignored, in fact. Matsuko, Takeko, and Umeko were Sahei's blood daughters, but they had been totally left out in the cold.

Sahei was said to have been cold to his daughters in life, but that his coldness would be this extreme... Kindaichi, swept by a horrible, powerful sensation, sat studying the faces of the family members.

The sinister mask with its supernatural aura prevented Kindaichi from reading the expression on Kiyo's face, but the intensity of the shock he had received was apparent in the fine trembling of his shoulders. The hands he held on his knees shook violently as if with fever, and sweat began to pour from beneath his mask, streaming down from his chin over his throat.

Také, with his squarish build, stared at a point on the floor in front of him, in a wide-eyed daze. Even this arrogant and insolent man seemed overwhelmed by his grandfather's peculiar will. His face, too, was covered with sweat.

Tomo, sly and insincere, could not be still for a moment. He shook his leg incessantly in a way that would irritate even a casual observer, and he rapidly glanced now here, now there, spying on the faces of the others in the room. His eyes were drawn, as if by a magnet, to Tamayo, and his thin lips curved upward in a faint smile that contained both hope and anxiety.

Také's younger sister, Sayoko, sat with her attention riveted on Tomo. With bated breath, her entire body tense, she watched her cousin's insincere manner, sending silent prayers and appeals in his direction. Realizing their ineffectiveness and seeing him again ogling Tamayo, however, she bit her lip hard and looked down sadly.

Matsuko, Takeko, and Umeko were fury incarnate. Their bodies seemed ready to burst with the darkest emotion— hatred, no doubt, for the dead Sahei. Then, when they remembered that the object of their hatred was no longer there to receive it, they redirected their animosity toward Tamayo. How their eyes blazed with anger at the poor girl!

Toranosuke, Takeko's husband, at first glance seemed collected, but his florid face, which grew even more flushed and oily, revealed that he, too, was consumed with wrath. He looked like he might be felled by a stroke at any time. His malevolent glare was like poisoned darts, directed at everyone except his wife and children.

Kokichi, Umeko's husband, had eyes like a stray dog that had been beaten and tormented all its life. Nervously, as if afraid, and apparently totally dejected, he studied the expressions of the others in the room. Yet, just below the surface, one could see a treacherous nature that could not be lightly dismissed. He seemed to harbor malice toward everyone except his son Tomo. He even glared at his wife.

Finally, there was Tamayo. Her attitude when the reading of the will was finally over was something to behold. She had gradually regained her composure as Furudate had gone through the articles, one by one, and by the time he had finished, she was still pale, but was in no way daunted or agitated. Tamayo sat perfectly poised, silent, and alone, like a beautiful clay figure. Did she not notice the looks of hatred the Inugamis shot at her like fiery arrows? She sat, poised and silent, yet in her eyes, there was a strange light, as if, in a trance, she were pursuing a dream.

Suddenly, someone shouted, "I don't believe it! I don't believe it! That will is a fake!"

Kindaichi looked in surprise toward the voice. It was Sahei's oldest daughter, Matsuko.

"No! No! That's not Father's real will. Someone… some-one…" She took a deep breath. "It's someone's plot to steal the Inugami fortune. It's a complete forgery!" Her shrieking voice filled the room.

Furudate's eyebrows twitched, and he began to cough and mumble at the same time. Promptly regaining his composure, however, he took out his handkerchief, wiped his mouth, and spoke in a deliberately calm, admonishing tone. "Mrs. Matsuko, I, too, cannot help but wish that this will were a forgery. Or that even if it does reflect Mr. Inugami's true wishes, there were some flaw in its format that would make it legally invalid. But Mrs. Matsuko—no, let me make this clear not only to Mrs. Matsuko but to all of you—this will is absolutely genuine and completely satisfies all legal requirements. If any of you have any objections to this will and intend to contest it in court, that's up to you. But let me tell you, you will probably lose your case. This will is perfectly binding. No matter what you say, the spirit of this will must be followed to the letter and its instructions carried out in full."

So Furudate explained, slowly and deliberately, looking one by one at all the family members, starting with the masked Kiyo. Finally, his gaze reached Kindaichi. Seeing the uneasiness, anxiety, fear, and, even more, the unspoken appeal that issued forth from Furudate's eyes, Kindaichi nodded slightly. Then, as he looked once again at the lawyer's hands clutching the document, he felt a nameless horror. It was as if blood were oozing from the pages of the will.

# The Family Tree

"Well…?" Like a lone raindrop that creeps along the eaves of a roof and then falls, the word dropped, forlorn and cheerless, from Kindaichi's lips.

"Well…?" After a while, Furudate echoed, with a voice as shadowed with a gloom as helpless as Kindaichi's.

That said, they both remained silent, gazing at the imposing structure of the Inugami villa down by the lake, as the fast-falling mountain twilight of autumn tinged the vast estate in a warm brown hue. Perhaps for Furudate it looked more like an evil veil of black that gradually cloaked it: Kindaichi noticed the fine shivers that crept up the lawyer's legs.

The wind must have picked up, for little ripples rose and scattered over the water's surface. Furudate, like anyone who had just lived through a crisis, had abandoned himself to a weary inertia, as if at any moment he would completely lose his capacity to concentrate. "Well…?" Once again he asked in a gloomy, mechanical voice.

They had taken leave of the Inugami house after the reading of the will. Their hearts unbearably heavy from the hopeless, deplorable enmity the will had generated, they had both automatically turned their steps toward the Nasu Inn without saying a word. Then, returning together to Kindaichi's room, they had seated themselves in the wicker chairs on the balcony and had remained sitting there in total silence for a considerable time.

Kindaichi had dangling from his mouth a cigarette that he had completely forgotten to smoke and, oblivious to the fact that it had gone out on him, had never even relit. Finally he hurled it into the ashtray and, with a squeak from his chair, he leaned forward.

"Alright, Mr. Furudate, tell me what you're thinking. You've read the will, so your duties are over for now. Nothing's secret any more, so please let everything out. Tell me everything you've been holding back about that will."

Furudate looked at Kindaichi's face with a dark, almost frightened expression. "Mr. Kindaichi, you're absolutely right. There's no need to keep anything secret now. But where should I begin?"

"Let's continue where we left off," Kindaichi answered in a soft but firm voice, "what we were talking about in this room before you left for the Inugamis' villa. Mr. Furudate, you suspect Tamayo of being the one who bribed Mr. Wakabayashi and who secretly read the will, don't you?"

Furudate started as if someone had touched a painful nerve, but breathlessly he countered at once, "Why do you say that? No, I haven't the faintest idea who bribed Wakabayashi or who read the will. I'm not even sure anybody did anything of the kind."

"Oh, come now, Mr. Furudate, it's too late to take back what you said. You know Tamayo's repeated mishaps couldn't really be accidents. Surely you don't think..."

"Right, exactly." Furudate seemed to regain his energy somewhat. "That's exactly what I mean. Don't those so-called accidents prove that Tamayo isn't the one who bribed Wakabayashi? Supposing, that is, there really was someone who bribed Wakabayashi and read the will."

Kindaichi smiled meaningfully. "But then, why has Tamayo been in danger so many times and had so many misadventures that very well could have proved fatal?"

"Because the person who read the will was trying to kill her. After all, Tamayo is like a thorn in the side for the Inugami clan. So long as she's alive, she's the one who'll decide the heir to the family fortune."

"But if that's the case, why have the attempts always failed? The viper in the bedroom, the faulty brakes, and the third accident of the other day with the boat—the attempts on her life have never succeeded. Why isn't the culprit doing a better job?"

Furudate stared at Kindaichi with a wild look, his nostrils wide and his brow wet with perspiration. Finally, he whispered in a throaty voice, "Mr. Kindaichi, I don't know what you mean. What on earth are you…?"

Kindaichi slowly shook his head. "Yes, you do, Mr. Furudate. You know, but you're denying it. I know you must have thought this way, too, that the person who threw the viper into the bedroom, the person who tampered with the brakes, the person who bore a hole in the boat and plugged it with putty was none other than Tamayo herself."

"But what for? Why would she do such a thing?"

"To set the scene for future events."

"Future events?"

"The triple murders of Kiyo, Také, and Tomo."

Furudate began perspiring even more freely, the sweat pouring from his brow and over his cheeks in numerous little rivulets. Without even thinking to wipe his face, he sat grasping both arms of the wicker chair tightly, as if he would spring out of it at any moment.

"The triple murders of Kiyo, Také, and Tomo? Who are you suggesting is going to kill them? And what does this have to do with Tamayo's accidents?"

"Listen to me, Mr. Furudate. Tamayo has been given an enormous fortune. She has been bequeathed tremendous power. But there is a condition attached: she has to marry Kiyo, Také, or Tomo—that is, unless all three of them die or all three refuse to marry her. The last possibility, of course, would never happen. With Tamayo being so beautiful and, what's more, with the person who marries her being entitled to the enormous wealth and power of the Inugami clan, one would have to be crazy or stupid to refuse such a marriage. Already today, in that room where we all sat, I clearly saw Tomo making a move on Tamayo with my very own eyes. So…"

"So?" Furudate retorted. He seemed to be challenging Kindaichi.

"So, what if Tamayo dislikes all three of them? Or has some other lover? Let's say Tamayo doesn't want to marry any of the three, but of course she doesn't want to lose the Inugami fortune, either. If so, Tamayo is doomed unless those three die. So, she decides to kill them, one by one, and she stages those repeated accidents as a preparatory move, so she can assume the role of another intended victim when the murders eventually take place."

"Mr. Kindaichi." Furudate breathed rapidly, as if trying to expel some red hot mass from inside him. Then he said with emotion, "You're a terrible man. How can you let such horrible thoughts dwell in your mind? Is everyone in your line of work so suspicious?"

Kindaichi smiled sadly and shook his head. "No, I'm not being suspicious. I'm just pursuing possibilities, that such a scenario could be the case. We can pursue the opposite possibility as well. Say Tamayo's strange accidents in fact do not involve pretense or deception on her part, but that someone really is trying to kill her. In that case, then who's the culprit and what does he or she have in mind?"

"Alright," Furudate repeated, "in that case, who is the culprit and what does he or she have in mind?"

"In that case, all three men—Kiyo, Také, and Tomo—are suspect. In other words, if one of the three has no confidence at all of winning Tamayo for himself, would that person stand by twiddling his thumbs while Tamayo marries one of the other two? As soon as any one of the three marries Tamayo, the other two are totally deprived of any of the Inugami fortune. So, killing Tamayo would mean he would at least come into some of the money."

"You're a terrible man, Mr. Kindaichi. Terrible. But what you're saying is all just fantasy. It's only in a novel that a person could be so cold-blooded."

"No. Whoever it is has already shown how cold-blooded he or she can be. Remember, someone has already murdered Mr. Wakabayashi in a very cold-blooded way. Incidentally, if we pursue the possibility I just mentioned, it's not just Kiyo, Také, and Tomo who are suspect but also their parents and even Také's sister as well. By making sure their son or brother receives a share of the inheritance, they're letting themselves in for a share, too. The question then is, who had the best, surest chance to toss a viper into Tamayo's bedroom, tamper with her car, and bore a hole in her boat. Mr. Furudate, don't you have any ideas?"

Furudate glanced again in consternation at Kindaichi,

and a look of obvious confusion quickly began to spread over his face.

"Ah-hah, Mr. Furudate, I see you're thinking of a particular name. Who is it?"

"No, no, I don't know. As for who had the chance, all of them did."

"All of them?"

"Yes, except for Kiyo, who just came back. Mr. Kindaichi, the family members have been gathering here in Nasu every month for Sahei's memorial services. Of course, they don't come to pay homage to the old man. They come here once a month because they want to find out what the others are up to and because they don't want to lose out on anything. And Tamayo's accidents invariably happen when they are here. This time, too…"

Kindaichi gave a shrill whistle and started to scratch his head vigorously.

"Th-th-this certainly is a very interesting case, Mr. Furudate. No matter who the perpetrator is, he or she keeps us guessing."

Kindaichi remained lost in thought, violently scratching his head, with its increasingly tangled mop of hair. Finally he remembered Furudate's presence. He turned toward the lawyer, who was staring at him aghast, and smiled sheepishly.

"Excuse me," he laughed. "It's a habit of mine when I'm excited. I hope you won't hold it against me. Anyhow, as I was saying, we've considered two possibilities—the possibility that Tamayo's strange accidents are staged performances and the possibility that they are not. By the way, if the latter is the case, then there is another strong suspect. Of course, whether he would have had a chance to read the will is another question."

"Who's that?"

"Shizuma Aonuma."

A faint cry escaped Furudate's taut lips.

"Setting aside whether he had the chance or not, Shizuma has the strongest motive of any to want Tamayo dead. Unless she dies, he won't be included at all in this scheme of inheritance. Since he can't make Tamayo reject Sahei's grandsons, he has to kill her first if he wants to be assured of a share of the money. Then, if the three grandsons die after that, he would get everything—all Sahei's fortune and businesses. Mr. Furudate," Kindaichi spoke with emphasis, "who is this Shizuma Aonuma? What connection does he have with Sahei? And why is he being shown such generosity?"

Furudate sighed deeply. Wiping his clammy brow with his handkerchief, he nodded with a gloomy expression. "Shizuma Aonuma was the reason Sahei had so much bitterness and anguish in his heart in his later years. It's no wonder he gave Shizuma such an important role in the will. Shizuma is…" The words seemed to stick in Furudate's throat. Then, clearing his throat, he murmured almost in a stammer, "Shizuma is Sahei's illegitimate son."

Kindaichi raised his eyebrows high in surprise. "His son?"

"Yes. His only son."

"But then, why…? I mean, that wasn't even mentioned in his biography."

"Of course not. Writing about that would mean exposing what Matsuko, Takeko, and Umeko did—their cruel, evil deed." Furudate began his tale in an emotionless voice, as if reciting something from memory. "When he was in his fifties, Sahei fell in love for the first time in his life. He already had three mistresses, with whom he had sired

Matsuko, Takeko, and Umeko, but he did not particularly love any of them. He just kept them by his side to satisfy his physical needs. But then, when he was past fifty, he fell deeply in love with a woman for the first time in his life. Her name was Kikuno Aonuma, and she worked at the Inugami silk mill. They say she was even younger than Matsuko. After a while, Kikuno became pregnant, throwing Sahei's three daughters into a panic. Having different mothers as they did, they'd never been close, even as children. No, in fact, they had constantly fought and feuded with each other like sworn enemies. But now, at least in regard to Kikuno, they joined forces in a united effort—they were that dismayed by her pregnancy."

"Why? Why would they care if she was pregnant?"

Furudate smiled wearily. "Isn't it obvious? What if Kikuno had a boy? Sahei was totally infatuated with her, and if she were to give him the son he had always wanted, he might decide to marry her legally. Then, the boy would steal the entire Inugami fortune from them."

"I see." Kindaichi controlled the shudder he felt rising within him. He nodded slowly and deeply.

"So the three daughters formed an alliance and began to hound Kikuno, tormenting her, abusing her fiercely in unspeakable ways. Kikuno finally found it unbearable. She thought that if this continued, the three would torment her to death in the end. So she ran away. Matsuko, Takeko, and Umeko were relieved, but then they found out, after Kikuno had left, that Sahei had given her the three Inugami heirlooms: the ax, zither, and chrysanthemum."

"Yes, I was going to ask about those. What are the ax, zither, and chrysanthemum?"

"Let me explain that later. As the will said, though, they are the Inugami family treasures, which signify the right of inheritance. The three half-sisters found out that Sahei had given them to Kikuno and had told her that if she had a son, she should come back with the heirlooms and demand her rights. It's no wonder the three panicked even more. When they heard that Kikuno had indeed safely given birth to a boy, they could no longer hold back their fury and rushed to Kikuno like demons from hell. Even though she had just given birth, they forced her to sign a statement saying that Sahei was not the father of her child. They then retrieved the three heirlooms and went triumphantly on their way. That's why Sahei was as cold as ice to Matsuko, Takeko, and Umeko in his latter years."

Kindaichi recalled the malicious features of the three women. Imagining how they might have been in their youth, when they would have had even more spirit and spite, he felt his flesh crawl. "I see. What happened to Kikuno and the baby?"

"Well, the terrifying experience must have made quite an impression on Kikuno. She had signed that statement, but who knew what other harm could come to her? So, she took her baby, Shizuma, and disappeared without a trace. Even now, we have no idea where mother and son are. If he's living, Shizuma should be twenty-nine, the same age as Kiyo."

Furudate finished his tale and sighed morosely.

A dark thought overwhelmed Kindaichi. Perhaps Sahei's will was written with a horrible purpose in mind from the first. Did the old man deliberately write such an extra-ordinary will to cause discord among Matsuko, Takeko, and Umeko—a blood feud that would continue for years and years to come? Kindaichi pondered what he had heard, crushed by depressing thoughts, but eventually, taking out a pen and paper, he began sketching the Inugami family tree. For a long time, he sat staring at the chart, as if there were something to discover there.

So this was the inception of the unearthly series of murders that befell the Inugami clan. The curtain had risen on the first act of this blood-soaked tragedy.

# THE INUGAMI CLAN

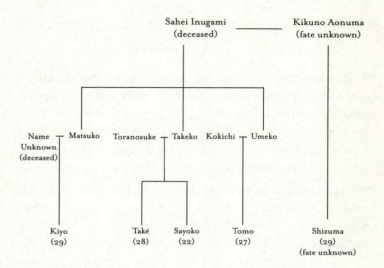

Sahei Inugami (deceased) ——— Kikuno Aonuma (fate unknown)

Name Unknown (deceased) ┬ Matsuko   Toranosuke ┬ Takeko   Kokichi ┬ Umeko

Kiyo (29)   Také (28)   Sayoko (22)   Tomo (27)   Shizuma (29) (fate unknown)

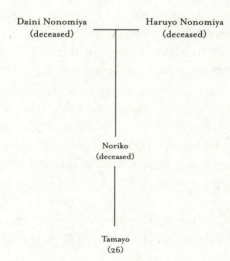

Daini Nonomiya (deceased) ——— Haruyo Nonomiya (deceased)

Noriko (deceased)

Tamayo (26)

# The Mysterious Monkey

Sahei's unusual will quickly became a hot topic for greedy journalists. Thanks to the efforts of a certain news agency, the will's contents and accounts of the bitter enmity it had caused among the family members were scattered far and wide to newspapers throughout the country. Of course the major dailies did not choose to publish articles about such private matters, but the second- and third-rate tabloids, without exception, splashed the story all over their pages with sensational and misleading exaggeration. As a result, the inheritance of Sahei Inugami's fortune was no longer just a topic of local interest but had ballooned into a national concern. Anyone who was even the least bit inquisitive watched with curiosity, waiting to see whom this Tamayo Nonomiya would choose for a husband. Some even made wagers among themselves.

The Inugami villa, while thus basked in the national spotlight, stood as hushed in suffocating silence as ever by the shores of Lake Nasu. Takeko, Umeko, and their families were still at the villa, but there was almost no communication between them and Matsuko or Kiyo. Each family, when not secluded in its own quarters, tried to read the others' faces and minds. Inside the mansion there now brewed four separate storms, with interests interlocking in complex ways: Matsuko and Kiyo, Takeko's family, Umeko's family, and Tamayo. Imagine Tamayo's miserable situation. Matsuko, Takeko, Umeko, and their families hated each other like bitter enemies, but even so they were united in their hatred for Tamayo. Not one of them, however, would express that animosity openly. Though they concealed daggers of jealousy in their hearts, the three half-sisters were all flattery and smiles toward Tamayo. Then, bitterly resenting being forced to lavish such false compliments on this young orphan, their hatred toward her doubled in intensity.

No doubt egged on by their parents, Také and Tomo went daily to pay their respects to Tamayo. Také, being the epitome of arrogance, appeared exceedingly confident from the first and did not jabber on with obviously insincere flattery, but Tomo, sly and smart, was like a dog nearly wagging its tail off. He would run around Tamayo, sit up, shake hands, and whimper obligingly, trying to curry favor with her.

Through all this, Tamayo was magnificent. She could feel the family's hatred and curses directed against her with her whole being, as sensitively as moist skin would feel electricity, yet she seemed not in the least daunted. She remained elegant and noble, and her attitude toward both the self-confident Také and the shifty Tomo seemed to have changed little if at all with the reading of the will—except that now she never forgot to have Monkey in an adjoining room when either one of them visited her in her quarters.

Neither did Tamayo shrink from the masked Kiyo. Since he never came to visit her of his own accord, she would sometimes call on him in his room, in encounters that were rumored to be extremely strange. Again, Tamayo was always accompanied by Monkey. Kiyo, too, was never alone, always having his mother by his side when he met with Tamayo. Thus, the meetings between Kiyo and Tamayo would take place with Matsuko and Monkey present. Invariably they would lapse into an uncomfortable silence.

Kiyo, with his sinister mask, perhaps self-conscious of his hideous appearance, hardly ever said a word. It was therefore mostly Tamayo who would speak. But when her words seemed to end in a question or referred to Kiyo's past, Matsuko would always intervene and answer for her son, responding with seeming frivolity and deftly maneuvering the subject in another direction. When this happened, Tamayo would pale visibly, and she would sometimes begin to tremble slightly.

Be that as it may, it was only thanks to Monkey that nothing untoward happened to Tamayo while living in the same villa as Také and Tomo, both of whom were noticeably impatient to secure her love. The easiest and fastest way to possess Tamayo would be to take her physically, by force if necessary—it was not beneath either of these men to consider such a plan. More than a few times in fact, they had wanted to make lewd advances. That they failed to carry out their intentions was due only to Monkey's presence. If Také or Tomo had tried anything so outrageous, the ugly giant would no doubt have broken his neck.

"You want to know about Monkey?" Furudate began explaining about this mysterious character one day. "That's not his real name, of course. As you know, he looks just like one, though, so people have called him that since he was a boy. It's come to seem like his real name. I for one don't even remember what his real name is. He was orphaned when he was still very small, so Tamayo's mother, feeling sorry for him, took him in and raised him. Yes, he and Tamayo were brought up together from a very young age. So when Tamayo's parents died and Sahei brought her to the Inugami home, Monkey came with her. He's slightly mentally handicapped, and is blindly loyal to Tamayo and serves her with the utmost devotion. He'd do anything she asked him to do. If she asked him to kill, he'd do it gladly."

These last words must have popped out of Furudate's mouth inadvertently. Surely he only wanted to describe how dedicated Monkey was to Tamayo. The moment they were uttered, however, both speaker and listener looked up as if jerked awake and stared at each other.

Furudate, obviously regretting his choice of words, coughed awkwardly, and Kindaichi changed the topic for him. "By the way, I heard Monkey is in charge of the chrysanthemums at the Inugami estate."

"Yes, yes, did you see them? He might not be very bright, but he has a remarkable talent for growing chrysanthemums. Tamayo's father, who was the priest of Nasu Shrine, taught him how because the chrysanthemum is historically significant to both Nasu Shrine and to the Inugami clan. Remember the ax, zither, and chrysanthemum?"

"Yes, I wanted to ask you about those. What is the story behind those three objects? Are they related in some way to Nasu Shrine as well?"

"Oh, yes. The ax refers to the *yoki*, the small hatchet used to chop firewood; the zither to the *koto*, the thirteen stringed musical instrument; and the chrysanthemum is the flower *kiku*. Originally, they were the three sacred treasures of Nasu Shrine. As you can see, when the words are spoken together, *yokikotokiku*, they are homonymous with 'we hear good tidings.' I understand that this phrase is also the family motto of the famous kabuki actor Kikugoro. Well, I'm sure the treasures of Nasu Shrine have nothing to do with any kabuki actor, but Daini Nonomiya—you know, Sahei's benefactor and Tamayo's grandfather—had thought of this same auspicious phrase and had a craftsman make a golden ax, zither, and chrysanthemum to be consecrated as the sacred treasures of the shrine. Then, later, when Sahei started his business, Daini presented them and the motto to Sahei to wish him success, so that now they've become the heirlooms of the Inugami clan."

"And where are they now?"

"The Inugami Foundation has them in its safekeeping. Eventually, when Tamayo selects a husband from among Kiyo, Také, and Tomo, they will be given to him. The heirlooms themselves are only little gold miniatures, each about thirty centimeters in height."

Furudate continued with a frown, "You know, since it was Daini who originally presented the ax, zither, and chrysanthemum to Sahei, I suppose I can understand why the old man might have wanted to return them to Daini's descendant after his own death. But things get terribly complicated because the Inugami fortune and businesses are attached to them. I have to wonder why Sahei ever devised such a will," Furudate murmured with a sigh.

Kindaichi looked thoughtful and said, "I see. So, the words for ax, zither, and chrysanthemum, *yokikotokiku*, and the miniatures themselves have no particular significance—that is, if they didn't represent the right to inherit the Inugami fortune."

"Exactly. The heirlooms are golden, but only gold-plated, so they're not worth much in and of themselves. It's what the ax, zither, and chrysanthemum represent that gives them their value." So Furudate quickly affirmed, but in retrospect, his answer could not have been more off the mark, for the ax, zither, and chrysanthemum—*yokikotokiku*—those very words would come to haunt them with their horrible significance.

*Yokikotokiku.* That auspicious motto indeed had watched over the Inugami clan while Sahei had been alive. Did it still protect them with its power now that the old man was dead? No, looking back on all that was to occur, we can say it no longer protected, but in fact now cursed the Inugami clan. Yet, even our astute Kindaichi remained completely unaware of this, at least until those series of nightmarish incidents gradually opened his eyes.

"By the way, does it look like you'll be able to locate Shizuma Aonuma?"

"I don't know. Even before I read the will, I made arrangements all across the country to search for him, but so far, we haven't a clue. Even if he safely reached adulthood, who knows if he's still alive or not, after the war we've just gone through?"

Perhaps the demons of hell were in a mischievous mood, for all at once, Kindaichi was struck by an extraordinary thought. Disconcerted at the seeming ridiculousness of his own notion, he nonetheless could not get it out of his mind.

"Mr. Furudate, you said that Monkey was an orphan, didn't you? And in age he would be just about right. Is Monkey's family background clearly known?"

Hearing Kindaichi's question, Furudate widened his eyes, appalled. He remained staring at Kindaichi for a while, but then gasped, "What are you saying, Mr. Kindaichi? Are you saying that Monkey is Shizuma? That's preposterous."

"No doubt you're right. The thought just popped into my head. No, I'm more than happy to retract my question.

I'm not thinking straight today. I just thought, perhaps Sahei asked Tamayo's mother to raise his illegitimate child. If that were the case, though, I'm sure someone would have noticed by now."

"Of course. Besides, as I've often told you, Sahei was an extremely handsome man. Kikuno, too, although I've never met her, must have been attractive, considering how Sahei lost his head over her. There's no way such an ugly child as Monkey could have been born between them. He's just a master chrysanthemum grower who's not very bright. And now, he's engrossed in making chrysanthemum dolls."

"Chrysanthemum dolls?" Kindaichi screwed up his face.

"Yes, you know, those dolls on which they arrange chrysanthemums of different hues to represent the kimonos and so forth. Once before, at Sahei's command, Monkey made a whole series of chrysanthemum dolls to depict scenes from Sahei's life. He must have remembered that, because he proclaimed to everyone that he would make chrysanthemum dolls again this year, though not, of course, on as large a scale as before. Monkey is alright—neither harmful nor helpful—so long as he isn't angered. Now that I think about it, though, I haven't once heard about his family background. Alright, then, if you have even an ounce of doubt, I'll find out the circumstances of his birth."

Furudate's expression, too, had gradually grown troubled.

# The Votive Hand Print

November 15. A half month since Kiyo's return and almost one month since Kindaichi's arrival in Nasu. The day when Inugami blood first flowed and the day when the devil finally commenced to act. Before turning to the subject of death, however, let us first recount an incident that might have been a prelude to murder.

"Mr. Kindaichi, you have a guest."

It was about three in the afternoon. Having dragged his wicker chair onto the balcony as usual, Kindaichi sat lost in thought, almost nodding off, when his drowsy musing was interrupted by the maid's voice.

"A guest? Who is it?"

"It's Mr. Furudate."

"If it's Mr. Furudate, tell him to come up."

"No, he's waiting for you in his car. He says he's going somewhere and would like you to accompany him, if you don't mind."

Kindaichi sprang out of his chair. Then, changing from his robe into his tired kimono and hakama trousers, he thrust a bowler, crumpled beyond recognition, over his tousled hair and rushed out the front door of the inn. A car was parked in front, and poking his head out of one of its windows was Furudate.

"Sorry to keep you waiting. Where are we going?" Trotting up to the car, Kindaichi nonchalantly placed his foot on the running board but then caught his breath in surprise. Furudate was not alone. Sitting in the car with him were the thickset Také and the fox-like Tomo.

"Well, hello. I didn't know you two were going, too."

"Get in, get in," said Furudate, moving to the spare pull-down seat so Kindaichi could sit next to Tomo. The car started moving immediately.

"So where are you off to together?" Kindaichi asked.

"To Nasu Shrine."

"The shrine? What for?"

"Yes, well, let me tell you about that when we get there." Perhaps concerned about the driver's presence, Furudate coughed awkwardly, avoiding the question. Také sat silently with arms crossed, his lips pulled tight in a scowl, while Tomo kept shaking his leg incessantly, whistling a tune in the direction of the window. The vibrations from Tomo's twitching augmented the jolts of the car and made Kindaichi squirm on his seat.

Nasu Shrine was located about four kilometers from the center of town. Already the car had gone past the town limits and was speeding through fields of bare-branched mulberry shrubs. Acres of rice paddies extended beyond the fields, but with the harvest over and the water drained, they were a sorry sight, black stubble sticking out of the mud. Still further, beyond the rice paddies, one could glimpse the lake, its waters glistening like a mirror. Biting cold gusts blew from its direction. Winter was quick to come to the Shinshu region. The peak of Mt. Fuji, soaring in the distance above the mulberry fields, was already white with snow.

The car soon pulled up in front of the large, plain wood gate of the shrine.

Nasu Shrine had a long and distinguished history. Towering cedar trees loomed over its extensive grounds, and deep-colored moss covered its rows of stone lanterns. As Kindaichi proceeded up the path of pebbles that crunched under his feet, he felt the bracing tension of the atmosphere overtaking him. Také frowned as sourly as usual, Tomo's eyes still darted in all directions, but no one said a word. They soon reached the shrine office.

"Hello. I heard the car, so I thought it might be you." A middle-aged man wearing a white kimono and a pair of pale-yellow hakama trousers came out of the office. With his short hair and wire-rimmed glasses, he looked unremarkable, but as Kindaichi soon learned, this was Taisuke Oyama, the priest of Nasu Shrine.

The priest led them deep into the building, to an aseptically clean, eight-mat tatami room. In the middle of it was a brazier filled with a warming fire. The garden outside was filled with magnificent chrysanthemum blooms, which scented the air with a faint fragrance.

As soon as they had seated themselves and exchanged greetings, Tomo impatiently leaned forward and said, "Mr. Oyama, I don't mean to rush you, but could you show us what we came to see?"

The priest, looking uncertain, glanced toward Kindaichi. "And this gentleman is...?"

"Oh, you don't need to worry about Mr. Kindaichi," Furudate interjected. "This is Mr. Kosuke Kindaichi, and he has been helping us in regard to the current matter. Now, since the two gentlemen are quite eager, could you please...?"

"Yes, of course. Please wait here for a moment."

The priest left the room but soon returned, reverently holding a small, plain wood offering stand on which lay three handscrolls with gold brocade covers. The priest placed the stand before the assembled group and took up the scrolls one by one. "This is Mr. Také's scroll, and this is yours, Mr. Tomo."

"We don't care about our own scrolls. Show us Kiyo's," Tomo urged irritably.

"This is Mr. Kiyo's scroll. Please have a look."

In sullen silence, Také took the scroll from the priest, unrolled it, and studied it, then quickly passed it to Tomo. It was a scroll about 40 centimeters wide and 60 centimeters long, and as he took it from Také, Tomo's hands quivered with excitement.

"Také, you're certain this is Kiyo's scroll, right?" said Tomo to his cousin.

"Absolutely. The handwriting at the top is Grandfather's, and without a doubt this is Kiyo's signature."

"Good. Have a look, Mr. Furudate."

As Tomo passed the scroll to the lawyer, Kindaichi, who was sitting next to him, was able to discern its contents for the first time. What he saw left him thunderstruck.

Pressed on the white silk of the scroll was a right hand print. Above it, in artistic brushstrokes, was written "Success in Battle," while along the left side, in another hand, were the words "July 6, 1943, Kiyo Inugami, age 23, male, born in the year of the rooster."

The hand print belonged to Kiyo—the man who had lost his face! For the first time, Kindaichi understood why they had come to the shrine, and he felt his heart racing with excitement.

"Mr. Kindaichi, I want you to have a good look at this, too." Furudate pushed the scroll toward Kindaichi.

"Yes, I saw it just now. But what do you intend to do with it?"

"Isn't it obvious?" said Tomo. "We're going to see if that masked man who returned the other day really is Kiyo or not. No two people have the same fingerprints, and a person's fingerprints are the same for life. Even you must know that."

Kindaichi watched Tomo speak, observing his animal-like cruelty, like that of a beast that had spotted its prey and was licking its chops in anticipation. Kindaichi felt his forehead grow clammy with a cold sweat. "I see, but why does the shrine possess this hand print?"

"In this part of the country, Mr. Kindaichi," Furudate took over and explained, "it's a custom for anyone going off to war to come to this shrine and to offer a votive tablet stamped with his hand print as a prayer for success in battle. Mr. Také and Mr. Tomo here, as well as Mr. Kiyo, did likewise, but since they're so closely connected with Nasu Shrine, they dedicated these scrolls instead of tablets. They were stored deep inside the shrine and we had completely forgotten about them, but Mr. Oyama here remembered and was kind enough to let Mr. Také and Mr. Tomo know, in case it should be of some use."

"Mr. Oyama told them?"

Noticing how Kindaichi cast a sharp glance in his direction, the priest became flustered. "Yes... well, actually... since there's been some gossip about Mr. Kiyo after his return, I thought if things could be made certain, it would be better..."

"So all of you suspect that man might not be the real Kiyo?"

"Of course. How can we trust a man with his face torn apart like that?" said Tomo.

"But his mother, Mrs. Matsuko, declared absolutely…"

"Mr. Kindaichi, you don't know my aunt. If Kiyo was dead, that woman wouldn't hesitate to find a stand-in. She doesn't want Také or me to have the Inugami fortune. To prevent that, she'd do anything, even swear that an imposter is her real son."

Kindaichi felt a shiver crawl up his spine.

"Alright, Mr. Furudate, I want you to sign your name beside this hand print. Mr. Kindaichi, if you would, too. We're going to take this back, get that masked man's hand print, and then compare the two, so we don't want anyone to say we've done anything fraudulent. Please sign here as witnesses."

"But… but what if Kiyo refuses to give you his hand print?"

"Oh, he won't refuse," Také stirred and spoke out at last. "If he does, I'll get it by force." His voice was no longer human, but the growl of a beast with blood dripping from its fangs.

# Evil Tidings

November 16. That morning, Kindaichi had overslept as never before, and although it was past ten o'clock he was still cuddled between the sheets of his futon. He had overslept because he had been up so late the night before.

The previous day, having obtained Kiyo's hand print at Nasu Shrine, Také and Tomo had blustered that they would return to the villa, get a hand print from the man in the strange mask and ascertain his identity, once and for all. They had asked Kindaichi to be present as a witness, but he had refused. If some incident requiring his professional services had already occurred to a member of the Inugami family, he would have felt differently, but at this point he did not want to risk earning the distrust of anyone, no matter whom, by sticking his nose into their private affairs.

"Fine. It's alright, we have Mr. Furudate." The hulking Také yielded immediately. Tomo the fox, however, insisted, "But should the authenticity of this scroll be called into question, you will testify that we retrieved it from Nasu Shrine, won't you?"

"Of course. So long as my signature is there where I placed it, I will stand by it. By the way, Mr. Furudate…"

"Yes?"

"As I just said, I feel it wouldn't be proper for me to be present as witness at this event, but I would like to know as soon as possible what happens. Could you let me know the results—whether that man in the strange mask is indeed Kiyo or not—as soon as you can?"

"Certainly. I'll stop by your inn on my way back."

After dropping Kindaichi off at his lodgings, the car headed straight to the Inugami estate.

It was about ten in the evening when Furudate, true to his word, came to Kindaichi's room. The instant Kindaichi saw the lawyer's face, he asked, "What happened?" He was taken aback by Furudate's dark, stern expression.

Furudate shook his head slightly and spat out, "No good."

"What? What do you mean?"

"Matsuko wouldn't let Kiyo give us his hand print."

"She refused?"

"Yes, absolutely. She wouldn't listen to Také or Tomo at all. I'm sure she's not going to change her mind—not for a while anyway. The only way we could get a new hand print from Kiyo now would be by force, like Také said, but I don't think anyone is willing to go that far. So we weren't able to learn anything definite at all."

Kindaichi had a heavy feeling in the pit of his stomach. "But… but…" He licked his parched lips. "But that would make Také and Tomo even more suspicious."

"Exactly. That's why I tried to persuade Matsuko till I was blue in the face. But she's not the type to listen to anyone. On the contrary, she grew infuriated with me and made all sorts of nasty remarks. She's a stubborn woman, and once she sets her mind on something, she won't be easily persuaded to change it."

Furudate sighed a deep, dark sigh. Then, as if spitting out something distasteful, he began to relate to Kindaichi the events of the evening. Listening to the lawyer's account, Kindaichi was able to paint the scene vividly in his mind.

It was the same twelve-mat room where the will had been read. The members of the Inugami clan were assembled in front of Sahei's photograph on the plain wood altar—Kiyo, with his sinister rubber mask, Matsuko, and facing them in a circle, Také, Tomo, their parents, and Také's sister. Also part of the circle were Tamayo and Furudate.

The scroll that had just been retrieved from Nasu Shrine had been placed in front of Kiyo, along with a blank sheet of paper, an inkstone with red ink, and a brush. Kiyo's mask prevented anyone from seeing his expression, but the fine trembling of his shoulders revealed his profound agitation. The eyes of the family members that were turned toward the masked face were full of suspicion and hatred.

"So, Aunt Matsuko, are you saying that you absolutely refuse to let Kiyo give us his hand print?" After a long, dangerous silence, Také spoke as if upbraiding her. His voice was that of a beast with blood dribbling from its fangs.

"Absolutely." Matsuko answered in a suppressed manner. Then, with blazing eyes, she looked around at the others in the room. "This is outrageous. Even if his face has changed, there is no doubt this is Kiyo. I guarantee it—I'm his mother and I should know. What better proof is there? And you go and listen to those ridiculous rumors. No, I refuse to allow it. I won't have it."

"But Matsuko," Také's mother, Takeko, interjected from nearby. It was a calm, quiet voice, but one that reverberated with ample malice. "That's all the more reason for Kiyo to give us his hand print. No, I'm not saying I have doubts about his identity. But it's so hard to keep people from gossiping. So to stop these silly rumors, too, I think it best if Kiyo simply gives us his hand print. Umeko, what do you think?"

"Oh, yes, I agree with Takeko. If you and Kiyo refuse now, I think people would become even more suspicious. Isn't that right, everybody?"

"Of course, that's right," Takeko's husband, Toranosuke, chimed in. "And not just the people outside. If you and Kiyo continue to refuse this now, we would be tempted to get suspicious, too. Kokichi, how about you?"

"Y-yes, that's true." Umeko's husband, Kokichi, stammered as if intimidated. "We certainly don't want to doubt a member of the family, but if Matsuko and Kiyo insist on saying no, we..."

"Have to believe you have something to hide." Takeko drove in the point with a venomous sneer.

"Shut up! Shut up, shut up, shut up!" At that moment Matsuko shrieked, her voice quivering with rage, "Do you realize what you're saying? At least for now, Kiyo is the head of the Inugami clan. If Father hadn't written such a ridiculous will, all the Inugami fame and fortune would be Kiyo's alone. He's the head of the clan. In the old days, he'd have been your lord and master. And you, Také and Tomo, you'd have been just like vassals, yet you... yet you... How dare you tell him you want his hand print, his fingerprints, like some sort of common criminal? No, no, there's no way I'll allow my son to do such a disgusting thing. No, never. Kiyo, come on, we don't need to stay here."

Matsuko stood up indignantly.

Také's expression changed to one of fury. "Aunt Matsuko, then do you refuse absolutely—"

"Absolutely, absolutely! Come, Kiyo."

The masked Kiyo stood up falteringly. Matsuko took his hand.

"Then, Aunt Matsuko, we—" Grinding his teeth, Také shot a vicious remark at the backs of Matsuko and Kiyo as they were leaving the room. "We can no longer recognize that man as Kiyo."

"Do as you like!" Leading the masked man by the hand, Matsuko stomped out the sliding door.

"Hmm…" Having heard Furudate's account, Kindaichi began vigorously scratching his head this way and that. "A tense situation."

"Indeed," Furudate answered gloomily. "I have to wonder why Matsuko refuses so obstinately. It's true, Také could have broached the subject more tactfully. He did treat Kiyo like a criminal from the start. Matsuko, proud as she is, became incensed, and since she's the type that once she gets her back up is hopelessly stubborn, I guess she couldn't help herself. But the issue being what it is… if that's the real Kiyo—and of course I believe it is—it would have been much better if she had just been a good sport and let them have what they wanted."

"In other words, we can interpret Matsuko's reaction tonight in one of two ways. Either Také's and Tomo's attitude offended her and made her stubborn, or, as Také and Tomo suspect, that masked man is in fact not Kiyo, and, what's more, Matsuko knows it."

Furudate nodded with a dark look in his eyes. "Of course, I choose the first interpretation, but unless Matsuko gives in and lets us take Kiyo's hand print, I can't erase that second interpretation, that horrible suspicion, from my mind, no matter how distasteful the thought."

Furudate stayed until near midnight talking. Soon after he left, Kindaichi lay down on his futon, but even after he had turned off the lights, his eyes refused to close for a long time. The surreal figure of the man in the rubber mask and the right hand print pressed on the silk scroll kept floating before him in the darkness, tormenting him until late into the night.

Suddenly, the phone he had placed beside his pillow started ringing loudly, and Kindaichi awoke with a start. Still lying prone between the sheets, he drew the telephone toward him and put the receiver to his ear. It was the manager at the front desk.

"Room number 17? Mr. Kosuke Kindaichi? Telephone call from Mr. Furudate."

"Yes, please put him through."

Immediately, he heard Furudate's voice on the other end. "Hello? Mr. Kindaichi? Sorry to wake you, but I need you to come quickly… very quickly… immediately."

Furudate's voice sounded unusually high-pitched and shaky. Kindaichi's heart skipped a beat.

"Come? Come where?"

"The Inugamis'… the Inugamis' villa. I'll send a car for you. Please come right away."

"Alright, I understand. Mr. Furudate, has something happened?"

"Yes, something has happened. Something terrible has happened. Wakabayashi's prediction has come true, and… and… in a very peculiar way. Anyhow, please come immediately. You'll understand everything when you get here. I'll see you soon."

A loud click from the receiver, the sound of Furudate hanging up hurriedly. Kindaichi sprang up from his futon and opened one of the shutters to peek outside. It was dark and overcast, as if a gray veil had descended upon the world, and a cold rain beat mournfully on the waters of the lake.

# The Chrysanthemum Garden

In his experience as a private investigator, Kindaichi had been involved in all sorts of cases, and more than a few times he had come face-to-face with ghastly corpses—the stuff that nightmares are made of. He saw a couple lying drenched in their own blood on their wedding night in *The Honjin Murders* case and the body of a young girl hung upside down from an old plum tree and her dead sister stuffed inside a huge temple bell in the *Gokumon Island* case. In the *Nightwalker* case, he saw the decapitated corpses of a man and a woman, while in the *Yatsuhaka Village* case he witnessed many people poisoned or strangled. By now, therefore, Kindaichi should have grown insensitive to corpses, no matter how different or terrifying, but this bizarre murder in the case of the Inugami clan still left him in shock.

A car from the Inugami estate arrived not long after Furudate's phone call, so Kindaichi wolfed down his bowl of rice and hurried outside. On the way to the villa, he tried his best to pry something out of the driver, but either because of someone's gag order or true ignorance, his answers were not very informative. "I really don't know much myself, sir. I did hear that someone was killed, but I have no idea who it was. Anyhow, the whole place is in an uproar."

The car soon pulled up by the front gate of the estate. Apparently the police had already arrived, for uniformed policemen and plain-clothes detectives with grim expressions on their faces were passing in and out of the gate.

Furudate came running out immediately. "Mr. Kindaichi, thank God you're here. It's happened, it's finally…" Having grabbed Kindaichi's arm, he was so agitated he could not go on. Kindaichi's heart turned over, wondering what could have so upset this normally self-possessed lawyer.

"Mr. Furudate, what on earth…"

"Come this way. Just come take a look. It's horrible… just horrible… no sane person… must be a lunatic or the devil himself. Why such a horrible prank…"

Furudate was incoherent. With his eyes wild and blood-shot, he seemed possessed, as if he would start foaming at the mouth at any moment, and the hand that grasped Kindaichi's wrist was burning hot. Kindaichi remained silent as he was half-led, half-dragged forward by Furudate. Inside the gate, a long driveway extended toward the front door. It was not in that direction that Furudate turned his steps, however, but through a side gate into a garden.

The original villa, built when Sahei first felt his company was safely established, was a small structure. Later, however, as the Inugami businesses expanded and Sahei amassed a fortune, he gradually bought up the surrounding land and continued to add to the building, until in the end, it had become a complex maze with numerous annexes. It was so complex, in fact, that had Kindaichi wandered onto the estate alone, he would surely have become lost.

Furudate, however, seemed thoroughly acquainted with the grounds and dragged Kindaichi deeper and deeper without any hesitation. Finally, after passing through a European-style outer garden, they entered the Japanese-style inner garden, where a crowd of policemen, soaked in the rain, milled about searching for something.

Past this inner garden and then through a stylish bamboo wicket they went, when suddenly, a magnificent chrysanthemum garden appeared before Kindaichi's eyes. Although Kindaichi was not given to aesthetic appreciation, even he could not help but marvel at its splendor.

On the other side of a neatly swept carpet of white sand stood a tastefully designed traditional building, probably a teahouse. It was surrounded by rows of chrysanthemums covered by a latticed awning. Large blooms of various types—spherical, cascading, and single-layered—filled the melancholy, rain-drenched garden with their fragrance.

"It's over there. A horrible sight…" Furudate whispered in a high-pitched, nervous voice, still holding Kindaichi's arm.

In front of the chrysanthemums just facing the entrance of the teahouse stood several policemen, frozen in silence. Furudate dragged Kindaichi to the spot.

"Look, Mr. Kindaichi. Look at that face."

Pushing the policemen aside, Kindaichi made his way to the front and stood in front of the chrysanthemums. He recalled what Furudate had said once before: "Monkey? He's a master chrysanthemum grower. And now, he's engrossed in making chrysanthemum dolls." Yes, these were Monkey's chrysanthemum dolls alright, and they were arranged to represent a scene from *The Chrysanthemum Garden*, a kabuki play about a legendary hero of medieval Japan.

In the center stood the former general Kiichi, his long hair tied behind him. Next to him was his daughter Princess Minazuru in a flowing, long-sleeved kimono. The young servant Torazo and another servant Chienai were crouched in front of Kiichi, to the right and left, respectively, while the villain Tankai stood like an evil spirit in semi-darkness toward the back.

Taking in the scene at a glance, Kindaichi quickly realized that the faces of the chrysanthemum dolls had all been made to resemble members of the Inugami household. The protagonist Kiichi was the deceased Sahei, and Princess Minazuru was Tamayo. The young servant Torazo, in the story actually the hero Lord Ushiwaka in disguise, looked just like the masked Kiyo, and the servant Chienai, in fact the young lord's retainer, was Tomo. And Tankai, the villain, looked like...

As Kindaichi peered into the shadowy gloom at the back, he felt his body convulse and become numb, as if shocked by a jolt of electricity.

Tankai, the villain—of course, the features were those of the hulking Také. But... but... but while Tankai should have long hair, this Tankai had his hair cut short and neatly parted on the left as if he belonged to the modern age. And what a realistic pale, dark face!

Kindaichi jerked as if another jolt of electricity had passed through him, and he unconsciously moved a step closer.

"That's... that's..." He could not get the words out; his tongue seemed stuck to the roof of his mouth.

Kindaichi leaned forward over the railing, squeezing its green bamboo stalks as if he would tear them asunder. But at that instant, Tankai's head tottered once, twice, as if nodding, and rolled off his shoulders to the ground.

Kindaichi cried out, croaking like a frog being crushed, and jumped back in spite of himself.

Tankai's—no, Také's—severed head lay on the ground, the cut surface covered with congealed reddish-black blood and revealing a shapeless mass inside. It was a nauseating, nightmarish head straight from hell.

"It's, it's…" After several seconds of frozen silence, Kindaichi gasped breathlessly. "S-s-so Ta-Také has been murdered."

Furudate and the policemen nodded once in silence.

"A-and the murderer cut off his head and switched it with the head of the chrysanthemum doll."

The lawyer and the policemen nodded again.

"B-but why go to such t-trouble?"

No one said a word.

"It's not like it hasn't been done before, decapitating the victim. We find headless corpses once in a while. But in those cases, the murderer cuts off the head to conceal the identity of the corpse and invariably hides it somewhere. But this—why is this head displayed so conspicuously in a place like this?"

"That's the question, Mr. Kindaichi. The murderer, who-ever it is, murdered Také, and for some reason decided not to leave the body untouched, but cut off the head, brought it all the way here, and exchanged it with the head of the chrysanthemum doll. But why?"

"Why indeed?" echoed Kindaichi. "Whatever for?"

"I wish I knew." It was the chief of the Nasu Police Department. His name was Tachibana—a pot-bellied man of rather short but imposing build, with a small, grizzled head on top of his stocky body. His nickname was Badger.

Chief Tachibana and Kindaichi were already acquainted, for, as the reader knows, our detective was questioned by the Nasu police after Toyoichiro Wakabayashi was murdered. Chief Tachibana had subsequently made inquiries to the

Tokyo police regarding Kindaichi's background and must have received answers exceedingly flattering to the private investigator, for ever since then, though still half in doubt, he had regarded this inconsequential-looking, stuttering man of smallish build and uncombed hair with curiosity and a certain awe.

Kindaichi looked once again at the ghastly chrysanthemum dolls—the now headless Tankai, standing like an evil spirit in the shadowy depths at the back of the stage, Také's grotesque head lying by Tankai's feet, and, what was more, beside them the dolls resembling Sahei and Tamayo and even Kiyo and Tomo, decked out in kimonos of colorful chrysanthemums and standing prim, proper, and aloof. The dismal sound of raindrops striking the oilpaper of the latticed awning provided accompaniment to the unearthly scene.

Kindaichi wiped the perspiration that had risen to his brow. "So…"

"So?"

"So, where's the body? What's happened to the body from the neck down?"

"We're looking for it right now. It shouldn't be far off. As you can see, this *Chrysanthemum Garden* set has not been disturbed much, so the crime must have been committed elsewhere. If we can find that…"

Chief Tachibana stopped in mid-sentence, for he saw several detectives hastening noisily toward him. When one of them ran up and whispered something in his ear, the chief lifted his eyebrows sharply, then quickly turned to Kindaichi. "We've found the scene of the crime. Come with us."

With the chief and his men leading the way, Kindaichi and Furudate followed, walking shoulder to shoulder.

"Mr. Furudate?"

"Yes?"

"Who first found that… Také's head?"

"It was Monkey."

"Monkey?" Kindaichi looked apprehensive.

"Yes. Once every morning, Monkey goes around the grounds tending to the chrysanthemums. But this morning, when he came to the garden—well, you saw what he found. So, he called me immediately. It must have been a little past nine. When I heard, I rushed here at once and found an unbelievable commotion. All the members of the clan were gathered in front of the chrysanthemums, and Takeko was crying and screaming like she had gone mad. But then, of course, who could blame her?"

"What about Matsuko and Kiyo?"

"Oh, yes, they were there, too. But as soon as they saw Také's head, they went straight back to their quarters without saying a word. I tell you, I have trouble dealing with those people. Kiyo's face is always hidden behind that mask, and Matsuko, as you know, is so strong-minded she hardly ever lets her emotions show. I haven't the faintest idea what they felt when they saw Také's head."

Kindaichi remained pondering the situation in silence, but soon, as if remembering something, said, "By the way, that scroll, the one with Kiyo's hand print. Could it be that Také had that scroll on him last night?"

"Oh, no. They gave that to me for safekeeping. It's right here in my portfolio." Furudate tapped the portfolio under his arm and continued, suddenly in a raspy voice, "Mr. Kindaichi, are you thinking that Také was killed on account of that scroll?"

Kindaichi did not answer but said, "Did the members of the Inugami clan all know that you had that scroll in your possession?"

"Yes, except for Matsuko and Kiyo. It was after those two had left that we had a discussion and decided that I should keep the scroll."

"So Matsuko and Kiyo did not know."

"That's right. Unless someone told them."

"Told them? No, I think we can put that possibility aside. After all, they had just had a very emotional confrontation with the others, hadn't they?"

"Yes, that's true. But I can't believe they would…"

By this time, Chief Tachibana and his men had reached the boathouse by the lake. It was where Kindaichi, in the boat rowed by Monkey, had first arrived at the Inugami estate on the day Sahei's will had been read. The boathouse was a rectangular, box-like building made completely of reinforced concrete, and its roof had been converted into a covered observation deck.

The chief and his troop climbed up the narrow staircase leading to the observation deck. Kindaichi and Furudate followed, but as soon as they reached the top of the stairs, Kindaichi's eyes widened at what he saw. There was a round wicker tea table surrounded by five or six matching chairs, one of which lay overturned. A huge pool of blood covered a part of the floor.

There was no mistake; the murder had been committed here. The body, however, was nowhere to be found.

# The Chrysanthemum Brooch

"Chief, the crime was committed here. The murderer must have killed Také, cut off his head, and then thrown the body into the lake from here. See?"

There was indeed a thin, red trail that led from the pool of blood to the edge of the observation deck. Following the trail and standing at the edge, one could see the waters of the lake directly below, as the rain carved dismal circles on the waves lapping against the wall of the building.

"Damn," Chief Tachibana muttered in disgust as he peered into the water. "We're going to have to drag the lake."

"Is it very deep around here?"

"No, it's not that deep, but look over there," said the chief, pointing to a spot on the lake about fifty meters away, "there where you see those large wave patterns. That's called 'Seven Cauldrons' and it's got a hot spring bubbling up from the bottom. It causes a slow but constant circular current in this part of the lake, so that if the body were thrown into the water from here, it's no doubt been carried off far away by now."

Just then, one of the detectives came up to Tachibana. "Chief, we found this." It was a gold, chrysanthemum-shaped brooch about three centimeters in diameter with a large ruby in the middle. "We found it over there, near the overturned wicker chair."

Chief Tachibana and Kindaichi heard a strange cry escape Furudate's lips, and whirling around in surprise, they found him staring intently at the brooch.

"Mr. Furudate, do you know anything about this brooch?"

Furudate took out his handkerchief and hurriedly wiped his brow. "Well, yes…"

"Whose is it?" pressed Tachibana.

"I think it belongs to Tamayo."

"Tamayo?" Kindaichi took a step forward. "But even if the brooch belongs to Tamayo, that doesn't necessarily mean she's connected with this murder, does it? She could have dropped it long before last night."

"But…"

"But, what?"

"But that can't be. I clearly remember her having this brooch on last night. Yes, clearly. Last night, as I was leaving, I accidentally bumped into her, and this brooch got caught on my vest. That's why I remember it so well."

Furudate nervously wiped the sweat from his neck, as the chief and Kindaichi exchanged meaningful glances.

"About what time was that?"

"Oh, a little before ten. It was just as I was leaving."

So Tamayo must have come to the observation deck after the little incident with Furudate, but what business could she have had here at such a late hour?

Just then, they heard footsteps from the direction of the stairs, and up popped Monkey's ugly face.

"Uh, Mr. Furudate?"

"Yes? What do you want?" Furudate approached Monkey and exchanged a few words with him, but returned immediately. "Matsuko wants to see me," he said. "I'll be right back."

"Alright," said Chief Tachibana. "Oh, and if you're going, would you mind asking Tamayo to come here?"

"I'll do that."

Furudate departed, but Monkey showed no signs of leaving and remained standing midway up the flight of stairs, glancing nervously around the observation deck.

"Monkey, is there anything else you want?"

"Yeah, well… something a little strange's happened."

"Strange?" asked Chief Tachibana.

"Yeah, one of the boats is gone."

"A boat?"

"Yeah. Every morning I go and look around the grounds, checking to see everything's alright, like. But this morning, as soon as I got up, I came downstairs here, and the sluice gate was open. I remember closing that gate for sure yesterday before it got dark, so I thought something strange's going on. I looked inside the boathouse and, sure enough, one of the three boats was gone."

Chief Tachibana and Kindaichi looked at each other in surprise.

"So, you're saying that someone must have rowed out in that boat during the night."

"Don't know that. I just know one of the boats is gone."

"And the sluice gate was open."

Monkey nodded sullenly.

Instinctively, Kindaichi looked back toward the lake, but there was nothing like a boat anywhere on the rain-splattered waters.

"Do your boats have any kind of mark on them?"

"Yeah, they've all got INUGAMI printed in black on the side."

At the chief's whispered command, three detectives rushed down the stairs, no doubt to search for the missing boat.

"Monkey, thank you very much. If you notice anything else, please let me know."

Monkey bowed awkwardly and padded down the stairs.

Chief Tachibana turned toward Kindaichi. "Mr. Kindaichi, what do you think? Do you think the murderer put Také's headless corpse into the boat and transported it somewhere?"

"I'm not sure," said Kindaichi, looking out over the misty lake. "If so, that would mean the murderer is an outsider, since whoever it is has left in the boat and hasn't come back."

"Not necessarily. The murderer could have weighted the body and thrown it into the lake, rowed to shore somewhere, and then hiked over the hills to return here."

"But that would be awfully dangerous. If the killer's going to put the severed head so ostentatiously on display like that, there's no reason to take such a risk hiding the body."

"Hmm. I guess that's so."

Chief Tachibana stood staring abstractedly at the gruesome pool of blood, but all at once shook his head fiercely. "Mr. Kindaichi, I don't like this case. Why decapitate the body? Why put the head on the chrysanthemum doll? I don't like it at all. It just gives me the chills."

Just then, Tamayo came up the stairs. She was pale and her eyes wide and sharp, but her loveliness was unchanged. No, her frightened, somewhat helpless air even seemed to enhance her beauty—a tender, melancholy beauty like that of a fragile flower languishing in the rain.

Tachibana coughed lightly and said, "Thank you for coming. Please sit down."

Tamayo glanced at the grisly pool of blood and grew wide-eyed in fear for an instant, but quickly averting her face, sat down awkwardly in one of the wicker chairs.

"I asked you to come because I want to know if you recognize this brooch."

When she saw the chrysanthemum brooch in the palm of Tachibana's hand, Tamayo stiffened for a moment. "Yes, I do. It's… it's mine."

"I see. And do you have any idea when you misplaced it?"

"Yes. Probably last night."

"Where?"

"I believe it must have been here."

Tachibana and Kindaichi quickly exchanged glances. "Then you came here last night?"

"Yes."

"Around what time?"

"About eleven, I think."

"What made you come to a place like this at such a late hour?"

Tamayo was kneading her handkerchief in her hands, kneading and kneading until it seemed she would tear the cloth in two.

"Listen, now that we've come this far, why don't you just let it out. Tell us everything. Exactly why did you come up here?"

Seeming to come to a decision, Tamayo lifted her face with determination. "To tell the truth, I met with Také here last night. There was something I wanted to discuss with him in private."

The blood had drained completely from her cheeks.

Tachibana threw another glance at Kindaichi.

# The Fingerprint on the Watch

"You met with Také here last night?"

All at once a slight hint of suspicion flickered in Chief Tachibana's eyes. Kindaichi too frowned with a puzzled look and stared at Tamayo's pale, bloodless profile, sphinx-like in its inscrutability.

"What business did you have with him? Or, no, I suppose it was Také who asked you to come."

"No, that's not right," Tamayo stated crisply. "I was the one who asked him to come and meet me here about eleven last night." Having said that, she turned her eyes hesitantly toward the surface of the lake. The wind must have picked up, for the rhythm of the rain beating on the waters grew more violent and chaotic, portending a storm.

Tachibana and Kindaichi looked at one another again.

"Oh, I see." Tachibana cleared his throat with effort. "And? What business did you have with him? You said you had something you wanted to discuss with him in private."

"Yes, that's correct. There was something I wanted to tell Také in secret, without letting anyone else know."

"And that was?"

Tamayo suddenly turned her eyes from the lake back to the chief's face. "Yes, with all that has happened, I will tell you everything, frankly and honestly," she said with a steady gaze, as if she had made up her mind, and began her curious tale.

"Mr. Inugami was very good to me. Ever since I was a child he always treated me with love and kindness, as if I were his granddaughter. I'm sure both of you know that already."

Indeed Kindaichi and Tachibana knew it very well. The old man's affection for Tamayo was obvious from the contents of his will.

Seeing the two of them nod in silence, Tamayo continued, a faraway look coming to her eyes. "One time, Mr. Inugami gave me a watch. Not recently—it was when I was still in pigtails. A Tavannes pocket watch, a hunter, that Mr. Inugami had. It wasn't a lady's watch, but child that I was, I had fallen in love with it for some reason, and whenever I was near Mr. Inugami I would ask him to take it out of his pocket and let me touch it. Then, one day, he laughed and said, 'If you like it so much, Tamayo, I'll give it to you. It's a man's watch, though, so you won't be able to carry it with you when you grow up, but… Yes, I know, you can give it as a gift to the man you marry. Until then, you take good care of it, alright?' He was joking, of course, but saying that, he gave the pocket watch to me."

Chief Tachibana and Kindaichi, looking confused, stared at Tamayo's profile. What connection did this watch have with the events of last night? Both men, however, hesitated to interrupt her. Instead they waited silently, for they saw that despite the grisly situation they were involved in, a look of indescribably tender love had flooded over Tamayo's brows, eyes, and lips as she had spoken about the late Sahei.

Still with a dreamy look, Tamayo continued her strange tale. "I was so thrilled. I always kept the watch with me, even putting it by my pillow when I went to bed. Tick-tock, tick-tock—listening to that clear, sharp sound was such a delight.

110

I treasured it. But being a child, I'd sometimes damage it—winding it too tight or accidentally getting it wet. When that happened, it was always Kiyo who would fix it for me."

At the mention of that name, Tamayo's fairy tale of long ago gradually began to acquire an air of reality. The two men's expressions became more tense.

"Kiyo and I are only three years apart, but he was always very skillful with his hands, even as a boy, and he loved working with mechanical things. He was very good at doing things like assembling a radio or building an electric train, so repairing my watch was a piece of cake for him. 'Tamayo, did you break your watch again? Shame on you,' he'd scold me. But when he saw me looking so sad, he'd say, 'Okay, I'll fix it. It'll be ready tomorrow; I'll fix it for you tonight.' And the next day, he'd place the watch in my hand, as good as new, always smiling, laughing teasingly, saying, 'Tamayo, you have to take better care of your watch. After all, you're going to give it to the man you marry when you grow up, aren't you? You have to treat it with more tender loving care,' he'd say, poking my cheek gently with his forefinger."

As she told her tale, Tamayo's cheeks colored ever so slightly, and her beautiful eyes glistened more brightly, as if they had become moist.

Kindaichi pictured Kiyo, with his sinister rubber mask. Today, there was no trace of the past in that hidden, disfigured face, but the features of the mask that had been made identical to his former self were indescribably handsome even in their eeriness. His photograph in *The Life of Sahei Inugami*, too, showed that Kiyo had been an extremely attractive young man. No doubt he had inherited his looks from Sahei, who had even aroused homoerotic passions in Tamayo's late grandfather, Daini Nonomiya.

The episode Tamayo related had probably taken place when she was still in elementary school and Kiyo in junior high. What emotions had stirred between this young, doll-like pair? And what plans had Sahei made for them as he watched them?

Kindaichi suddenly remembered the scene with Monkey's chrysanthemum dolls. In the kabuki play *Chrysanthemum Garden*, the former general Kiichi presented the young lord and warrior Ushiwaka, who had entered his household disguised as a servant, not only with his secret book of military tactics but with his daughter Princess Minazuru as well. Among Monkey's chrysanthemum dolls, Kiichi had been made to look like Sahei, while the young hero Ushiwaka resembled Kiyo, and Princess Minazuru, Tamayo. Did this mean that Sahei had planned from long ago to make Kiyo and Tamayo husband and wife and to bestow upon them not the secret book of military tactics, as in the play, but the ax, zither, and chrysanthemum—the right to inherit the Inugami fortune?

Of course, it was Monkey, not Sahei, who had made the chrysanthemum dolls, so Kindaichi could not be certain that they reflected Sahei's wishes. Besides, Monkey was not a man of normal intelligence. Could it not be, however, that with the God-given instincts of such individuals, instincts that are so often sharper than those of ordinary people, Monkey had subconsciously guessed Sahei's feelings? Or perhaps, fond of Monkey's naive directness, had Sahei secretly told him his plans? If that were so then Monkey might have made the dolls as a comment on the Inugami clan's recent

situation. Laying aside the question of Sahei's possible intentions, therefore, Monkey, for one, must have felt that Kiyo
should be Tamayo's husband and that the three heirlooms
should be presented to them and them alone. But Kiyo...

But Kiyo was no longer the Kiyo of yesteryear. Those
handsome features had been totally destroyed.

Remembering that horribly mutilated, disgusting mass of
flesh he had seen that day, Kindaichi felt a shudder of horror
and was overwhelmed by a hopeless gloom. His meandering
thoughts, however, were soon interrupted when Tamayo,
after a period of silence, once again began to speak.

"During the war, something went wrong with my watch
again, but by then Kiyo, who had always fixed it for me, was
no longer in this house. He had been drafted and was fighting on the battlefields somewhere in Southeast Asia."

Tamayo's voice faltered a bit, but quickly clearing her
throat, she continued. "I just couldn't bear to take that watch
to a shop to be repaired. For one thing, I had heard from
time to time that with such a fine watch, there was a danger
they would switch the movement for something inferior.
The other reason was that I had come to feel that the only
person who should ever repair that watch was Kiyo. I didn't
want to hand it to anyone else, even for a short while. So,
for a long time now, the watch has not kept accurate time,
but since Kiyo has finally returned..." Tamayo hesitated a
moment but quickly seemed to urge herself on, "and seems
to have gotten quite settled now, I took the watch to him
several days ago and asked him to repair it."

Kindaichi suddenly became very interested. As was his
habit when thus aroused, he began enthusiastically scratching his head. He did not yet understand what exactly Tamayo

wanted to say or what thoughts lay in her mind. Nevertheless, there was something that was exciting him intensely, and he continued scratching his head with wild abandon. "A-a-and did K-K-Kiyo repair the watch for you?"

Tamayo slowly shook her head. "No, he took it in his hand and looked at it for a while, but said he didn't feel like repairing it then and would do it some other day. Then he handed the watch back to me." Having spoken thus, Tamayo fell silent. Chief Tachibana and Kindaichi, expecting more, watched Tamayo's face with bated breath, but she remained turned toward the lake and seemed loath to open her mouth again.

Tachibana looked confused and scratched the side of his head with his little finger. "I see. And what does this have to do with the events of last night?"

Tamayo did not answer his question, but abruptly turned her account in another direction. "I'm sure you both know what happened in this villa last night. There was a big fuss because Také and Tomo brought back Kiyo's hand print from Nasu Shrine and tried to use it as, what's the right word…" Tamayo shuddered slightly, "evidence?—yes, though that's an unpleasant word—as evidence to check Kiyo's identity. For some reason, Mrs. Matsuko obstinately refused to let Kiyo give them his hand print, and all Také's and Tomo's efforts came to naught. But then I suddenly remembered something. The other day, as I told you, I went to ask Kiyo to repair my watch, and he refused. After returning to my room, though, I just happened to open the lid, and saw Kiyo's right thumbprint pressed clearly on the back of it."

Kindaichi suddenly jerked as if struck by lightning. Yes, this was what had been exciting him so intensely. Kindaichi again began furiously scratching his head this way and that, his hair now a tangled mess. Chief Tachibana, appalled, stared at him for a while, but eventually turned back to Tamayo and said, "But how could you be certain that was Kiyo's fingerprint?"

Stupid question! Wasn't it obvious? Tamayo spoke as if Kiyo's fingerprint had been pressed there accidentally and she had later discovered it accidentally, but how could that be true? No doubt she had planned ahead and set a trap for Kiyo, intending from the first to get his fingerprint somewhere on the watch. Yes, this was what had been exciting Kindaichi so intensely—what an intelligent and, at the same time, what a cunning woman Tamayo was.

"I don't think there could be any mistake. I wiped and polished the watch completely before taking it to Kiyo, and the only two people who handled the watch were he and myself. Since that print is not mine…"

I'm right, Kindaichi thought. Tamayo had wiped the watch clean, planning to obtain Kiyo's fingerprint. How ingenious she was, though, to think of the back of the lid. What better place to preserve a fingerprint.

Tachibana, too, finally seemed convinced. "I see. And?"

"Yes, and…" Tamayo kept searching for words. "And, seeing Mrs. Matsuko's attitude last night, I knew we could not hope to obtain Kiyo's hand print any time soon. But to leave the situation as it was would mean making Také and Tomo, and their parents as well, even more suspicious. So, when I remembered Kiyo's thumbprint on the watch, I felt it best to make things certain as quickly as possible, and at the risk of being a little presumptuous, I decided to ask Také to compare it with the hand print on the scroll."

"I see, and you asked Také to come here to speak to him about that."

"Yes."

"That was about eleven last night?"

"It was exactly eleven when I left my room. I knew that if Monkey found out, he would insist on coming along. I couldn't have that, so I first retired to my bedroom and then waited until eleven to sneak out."

"Just a minute," Kindaichi interjected for the first time. "Could you please tell us what happened then in detail? If it was exactly eleven o'clock when you left your room, then that means it must have been about two or three minutes past eleven when you arrived here. Was Také already here?"

"Yes, he was. He was standing by the edge there, looking out over the lake and smoking a cigarette."

"When you came up the stairs to this observation deck, was there anyone else about?"

"I don't know. I didn't notice anyone. But it was so cloudy and dark last night, I don't think I would have noticed even if someone had been."

"I see. Then, you told Také about the watch."

"Yes."

"And the watch?"

"I gave it to him. He was very happy and said he would ask Mr. Furudate to bring the scroll over first thing tomorrow and compare the prints."

"What did Také do with the watch?"

"I think he put it in his vest pocket." Since Také's body had not been discovered yet, however, they had no way of knowing whether it was still there.

116

"And about how many minutes did you remain here talking?"

"Not more than five, I would think. I didn't want to stay alone with Také in a place like this for very long, so I said what I had to as quickly as possible."

"I see. So you went your separate ways by about seven or eight minutes past eleven. Who left first?"

"I did."

"Then, Také remained behind alone. What was he doing?"

Tamayo suddenly flushed. For some time, she stared straight ahead with blazing eyes, crumpling her handkerchief in her hands. Suddenly she shook her head fiercely, as if angry, and said, "Také acted very rudely toward me. As I started to leave, he suddenly pounced on me, and… I think it must have been then that I lost my brooch. If Monkey hadn't come just then, I don't know what would have happened to me."

Tachibana and Kindaichi exchanged glances. "So Monkey was here, too."

"Yes, I thought I'd managed to sneak out without him noticing, but he had found out and had followed me here. But I'm so thankful now that he did. If he hadn't come…"

"What did Monkey do to Také?"

"I'm not sure of the details. After all, Také had me in his arms and I was desperately trying to free myself. But all of a sudden, Také cried out and fell. Yes, that was when the chair was overturned. Také fell onto the floor. I looked up, and there was Monkey standing there. He helped me, and I ran away from this place as fast as I could. Také was still on the floor on his knees, muttering abuses."

"I see, then the murderer must have come after that,

117

killed Také, and cut off his head. Did you notice anyone as you were leaving?"

"No, I didn't. Like I said, it was pitch black outside. Besides, I was so upset." Tamayo's tale had come to an end.

"Well, thank you very much," Chief Tachibana said. "I'm sorry to have troubled you."

At his words Tamayo stood up, but Kindaichi stopped her. "Just a moment. One more question. What do you think about that masked man? Do you think that really is Kiyo or…"

The blood drained from Tamayo's cheeks. For a long time, she stood staring fixedly at Kindaichi's face, but soon answered in an emotionless voice, "Of course, I'm convinced it's Kiyo. Také's and Tomo's suspicions are absurd."

Yet, Tamayo had deliberately set out to trick him into giving her his fingerprint.

"Thank you very much. That's all, then."

Tamayo acknowledged Kindaichi with her eyes and descended from the observation deck. Almost simultaneously, Furudate returned.

"Oh, you're still here. Matsuko is asking all of you to come to the house."

"Any particular reason?"

"Yes," said Furudate, a slightly bewildered expression on his face. "It's about, you know, the hand print. She says she wants to have Kiyo make a hand print in front of everyone."

# The Abandoned Boat

The wind that had begun to gust earlier became increasingly stormy, and shadowy blasts and rain thrashed the waters of the lake in frenzied fury. As with all mountain storms, a peculiar sense of the surreal hung in the air. The clouds overhead were oppressively low, and the lake groaned as if possessed, while the dark, turbid waters surged, frothed, and tumbled with a fiendishness different from that seen at sea. Anyone daring to peer into the depths of the lake would have quaked at seeing the eerie masses of dark weeds intertwining, tangling, and rubbing against each other like a woman's hair. A single bird, propelled by the wind, darted diagonally across the lake like a spirit.

Surrounded by this raging storm, the twelve-mat room deep inside the Inugami villa was fraught with tension. Among the members of the clan once again assembled before Sahei's photograph, inner conflicts no less violent than the storm outside were seething in ominous silence. The masked Kiyo sat with Matsuko at the head of the room, with the hand-scroll from Nasu Shrine. In addition, a sheet of white paper, an inkstone with red ink, and a brush were placed in front of them. Takeko, the mother of the murdered Také, sat limp and dispirited, eyes red from weeping, but she shot looks in Matsuko's direction that bristled with inordinate hostility. Tomo, with frightened eyes, constantly bit his fingernails.

Kindaichi studied the faces of the people in the room, one by one, but it was Tamayo whom he watched with the most interest. Even he, however, could not fathom her true feelings, for she simply sat pale and icily beautiful. Surely she harbored serious doubts about the masked man, scheming as she had to obtain his fingerprint, and now that he had voluntarily stepped forward to give them his hand print, her mind must be racing. Yet Tamayo simply sat cold and exquisite.

A man immediately identifiable as a policeman entered the room and, acknowledging everyone with his eyes, seated himself next to Chief Tachibana. He was a forensics officer the chief had summoned, and his name was Fujisaki.

"Mrs. Matsuko," Tachibana said quietly, prompting her to begin.

Matsuko nodded and said, "Before I ask Kiyo to make a hand print, I would like you all to hear something." She cleared her throat softly. "I'm sure you have already heard, Chief Tachibana, but a scene similar to this one occurred last night in this very room. Také and Tomo tried to force Kiyo to give them his hand print. At that time, I refused flatly, because they were so rude, treating Kiyo like a common criminal. I was so mortified, I swore to myself that I would never, ever let Kiyo do anything so undignified. Now, however, everything has changed, since this terrible tragedy has befallen Také, and..." Matsuko glared at Takeko, "these people seem to think that Kiyo and I were involved in some way. Even though they say nothing, I can see it in their eyes. Thinking back, though, I guess I can understand their feelings. I admit we may be partly to blame. The fact that I refused so stubbornly last night to let Kiyo make a hand print—if that caused them to suspect that we might have something to hide, or caused them to think we might have killed Také, then that was bad judgment on our part. I regret the way I acted, and I realize that circumstances forbid my being stubborn any longer. So, I've decided to have Kiyo make a hand print in front of everyone, with Chief Tachibana as witness. I hope you all now understand how I feel."

Matsuko looked around at the others in the room, but no one gave an audible reply. Only Chief Tachibana answered with a nod.

"Alright, then, Kiyo."

The masked Kiyo held out his right hand, trembling with what was no doubt excitement. Matsuko dipped the brush deep in the red ink and spread it over his hand until it was bright red.

"Now, the paper." Kiyo spread his fingers wide and placed his hand full on the white paper. Pressing down firmly on his hand, Matsuko looked around at the others in the room with spiteful eyes. "Look, everyone," she said. "Kiyo's hand print. No fraud, no tricks. Chief Tachibana, you've witnessed it, alright?"

"Yes, of course. You can move your hand now."

Kiyo lifted his hand, and Tachibana approached and picked up the sheet of paper. "Where's the scroll?"

"I have it." Furudate took the scroll out of his portfolio and handed it to Chief Tachibana.

"Okay, Fujisaki, I'm giving these to you," said the chief. "How long before you'll know for sure?"

"Well, it will take some time for me to write an accurate scientific report, but just to determine if the two hand prints are identical or not, I should only need an hour."

"Good. Then, get to work. I should tell everyone in this room that Fujisaki here is an authority on fingerprints. He may be working in these rural parts, but you can rely on his expertise completely. Alright, Fujisaki, we're depending on you."

"Yes, sir."

As Fujisaki stood up to go with the two hand prints, Matsuko stopped him. "Just a minute. You said an hour?"

"Yes, I'll come back here to report in an hour's time."

"Fine. Then would everyone come back to this room in an hour? Chief Tachibana, Mr. Furudate, Mr. Kindaichi, I have some food prepared for you in another room, so please help yourselves. Kiyo, let's go." Matsuko took the masked Kiyo's hand and they stood up.

The others, too, left the room, with a variety of expressions on their faces. Tachibana looked relieved. "Well, that's that. I think the tension's made me a little hungry. Mr. Furudate, Mr. Kindaichi, let's avail ourselves of their hospitality."

Guided by the maid, the three men retreated to another room. They had just finished eating when two detectives, soaked to the skin, came bustling in. They were two of the men who had gone to find the missing boat.

"Chief, could I speak to you?"

"How's it going?" asked Tachibana. "You must be hungry. They've prepared some food for us, so why don't you two help yourselves, too."

"Yes, we will, but before that, there's something we'd like you to come see." From the expression on the detective's face, it appeared that they had found something.

"Okay. Mr. Kindaichi, why don't you come along, too?"

The storm had intensified further, and the wind blew the rain in torrents from the side. With the detectives in front, the men made their way to the sluice gate, holding their umbrellas at an angle. Two boats moored together with ropes, the one in the back covered with a large piece of canvas, were being tossed on the choppy waters like a couple of leaves.

"You found the boat."

"Yes, we found it abandoned near Kannon Point in Lower Nasu and towed it here. We were lucky. Any later, and the rain would have washed away an important piece of evidence."

Climbing into the front boat, one of the detectives tugged on the rope attached to the boat behind, drawing it closer, and then removed the canvas. Tachibana and Kindaichi stared aghast at the sight. Dark blood covered the inside of the boat and a heavy mass of liquid lay on the floor.

They remained staring with bated breath at this repugnant liquid for some time, but eventually the chief coughed awkwardly and turned to Kindaichi. "Mr. Kindaichi, I'm afraid you were wrong about this one. The murderer did transport the headless corpse in a boat."

Kindaichi stared abstractedly at the rain falling on the pool of blood. "Yes, you're right. I have to admit I was wrong. But, Chief," said Kindaichi, his eyes suddenly feverish, "why did the murderer see a need to do this? Why display the head so conspicuously on top of the chrysanthemum doll like that and yet feel a need to hide the body? I should think that's an awfully dangerous thing to do."

"I don't know. But now that we're sure it was transported in this boat, we're definitely going to have to drag the lake. Detective, will you see to that as soon as you've finished eating?"

"Yes, sir. By the way, Chief, we've learned something else rather strange."

"Strange?"

"Yes, Sawai's supposed to bring the eyewitness, but… Oh, there he is now."

Led by another detective through the pouring rain, there appeared a fortyish man wearing a dark-blue cotton kimono and a dark-blue apron. According to the detective, his name was Kyuhei Shima, and he ran a cheap inn called Kashiwaya in Lower Nasu.

Although now consolidated into a single city, Nasu had been divided into Upper Nasu and Lower Nasu until a decade or so ago. The Inugami estate was located at the edge of Upper Nasu and was separated from Lower Nasu by an unpopulated tract of land stretching along the lake for about two kilometers.

The proprietor of the Kashiwaya Inn began his account. "As I just told the detective here, we had an odd guest last night." According to the innkeeper, the man was clearly a repatriated soldier, for he wore a military uniform and military boots, and had a duffel bag slung over his shoulder. That in itself was not unusual. What was strange was that he had a field cap pulled down over his brow—so low as to hide his eyebrows—and a muffler wound around his neck and face, covering even his nose, so that the only visible part of his face was his two eyes.

At that time, however, neither the innkeeper nor the maid felt wary of him in any way, so he was provided with a room as he requested. After the maid had carried his dinner up to his room, however, she returned to the front desk with a disturbing report. "There's something strange about that man. He still has his muffler on even in his room, and when I tried to serve him his rice, he told me to go away. I think he doesn't want anybody to see his face."

The innkeeper was made a bit apprehensive by the maid's report. When he went up with the register, he found that the man had finished his meal and had again neatly put on his cap and buried his face deep in the muffler. Nothing else seemed out of the ordinary, but when the innkeeper placed the register in front of the stranger, he said, "You write it for me," and dictated the information.

"And here it is," said the innkeeper to Chief Tachibana, showing him the entry in the register: "Sanpei Yamada, age 30, unemployed, 3-21 Kojimachi, Tokyo."

"Sawai, did you make a note of this information?" Tachibana asked the young detective.

"Yes, I did."

"Check it out with Tokyo, although it's probably a fake. Please go on with your story."

Prompted by the chief, the innkeeper continued. "I forgot to tell you, but it was about eight o'clock at night when this man first arrived. Then, about ten, he said he was going to visit someone he knew living nearby, and he went out. Of course, he still had his face completely hidden with his cap and muffler. About two hours later, around midnight, I was thinking maybe I would go and lock the front door, and as I was doing so, he came back. It didn't bother me at the time, but now that I think about it, he was kind of flustered."

"Wait, just a minute," interjected Kindaichi. "Did he have his face hidden then, too?"

"Yes, of course. It turns out I never once got to see that man's face, because early this morning, about five o'clock, he suddenly said he was going and left. He had settled his bill the previous night, but we were all talking about what a strange guest he had been and how there must be something going on, when the maid who had gone to clean his room came back with this."

The innkeeper spread before them a thin cotton towel, the sight of which made Tachibana and Kindaichi grow wide-eyed in spite of themselves. Printed on it were the words "Hakata Friends of Returning Veterans," indicating that it was one of the towels distributed to repatriated soldiers in Hakata. It was smeared with thick, dark blood. Clearly it had been used to wipe a pair of bloody hands.

Kindaichi and Tachibana exchanged glances. The thought that had flashed through their minds was of the masked Kiyo, who had recently been repatriated through Hakata. From eight to ten last night, however, that same Kiyo was supposed to have been surrounded by the members of the Inugami clan in a room deep inside the villa.

# The Mysterious X

The eyewitness account given by the proprietor of the Kashiwaya Inn suddenly hurled a significant mystery into the midst of the first tragedy to befall the Inugami clan. In summary, the tale he told was as follows.

Last night, a man who appeared to be a repatriated soldier came to the Kashiwaya Inn in Lower Nasu, located about two kilometers from the Inugami estate. He wanted a room for the night. For now, let us call him X.

It was about eight o'clock at night when X arrived at the inn.

X made certain that no one saw his face.

X identified himself as Sanpei Yamada, unemployed, of 3-21 Kojimachi, Tokyo.

X went out of the inn at about ten o'clock saying he was going to visit an acquaintance living nearby.

X returned to the inn around midnight, seeming somewhat disconcerted.

X left the inn about five o'clock the following morning, saying he had remembered a sudden errand.

A bloody towel, printed with the words "Hakata Friends of Returning Veterans," was found in the room in which X had stayed.

This was what was known about X's actions from last night to this morning. Thinking about his actions in conjunction with the previous night's murder at the Inugami estate revealed various interesting correspondences. First of all, based on Tamayo's statement, Také's murder could be estimated as having taken place sometime after 11:10. X, who had left the Kashiwaya Inn around ten, could easily have arrived at the Inugami estate by then.

Second, there was the boat. The bloody boat was discovered in the vicinity of Kannon Point in Lower Nasu, not five minutes away from the inn. Therefore, supposing someone had placed Také's headless corpse in the boat and, leaving the boathouse around 11:30, made his way out to the middle of the lake, thrown the body into the water, and then turned toward Kannon Point, he would still have had plenty of time to reach the Kashiwaya Inn by around midnight. In other words, the timing of X's known actions matched the murderer's in many respects.

"Things are getting even stranger, Mr. Kindaichi. Maybe this man came to Nasu to kill Také."

"Chief, it's too early to come to that conclusion." With eyes that seemed to be peering into a deep abyss, Kindaichi continued, "But putting aside whether this man came to kill Také or not, one thing is certain: that he placed Také's headless body into the boat and rowed out from here. And that's what I find extremely interesting."

"What do you mean?" asked Chief Tachibana, looking searchingly at Kindaichi.

"I keep saying that I just can't think of any reason why the murderer had to hide the headless corpse. After all, with the head so ostentatiously displayed on top of the chrysanthemum doll, it's meaningless to hide the body. Yet the murderer has done this seemingly meaningless thing and at great danger to himself. Why? What was the need? I've been pondering that over and over all this time, but having heard the innkeeper's story, I think I finally know the reason."

"And that is?"

"Chief, why do you think the innkeeper came to the police so promptly about this X? It's because X had left behind an irrefutable piece of evidence, something that couldn't possibly be overlooked: that bloody towel. If he hadn't left that towel behind, I don't think the innkeeper would have been as quick to come to the police, even if X's actions were a bit suspicious. Those kinds of people dread getting involved in police matters more than anything. That being the case, it's likely that X left the towel on purpose, almost as if to tell the innkeeper to report him to the police immediately—isn't that the logical conclusion? After all, I can't believe he would forget such an important piece of evidence accidentally."

"I understand. You're saying that X is drawing attention to himself on purpose."

"That's right. The same thing can be said about that bloody boat—moving a headless corpse that needn't have been moved, and abandoning the blood-soaked boat at Kannon Point right by the inn."

Tachibana's eyes suddenly grew wide, and he stared intently at Kindaichi's face, for he had finally begun to realize what Kindaichi was implying. "Are you saying that man was trying to protect somebody?"

Kindaichi nodded silently.

"Who? Who is he protecting?" Chief Tachibana pressed eagerly, but Kindaichi shook his head lightly and said,

"That I don't know. But no matter who it is he was protecting, one thing's certain: it's someone living in this house, because all X's actions are designed to turn attention away from here. He's trying to make people think that the murderer came from somewhere outside. Thus we can guess that the murderer is someone inside this villa."

"X is a mere accomplice, then, and the real murderer is someone living in this villa."

"Yes, exactly."

"So, who is this X? And what connection does he have with the Inugami clan?"

Kindaichi lightly scratched his head all around. "Th-that's the question, Chief. Who is X? When we find that out, we'll find the murderer, too." Kindaichi faced Tachibana again. "Do you know what I'm thinking right now, though?"

Tachibana contorted his face and looked at Kindaichi, who smiled wryly. "Last night, the whole clan was gathered in that inner room trying to obtain Kiyo's hand print. They failed, but argued about it from about eight to ten. X, meanwhile, appeared at the inn about eight and is said to have stayed there until about ten. This is a very helpful fact. First of all, it saves us a lot of trouble. If he hadn't been at the inn all that time, I would have had to go and check out alibis for every single member of the clan, to see if one of them could have gone to the inn disguised as X."

The chief grew wide-eyed again. "Then you're thinking that X, too, could have been someone from this house."

"No, that's what I would have liked to think, but as I just told you, it's impossible; they've all got alibis. Still, I keep wondering why X was so determined to hide his face. The murder hadn't even occurred yet when X first appeared at the inn, so why was he so careful to hide his face? I can think of two reasons why someone might not want people to see his face. One, he has an ugly scar or some other disfigurement—in other words, someone like Kiyo. Or two, he has something to hide and he knows that people will recognize him."

"I see. The members of the Inugami clan would all be well known around here."

Chief Tachibana started biting his nails quietly. It seemed that this was his habit when he was deep in thought.

"So, Mr. Kindaichi, your guess is that two of the people in this house are accomplices, and that one of them appeared at the Kashiwaya Inn in Lower Nasu last night disguised as X. That X came back here around 11:30, placed Také's headless corpse in the boat and rowed out, disposed of the body in the lake, rowed to shore at Kannon Point, and went back to the inn for the night. That was all to suggest that the murderer had come from outside the house. Then, X left the inn early this morning leaving the bloody towel behind as evidence, returned unnoticed to this house, and has been sitting by as if nothing had happened. That's what you'd like to think."

"But, like I said, because of the family conference last night, everyone has an alibi."

Tachibana's face suddenly grew stern. "I wonder. I wonder if everyone really does have an alibi."

Kindaichi looked again at the chief's face in surprise. "Is there someone without an alibi?"

"Yes, there is. Well, actually, we would have to check it out, but there is someone who would probably find it hard to come up with an alibi."

"Who, Chief? Who's that?"

"Monkey."

Kindaichi felt as if he had been struck by lightning. His hands and feet trembled for a moment, and a chill swept over his body. For a while he remained staring intently at the chief's face, but soon whispered in a soft, almost inaudible voice, "But Chief, according to Tamayo, when Také tried to attack her, Monkey jumped in and…"

"Tamayo's story is unreliable," Tachibana declared flatly. Having said this, however, he coughed awkwardly, seeming to regret his extreme statement, and continued, "Of course, it's just a hypothesis. I'm just saying that if we pursue this line of thinking, such a hypothesis is possible. If, say, Tamayo and Monkey are accomplices, it goes without saying that her story can't be trusted, right? And even if her story is true, if Monkey left Lower Nasu around 10:00, he could have been back here at around 11:10. In any case, I'm sure Monkey didn't attend that family conference, and since everyone else was so involved with it, I doubt anyone paid any attention to what he was doing. Of course, I'll have my men check it out thoroughly just to be sure, but I'll bet there isn't a soul who can attest to where that man was last night. Except for Tamayo, that is."

Tamayo and Monkey! It was only natural for Tachibana to be suspicious. After all, Tamayo had the strongest motive to kill Také and, at the same time, had had a superb opportunity to do so last night. It was Tamayo who had summoned Také to the observation deck and she who had specified an hour that would have provided ample time for X, who had left the inn in Lower Nasu at ten, to reach the estate. Monkey, moreover, was more comfortable with boats than anyone.

Yet, it was not just these peripheral details that fueled Chief Tachibana's suspicion, but a bigger, more fundamental consideration—Tamayo herself. Tamayo had the cunning to formulate such a plan, and Monkey was so blindly devoted to her that he would do anything she commanded. Picturing the striking contrast between the elegant beauty and the ugly giant, Kindaichi felt a nameless fear that made his flesh creep.

# The Koto Teacher

The lakeside Inugami villa had an extremely complex, labyrinthine structure, and it was in an annex deep inside this maze that Matsuko and Kiyo lived. This annex resembled a cul-de-sac in structure, but it was in no way cramped, for it had five rooms, and although it was connected to the main building by a corridor, it even had a separate entrance. In other words, whenever relations became strained with the rest of the villa, all that the inhabitants of this annex had to do was to close off the corridor with what was literally an iron curtain and they could lead their lives completely independent of the others. Moreover, the annex had attached to it another section, a tea-house-like pair of smaller rooms that served as Kiyo's quarters.

Since his repatriation and return to the villa, Kiyo had hardly ever stepped out of his rooms. Day after day he remained there, speaking rarely, even to his mother, Matsuko. Handsome but devoid of all life or expression, the rubber mask always stared fixedly at a dark corner of the room, never allowing anyone to so much as guess what thoughts were brewing beneath. His presence blanketed the Inugami household with an ineffable feeling of dread.

Even Matsuko, his mother, felt her flesh crawl whenever she looked at this silent rubber mask. Yes, even Matsuko feared this masked man, although she tried her best to conceal her feelings.

Today, too, Kiyo was sitting at the low writing desk in his tatami-mat room, staring fixedly out a round window, its paper screen open and the water of the lake raging beyond. Although the rain and wind had grown fiercer, and the waters rolled and churned, a launch and several motorboats were out on the lake braving the elements, no doubt searching for Také's headless corpse.

After a short time, Kiyo unconsciously placed both his hands on the desk and stretched himself upward to better study the scene outside the window. Suddenly, he heard his mother's voice from the main part of the annex: "Kiyo, shut your window. The rain will come inside."

Kiyo jerked at her voice, but he obediently closed the glass window pane, his shoulders at once limp with despondence. As he did, however, his eyes caught sight of something that made his whole body tense. On the well-polished surface of the desk he could see clearly the ten prints his fingers had left when he had stretched himself to look out the window. For a long time, Kiyo remained staring at the fingerprints as if they terrified him, but soon he took a handkerchief from his kimono sleeve and began wiping them off—carefully, repeatedly, as if worried that once might not be enough.

As Kiyo was thus engaged, Matsuko was in the main part of the annex sitting across from an unusual figure: a woman about her age, perhaps a bit older, perhaps a bit younger, with her hair cut short, wearing a plain, dark coat over a plain, dark kimono. One eye protruded as if she had goiter, the other was sunken and blind, and, what was more, she had a large scar on her forehead. Her countenance could have been considered repugnant, yet no doubt because of the discipline and cultivation that emanated from her soul, she seemed refined and noble instead.

This woman was Kokin Miyakawa, a koto master of the Ikuta school, who visited the villa once every quarter-year or half-year from Tokyo. She had a considerable number of students in this area, all the way through Ina, and whenever she came to Nasu she used the Inugami villa as a base from which to visit their homes.

"So when did you arrive, Mrs. Miyakawa?"

"Last night. I considered coming here right away, but since it was a little late in the evening, I did not want to trouble you. I decided to stay at the Nasu Inn."

"Oh, you shouldn't have worried. You know you're always welcome here."

"I would have come if you had been by yourself, Mrs. Matsuko, but I heard that you have many relatives staying here right now." Wrinkling up her nearly sightless eyes, Kokin spoke quietly and calmly, in a thin and delicate voice. "But actually, I'm glad I decided to stay at the inn, because I heard that something horrible happened here last night."

"So you heard about it, too."

"Yes, I did. What an awful thing to have happen. I thought that since you must be frightfully busy, I would just go on to Ina, but I didn't want to leave without saying hello. Really, what a terrible shock."

"I'm so sorry to inconvenience you, but since you're here, I'd like to have a lesson. So even if you do go on to Ina, couldn't you stay in Nasu a little longer and see if things settle down?"

"Well, yes, I guess I could do that."

136

Just then, the maid in charge of Matsuko's annex appeared. "Excuse me, madam, but Chief Tachibana and Mr. Kindaichi would like to see you for a moment."

Taking her cue from the maid, Kokin stood up to go. "I'll be leaving now, Mrs. Matsuko. But even if I do decide to leave for Ina, I'll come see you or phone you before I go."

It was just as the koto teacher was leaving that Tachibana and Kindaichi came into the room. Regarding her diminutive figure from the back, Kindaichi remarked, "An unusual-looking guest."

"Yes, she's my koto teacher."

"She has trouble with her eyes?"

"Yes, it's not that she can't see at all, but…" Matsuko turned toward Tachibana, "Chief, do you have the results on that hand print?"

"No, not yet. But first, I wanted Mr. Kiyo to look at something."

Matsuko looked searchingly at their faces but soon called out to Kiyo. He immediately came from his room.

The chief turned to Kiyo. "Sorry to bother you, Mr. Kiyo, but I'd like you to take a look at this."

When Tachibana spread the blood-soaked towel in front of them, it was Matsuko, rather than Kiyo, who was taken aback. "My God, where did you find a thing like that?"

Chief Tachibana briefly summarized the innkeeper's story. "You see how it's been printed with the words 'Hakata Friends of Returning Veterans,' so I just wondered if Mr. Kiyo might know anything about it."

Kiyo sat silently, thinking, but after a while he turned to Matsuko and said, "Mother, where are the things they gave me at Hakata when I came back to Japan?"

"I put them all together in the closet."

Opening the closet, Matsuko took out a cloth-wrapped bundle and untied it, to reveal various articles—a military uniform, a field cap, and a cloth duffel bag. Kiyo opened the duffel bag and took out a towel from inside. "This is the one I was given." On it were the words "Hakata Fraternal Association for Returning Veterans."

"I see. So, the towels they give out are not always the same. But Mr. Kiyo, do you know anyone who might have had a towel like this? He called himself Sanpei Yamada and gave his address as 3-21 Kojimachi, Tokyo."

"What?" Matsuko cried out sharply. "3-21 Kojimachi?"

"Yes, that's right. Mrs. Matsuko, does that address mean anything to you?"

"Of course it does. That's our address in Tokyo."

Kindaichi suddenly whistled shrilly and began briskly scratching his head this way and that. Chief Tachibana's eyes, too, became tense. "I see. Now it's even more certain that the man at the inn is connected with last night's murder. Mr. Kiyo, do you have any idea who he might be? A war buddy, for example, who might have come to look you up after returning to Japan? Or, say, someone who might hold a grudge against you?"

Kiyo slowly shook his masked head and said, "No, I have no idea. Of course, we were there a long time, so I might have told someone my address in Tokyo, but I can't think of a soul who would come all the way to Nasu."

"Besides, Chief Tachibana," interjected Matsuko. "You said, someone who might hold a grudge against Kiyo. But remember, it was Také, not Kiyo, who was killed."

"Quite right." The chief scratched his head. "By the way, did Mr. Také serve in the military as well?"

"Yes, of course. But he was lucky and was stationed in Japan the whole time. At the end of the war, I think he was at an anti-aircraft artillery site in Chiba or somewhere like that. Takeko would know the details."

"Yes, I'll ask her later. One more thing, Mrs. Matsuko." Tachibana glanced quickly at Kindaichi and then inhaled deeply as if to gather strength. "It's about Monkey. I suppose he, too, was drafted."

"With his physique? Of course he was."

"And where was he at the end of the war?"

"I think he was in Taiwan. Lucky for him, he was able to return to Japan very quickly, though. I think he came back in November of that year. But what about Monkey?"

Tachibana did not answer but said, "If he was in Taiwan, then didn't he also come back through Hakata?"

"Maybe so. I don't really remember very well."

"Mrs. Matsuko," said Tachibana, changing his tone of voice a bit. "Last night's conference, was it only family members who attended?"

"Yes, of course. Well, Tamayo isn't a blood relation, but she's just like family. And Mr. Furudate was there."

"Mr. Furudate was there in a professional capacity. I don't suppose Monkey was there, was he?"

"What?" Matsuko stared at him as if he were out of his mind. "Why on earth would he be there? He's just a servant, and one who only works behind the scenes at that."

"I understand. I just wanted to know where Monkey was and what he was doing last night. I don't suppose you'd know."

"No, I don't. Yesterday evening, he asked for one of my old koto strings, so perhaps he was mending the nets."

According to Matsuko, Monkey was a skilled cast-net fisherman. When Sahei was still alive, Monkey would accompany him fishing, not only on the lake but even as far away as the Tenryu River. During the war, however, nets gradually became harder to come by, and eventually it even became difficult to find the right kind of string with which to repair them. Then, hitting upon an idea, Monkey had untwined some old koto strings into their thin fibers and used them to repair his nets. That had worked so well that he still used them even today.

"Believe it or not, he's very good with his hands. Was there something you wanted to ask Monkey?"

"Oh, no, nothing in particular."

Just then, one of the detectives burst in upon the scene. They had found Také's body.

# Tamayo's Silence

They had the storm to thank for the quick recovery of Také's body. The howling tempest had been hindering every attempt by the police at investigation, but as if to make up for the inconvenience it was causing, it pushed to the surface, much earlier than anyone had expected, the body that had sunk to the depths of the lake.

Hearing the news, Kindaichi and Chief Tachibana rushed to the sluice gate, arriving there just as a man, water streaming from his wide-brimmed waterproof hat and down his long raincoat, was making his way from his motorboat past the milling detectives and uniformed officers.

"Hi, there. Good to see you again."

Greeted unexpectedly by the man in this way, Kindaichi stared at him in surprise. He had seen the face with its wire-rimmed glasses before, but he could not place it. Seeing Kindaichi searching for an answer in confusion, the man chuckled and said, "Have you forgotten me? I'm the priest of Nasu Shrine."

Kindaichi finally remembered. Indeed, it was Oyama, the priest from the other day.

"P-p-please forgive me. You look so different."

"Everybody tells me that," the priest laughed. "But I certainly can't go about dressed in my priest's clothing in this rain. I learned this trick during the war," he said, tapping the traveling bag he was carrying under his arm. No doubt his priest's vestments were inside.

"You came by motorboat?"

"Yes, it's much faster. I debated whether I should in this storm, but you get wet either way. So, I decided to take my chances and come across the lake, and ended up bumping into something unbelievable on the way."

"Také's body?"

"Yes, I was the first to find it. What's more, it was headless. Talk about creepy…" The priest screwed up his face and shook himself like a dog.

"Yes, well, I'm sure the police are thankful you found it."

"See you later, then."

The priest shook the water off his body once more and was starting to leave, carrying his traveling bag, when Kindaichi called after him, "Mr. Oyama, wait."

"Do you want something?"

"There's something I'd like to ask you, so could I see you later?"

"Certainly, any time," the priest replied. "Later, then."

When the priest had gone, Kindaichi finally turned his eyes toward the lake. Outside the sluice gate were a police launch and several motorboats, bobbing on the water like scattered leaves. The body must be in the launch, for policemen with stern expressions, Tachibana among them, were climbing in and out of it.

Kindaichi debated for a moment what he should do, but since he was not particularly interested in the corpse itself, he decided not to board the launch. The doctor and Tachibana could do the forensics work well enough, and there was no reason to subject himself unnecessarily to such an unpleasant sight.

As Kindaichi stood there waiting, Tachibana came out of the launch wiping the sweat off his face.

"Pretty ugly, huh?"

"I know it's my job, but I really wish I didn't have to look at things like that." The chief contorted his face and kept rubbing his forehead with his handkerchief.

"It's Také's body for sure?"

"We'll eventually have to have one of the family members identify it, of course, but fortunately Dr. Kusuda has examined Také several times before and swears it's him." Kusuda was the town doctor who also doubled part-time as the police medical examiner.

"I see. So there's no mistake. Do you know the cause of death yet? There wasn't any particular damage to the head."

"Yes, a single stab wound in the back, toward the chest. The doctor says that, assuming Také was caught by surprise, he probably would have died instantaneously, without so much as uttering a sound."

"And the weapon?"

"He thinks it must have been a Japanese sword of some kind. There are supposed to be quite a few of them in this house. Sahei was an avid collector for a time."

"So, kill him with a thrust of the sword and then cut off the head later. What about the surface where the head was cut off?"

"It was an amateur job. The doctor says the murderer must have had a hard time with it."

"I see. By the way, Chief," said Kindaichi, suddenly speaking more emphatically, "your impression of the headless corpse. Did you see anything there that would make the murderer want to hide it?"

At Kindaichi's question, Tachibana made a wry face and scratched the side of his head. "No, there wasn't anything unusual. I can't think of any reason to go to all the trouble of disposing of that body in the middle of the lake."

"I suppose you've looked in the vest pocket. You know, for the watch Tamayo said she gave him."

"Of course, we looked for it, but it wasn't anywhere on the body. Maybe the murderer took it, or maybe it's lying on the bottom of the lake. Either way, though, I don't think the killer rowed all that way and threw in the body just to hide the watch. No, the reason may be just as you said, Mr. Kindaichi."

Tachibana stood rubbing his chin thoughtfully, when a detective trotted up to him in the rain.

"Chief, Mr. Fujisaki of Forensics is here. He's got the results on the hand print."

"Alright." Tachibana glanced at Kindaichi, with somewhat nervous eyes. Returning his look, Kindaichi, too, swallowed hard. "We'll be right there. Ask the members of the family to gather in the same room."

"Yes, sir."

Leaving his men with detailed instructions, Tachibana joined Kindaichi and they made their way back to the same room where they had previously met with the family. None of the family members had assembled yet, however. They found Oyama sitting alone in his priest's garb, calmly holding a wooden scepter.

As the two men entered the room, the priest squinted at them from behind wire-rimmed glasses and greeted them, "Hello again. Is something going to happen in this room?"

"Yes, but you're welcome to stay. You're concerned in this matter also."

"Wha-what is it? What's going to happen?"

"It's about that hand print, the one we got from your place. We're comparing it with one Kiyo made in front of us a while ago, and the results are about to be announced."

"Oh, I see." The priest squirmed on his seat a bit and coughed awkwardly.

Eyeing Oyama sharply, Kindaichi asked, "Concerning which, I've been wanting to ask you something. Was it your idea, Mr. Oyama, to compare hand prints?"

The priest, in consternation, cast a quick glance at Kindaichi. He immediately shifted his gaze, however, and taking out a handkerchief from the bosom of his kimono, hurriedly wiped the sweat from his brow. Kindaichi observed him steadily. "Just as I thought," he said. "So, there was someone who suggested it to you. I'd thought it strange from the first, how someone like you, who would seem to have no interest whatsoever in criminal investigations, detective novels, and the like, had thought of such things as fingerprints and hand prints. Who urged you to do this?"

"Oh, I wouldn't say anyone actually urged me to do it, but two days ago, a visitor to the shrine asked to see Mr. Kiyo's votive hand print. I myself had forgotten long ago that such a scroll existed and was reminded of it only then. I had no reason to refuse, so I brought out the scroll, and that person studied it in silence for a while and then thanked me and left. That's all. But actually, it was because that was all that happened that I thought it very strange. I kept thinking, what was the purpose of looking at Mr. Kiyo's hand print, when all of a sudden the word 'fingerprint' came to my mind. So, yesterday, I told Mr. Také and Mr. Tomo about the scroll."

Kindaichi's and Chief Tachibana's eyes met. "I see. So that person came to look at the scroll to suggest the idea to you. Who was this individual, Mr. Oyama?"

The priest hesitated a bit but soon said with decision, "It was Tamayo. As you know, she was born and raised at Nasu Shrine, so she often comes to visit."

The moment Tamayo's name was mentioned, Kindaichi and Tachibana exchanged intense glances that crackled with shared understanding. Tamayo again! No, not just again—everything involved Tamayo! What plot hid behind her tantalizing face?

Now, in that same room, Tamayo again sat, as impassive and enigmatic as a sphinx. Even though the other members of the Inugami clan seated around the masked Kiyo and Matsuko were all agitated to some degree, she alone remained prim, proper, and sublimely calm. Kindaichi found her calmness detestable, her impassiveness unpleasant, and what was more, her excessive beauty terrifying.

The room was hushed. The atmosphere was tense: even the forensics specialist Fujisaki seemed nervous and coughed awkwardly. "Now, I would like to announce the results of my investigation. I will submit a more detailed report to the chief here eventually, but at this time I would like to state my conclusions very simply, avoiding all complicated technical jargon."

Fujisaki again cleared his throat. "These two hand prints are identical. Therefore, the man who is sitting there is without a doubt Mr. Kiyo Inugami. These two hand prints attest to that most eloquently."

You could have heard a pin drop—how better to describe the scene? No one said a word. They all sat staring blankly ahead, as if they had not heard anything Fujisaki had said. But Kindaichi had seen her—Tamayo, at that very moment, half-opening her mouth as if to speak. The next instant, however, she had drawn her lips together tight and closed her eyes, reverting to the enigmatic and impassive sphinx. Kindaichi could hardly contain the unspoken impatience seething in the pit of his stomach. What was it that she had started to say?

# Inside the Chinese Chest

It was over. Comparison of the hand prints had proven without a doubt that the man in the strange mask was Kiyo Inugami. Také and Tomo had merely been building castles in the air when they had thought that maybe, just maybe, someone else had come back disguised as Kiyo. Yet why was it that dissatisfaction still hung heavy in the air, despite the clearly stated verdict? Why was it that everyone looked like they were suppressing something they wanted to say?

Alright, so the two hand prints were identical. Was it possible, though, to forge fingerprints in some way? Even if that could not be done, had some trick or gimmick been involved?

Although it was not surprising to see such doubts on the hostile faces of the other family members, why, strange to say, did even Kiyo's mother, Matsuko, seem confused? Why, at the moment Fujisaki declared that the man sitting beside her was without a doubt her son, did an incomprehensible look of agitation pass over her face?

Matsuko, though, was too cool to be disconcerted for long. She immediately composed herself and looked point-edly around at the others in the room with her usual malicious expression. Eventually, she said in her catty way, "You all heard the results. Does anyone want to raise any objections? If you do, please state them here and now."

Of course everyone had objections. They just did not know how they should phrase them. Because everyone remained waiting silently, Matsuko repeated, driving home her point, "Since no one seems to want to say anything, I assume you all have no complaints. In other words, you recognize that this man is Kiyo. Chief Tachibana, thank you very much. Kiyo, shall we go?"

Matsuko stood up, and after her, the masked Kiyo. Was it because his legs were numb from sitting rigid on the tatami so long that he seemed to totter a bit?

Just then, however, Kindaichi noticed it again: Tamayo half-opening her mouth to speak. Breathless, he stared intently at Tamayo's lips, but this time, too, she shut her lips tightly and lowered her eyes.

Matsuko and Kiyo were no longer in the room.

What had Tamayo intended to say? She had started to speak not once, but twice, and her expression and determination had indicated that she was about to say something most important. For that very reason, Kindaichi felt indescribably irritated at her hesitation. In hindsight, he should have insisted that she speak her mind, even if he had to force her, for if she had, he could have solved at least half of the case then and there. More than that, he might have been able to prevent the crimes that were to occur.

"Well," Chief Tachibana said with almost a sigh of relief after the family members had left the room, "at least we've made some progress by verifying that masked man's identity. In these kinds of cases, there's nothing you can do but peel away the mysteries, one by one, like the layers of an onion."

That same day, the body of Také, which had been fished out of the lake, was autopsied and returned to the Inugami villa. According to the autopsy findings, the cause of death was a single stab wound in the back, toward the chest, with death probably occurring sometime between eleven and twelve the previous night. What was interesting, however, was that from the appearance of the wound, it was concluded that Také had been fatally stabbed not with a Japanese sword, but with something like a dagger.

The moment he heard the contents of this report, Kindaichi's interest was aroused. True, a dagger would suffice to take someone's life, but decapitating a corpse with one would be impossible. Did the murderer then have two types of weapons ready, a dagger and something to cut off the head?

In any case, because Také's body had been returned to the family, a perfunctory wake was held that night at the Inugami villa, with Oyama, the priest of Nasu Shrine, performing the services in accordance with the Inugamis' Shinto beliefs. Kindaichi, too, ended up attending the wake, and it was there that he heard a strange story from the priest.

"Guess what, Mr. Kindaichi. I found something interesting the other day." Oyama must have been drunk from the liquor that had been served, for why else would he seek out Kindaichi expressly to tell him such a tale as he then related?

"What did you find?"

The priest grinned wickedly at Kindaichi's question. "Well, perhaps I shouldn't use the word interesting, but it's about old Sahei's secret. It's an open secret, since everyone in these parts knows about it, but recently I found proof."

"What is this secret of Mr. Inugami's you're talking about?" asked Kindaichi, his curiosity piqued.

Oyama contorted his oily face with a sleazy smile. "You know what I mean. Or maybe you don't. No, surely, you must. After all, whenever people tell the story of Sahei Inugami, they always tack this secret on at the end," said Oyama suggestively. "You know that there was a homosexual relationship between Sahei and Tamayo's grandfather, Daini Nonomiya, don't you?"

"W-w-what?" Kindaichi blurted out loudly, but immediately came to himself and glanced around. Fortunately, the others at the wake were all gathered together in a far corner of the room, and no one was paying Kindaichi any heed. Flustered, he gulped down all the tea in his cup.

For Kindaichi, the priest's revelation was a bolt out of the blue. This was one aspect of Sahei's life that was not mentioned in *The Life of Sahei Inugami*, and Kindaichi was hearing about it for the first time.

Surprised in turn by the intensity of Kindaichi's amazement, Oyama blinked and said, "Then you didn't know about this?"

"No, I didn't. *The Life of Sahei Inugami* said nothing about it, even though it went into quite a lot of detail about Sahei's relationship with Daini Nonomiya."

"Of course, it's not something people say out in the open, but everybody around here knows about it. Didn't Mr. Furudate say anything?" Furudate was a gentleman and no doubt had refrained from commenting on other people's private affairs indiscriminately. Yet perhaps this fact—that there had been a homosexual relationship between Daini and Sahei—was somehow affecting the current case.

Kindaichi remained lost in thought for some time, his eyes seeming to peer into a deep abyss. Eventually, however, he looked up and said, "You just said that you had discovered some proof of this. What kind of proof?"

Although the priest had at last begun to show some signs of embarrassment at his indiscretion, he still could not restrain himself from divulging his discovery to someone. "Yes, the proof..." he began, leaning forward and blowing breath reeking of liquor in Kindaichi's face.

According to Oyama, he had recently had to rearrange some articles stored in the shrine treasure hall and had discovered an old Chinese chest there. Hidden beneath dust and piles of junk as it was, he had never noticed it before, but the lid, he saw, had been carefully sealed shut with a strip of paper that had something written on it in ink. So old and black with soot was the paper, however, that he could not discern what was written at first, but after much effort, he finally made out the following characters: "Sealed in the presence of Daini Nonomiya and Sahei Inugami. March 25, 1911."

"March 25, 1911. The date struck a familiar chord. If you have read *The Life of Sahei Inugami*, you know that Daini Nonomiya died in May of 1911. The Chinese chest, therefore, was sealed by the two men a little before Daini passed away. Probably, Daini had realized he didn't have long to live and, together with Sahei, stored something in the chest. That's what I surmised."

"So you broke the seal?"

At Kindaichi's somewhat accusatory tone, the priest hurriedly waved his right hand in remonstrance. "No, no. It's misleading to say I broke the seal. Like I said, the strip of paper was quite old. It was completely moth-eaten, and seal or no seal, the chest came open, just like that, when I lifted the lid."

"I see, so you just happened to look inside. And what did you find?"

"An unbelievable number of documents, enough to fill up the whole chest. Letters, account books, diaries, notebooks—everything on washi paper, since it was a long time ago. I read a few of the letters and found they were, well, love letters that Daini and old Sahei had exchanged. Of course, back then, he wasn't old Sahei but a strapping young man." So Oyama said, and smirked as if someone had tickled him.

He immediately continued, however, as if to justify himself, "Mr. Kindaichi, I don't want you to think that I've been consumed by some kind of vulgar curiosity. I respect Sahei Inugami. I revere him. After all, he was not only a benefactor to all the people of Nasu but the most distinguished man in the Shinshu region as well. I just want to know what this great man was really like. In fact, I'd like to write his biography some day. I want to depict his real, undisguised self, not the glossed-over portrait they give in *The Life of Sahei Inugami*. I'm certain that it would in no way harm his memory but in fact would show his true greatness. For that reason, I intend to examine the contents of that Chinese chest thoroughly. I think I might find some valuable document that no one else has ever known about before."

It was just drunken spiel. Oyama was intoxicated on his own words, and he did not even believe himself. Yet long after everything was over, Kindaichi would still shudder every time he remembered the remarkable secret the priest would soon discover in the Chinese chest and how heavily it would weigh upon this case.

# Pomegranate

Nowadays, it is rare to find a full-scale, all-night wake. In most cases a wake will end in the evening around ten or eleven—a half-wake, if you will. With a family like the Inugami clan, moreover, in which the members despised each other, only the deceased's parents and sister saw any reason to keep vigil by his body throughout the night. Besides, it was not very pleasant to be near a corpse whose head and body had been sewn back together. So, as Furudate, the family lawyer, proposed, the wake was brought to a close at ten.

The storm had abated considerably by then, but ink-black clouds still rushed across the sky, and occasionally the wind, as if recalling its purpose, would blow the lingering rain in gusts from the side. It was after Kindaichi and Furudate had left in this rain that another incident occurred at the Inugami villa.

Compared to the murder of Také the previous night or the two killings that were to follow, this episode might at first glance have seemed trivial, but the full extent of its import was to become clear later on. The incident, again, revolved around Tamayo.

When the wake ended, Tamayo returned immediately to the sitting room in her annex. This annex, like Matsuko's and Kiyo's, was connected to the main part of the villa by a corridor and also had five rooms, its own entrance, and a bathroom, the only difference being that Tamayo's had been designed mostly in Western style. For several years now, Tamayo had lived here with Monkey.

As Tamayo reached her annex, Také's younger sister, Sayoko, came chasing after her, saying that she needed to talk. With all that had happened since morning, Tamayo was completely exhausted and wanted to take a bath and retire as quickly as possible, but she felt she could not refuse Sayoko's request. So, according to Tamayo, she showed Sayoko into her sitting room.

What was the subject of their conversation? "I just wanted to ask her about my brother," Sayoko said. "I heard that he had seen Tamayo right before he was killed, so I wanted to hear from her directly what she remembered about that night." Thus she explained when questioned by the police the following day, and Tamayo corroborated her story. Yet anyone with the least bit of inside knowledge about certain private matters in the Inugami household would have guessed that there must have been more.

Sayoko had come to find out how Tamayo felt—how she felt about Tomo. Sayoko was an unfortunate girl. She was in no way homely, and in fact, on her own, was quite above average in appearance. However, because there was a ravishing beauty, an incomparably exquisite creature, living in the same villa, Sayoko's attractiveness paled in comparison, just as the stars lose their sparkle before the glow of the moon.

Yet until the reading of Sahei's will, Sayoko had never considered herself at a disadvantage to Tamayo. In fact, it would be more correct to say she had thought Tamayo a nonentity. Granted, Tamayo was beautiful. But she was a penniless orphan, a freeloader living on charity doled out by strangers. Sayoko, in comparison, though admittedly less of a beauty, had factors on her side to compensate, and more— her social standing as Sahei Inugami's granddaughter and the guarantee that some day she would come into a share of his enormous fortune. So if a man were to compare her and Tamayo, she was dead sure that, unless he were a fool or a lunatic, he would choose her, Sayoko—as indeed Tomo had done without hesitation.

For some reason, Sayoko had always been fond of her cousin Tomo, even as a child. As she grew older, that emotion had gradually turned to love. Tomo, for his part, did not dislike Sayoko, but it was doubtful whether his feelings were as earnest or sincere as hers. Nevertheless, he accepted her love. Tomo's calculating parents, thinking that a marriage between the two would be the best way to grab hold of as much of the Inugami fortune as possible, in fact strove to ingratiate themselves with Sayoko and prevailed upon their son to do the same.

Now, however, the situation had changed. Sayoko, whom they had thought to be the goose that would lay the golden egg, became worthless to them, while Tamayo, whom they had not so much as noticed before, suddenly glittered with a halo of gold. Not surprisingly, the fickle-hearted Tomo and his parents immediately reversed their attitude and turned as cold as ice toward Sayoko, while they began to fawn shamelessly over Tamayo.

Sayoko probably came that night seeking to learn Tamayo's feelings. It must have been unbearably humiliating for her, yet she still could not keep herself from coming, for ever since morning she had been tormented by heart-wrenching anguish and worry. Now that Také was dead, the likelihood that Tamayo would choose Tomo for her husband had increased tremendously, for, after all, of the two remaining candidates, Kiyo had a face too dreadful to behold.

No doubt, however, it will forever remain a mystery to us what words were exchanged between the two women in Tamayo's sitting room. Wresting that information from Sayoko would be harder than making a stone statue speak; and Tamayo, always discreet, would not say anything that would disgrace Sayoko.

Be that as it may, the two women's conversation came to an end in about half an hour. Having seen Sayoko out, Tamayo immediately turned toward the adjoining bedroom. Her sitting room and bedroom were both Western-style rooms, and there was no way in or out of the bedroom except through the door connecting it to the sitting room. Tamayo could not wait to lie down and rest, so as soon as Sayoko had left, she opened the door to the bedroom and flipped on the light switch on the wall by the door. The moment she did, however, a terrible scream escaped from her throat.

The next day, Tamayo described the events to Chief Tachibana.

"Yes, that's right. The moment I turned on the lights, someone came tearing out of the bedroom. It was so sudden, I can't be precise as to details, but for sure, it was a man in a soldier's uniform. He had on a field cap pulled low over his brow and hid his face with a muffler. So even now, my clearest impression is of his two glinting eyes. He came at me like a whirlwind, and I screamed. Then, he knocked me aside and flew out of my sitting room into the corridor. The rest is as you heard from the others."

"Why was this man hiding in your bedroom? Do you have any idea?"

"I do have a theory," Tamayo replied to Tachibana's query. "I didn't notice last night when I came back to this annex because I was with Sayoko, but checking afterwards, I realized that someone had rummaged through the sitting room. There's nothing missing, though. I think he must have been there looking for something when Sayoko and I came back, so he hurriedly hid in the bedroom. As you can see, this bedroom has only this one exit, and since the windows were all closed, opening one of them would have caused a noticeable sound. So he could do nothing but wait in the bedroom until Sayoko left."

"I see. That would make sense. But what was this man looking for? Do you possess anything that he might want?"

"I have no idea. Whatever he was looking for, though, must have been very small, because he had opened up even tiny drawers that could only hold things like rings and earrings."

"And yet nothing is missing."

"Nothing."

Let us return the account to the actions of the intruder after he had rushed out of Tamayo's room. Tamayo's scream reached even the farthest ends of the extensive Inugami villa, and interestingly, this provided all the members of the family with alibis. Kiyo, first of all, was in his room in Matsuko's annex, a fact that was confirmed not only by Matsuko but by Oyama the priest as well. Oyama was staying at the Inugami villa for the night and had been deep in conversation with Matsuko in her room when they heard the scream.

The priest described what had happened. "Yes, it must have been about half past ten. Mrs. Matsuko and I were

158

talking in her room when all of a sudden, we heard a woman scream. Mr. Kiyo came running in from his room saying it was Miss Tamayo's voice, and then he leapt barefoot into the garden. We were astounded and followed him onto the veranda, but we could no longer see him by then. It was pitch black last night, and unfortunately it had started raining hard again at just about that time."

Toranosuke, on the other hand, was still keeping vigil by his son's corpse with Takeko, as attested to by three maids who were tidying up after the wake. Toranosuke did not even stir when he heard the scream.

Last, Tomo and his father, Kokichi, were preparing to retire in their own rooms. This was witnessed not only by Kokichi's wife, Umeko, but by two maids who had come to lay the futon. When Tomo heard the scream, he turned white as a sheet and dashed out, despite his mother's protestations. Kokichi raced after him.

The one who heard Tamayo's scream from the closest vantage point was, of course, Sayoko. She had come out of Tamayo's room and had reached the middle of the corridor leading to the main part of the house, but when she heard the scream she ran back in alarm. When she came to the entrance of Tamayo's sitting room, she saw two shadows struggling at the far end of the corridor. One of the shadows was a man in military uniform, and the other was Monkey.

"What? You're saying Monkey was struggling with the man in the military uniform?" asked Chief Tachibana. No wonder he was so surprised. The chief had suspected Monkey of being the man in the uniform, but now his theory had been shattered.

"Yes, without a doubt. Not only did I see them with my own eyes, I even talked to Monkey right after that," Sayoko explained.

As the two men struggled, their relative positions became reversed, and at that instant the uniformed man swiftly darted out the French window at the end of the corridor, beyond which was a balcony leading down into the garden.

"I could've run after him, but I was worried about Missy," explained Monkey, recounting his actions of that evening. Because of all the disturbing things that had occurred recently, Monkey had decided to make the rounds of the villa that night. He had mistakenly assumed that the wake would continue until the morning and so had not realized that it had already ended and Tamayo had returned to her annex. Then he heard the scream.

"Nearly jumped out of my skin, I did. I ran up the balcony, in through the French window, and smack into this guy dressed like a soldier. Nah, didn't see his face. He had it hidden with his muffler."

As Monkey and Sayoko, who had both hastened into the sitting room, were tending to Tamayo, Tomo and his father, Kokichi, came running in. They were all arguing about what they should do when they heard another scream—a high-pitched, trailing scream that pierced the driving rain. They looked at each other horror-struck.

"It sounded like a man's voice," Tamayo gasped.

"Yes," Tomo muttered with frightened eyes, "it came from the direction of the observation deck."

"I think it might have been Kiyo," Sayoko whispered with quivering voice, and Tamayo sprang to her feet.

"Let's go," she said. "Let's all go and see. Monkey, bring the flashlight."

It was pouring outside. As they ran together through the rain, Toranosuke and Oyama the priest came up to them from another direction.

"What happened? What was that scream?" barked Toranosuke.

"We don't know," answered Tomo. "We think it might have been Kiyo." They again began running toward the observation deck.

It had indeed been Kiyo's scream. Lying sprawled at the foot of the stairs to the observation deck, he was first discovered by Tamayo, as she stumbled over his prostrate body in the dark and lost her balance. "There's somebody lying here," she said. "Monkey, let me have the flashlight."

The moment the beam from the flashlight illuminated Kiyo's face, everyone cried out and edged back instinctively. Kiyo was not dead, but unconscious. His mask must have come off as he fell, however. Lying exposed for all to see was that hideous face—like a pomegranate that had ripened and burst, the reddish-black, formless mass of flesh extending from his nose to his cheeks. When Sayoko saw it, she screamed and covered her eyes. But Tamayo, for some reason, continued to stare intently into the horrifying countenance.

# Tomo Sharpens His Claws

The following day, Kindaichi was summoned to the Inugami estate, and as he heard the events of the previous night from Chief Tachibana, his face became very thoughtful.

"And what is Kiyo's story, Chief?"

"He says that when he heard Tamayo's scream and rushed out of the house, he saw somebody heading toward the observation deck. He ran after him but was suddenly punched hard at the foot of those stairs."

"I see."

"Now he's totally dejected this morning because they all got to look at his disfigured face to their hearts' content while he was unconscious. He might not care that the others saw him, but having been seen by Tamayo must have been quite a blow."

"Doesn't anyone know where the man in the military uniform went?"

"Not yet, but don't worry, it's such a small town, we'll find out soon for sure."

"Is there evidence that he sneaked in from outside?"

"Oh, yes. There are muddy footprints all over Tamayo's sitting room and bedroom, but finding traces outside the building is proving extremely difficult. As you know, it was still raining last night, and his footprints have been washed away, so we can't tell where he came in or how he escaped."

"Chief, this episode of last night may be very significant. This man who seems to be a repatriated soldier and insists on hiding his face—last night's incident has proven without a doubt that he in fact exists and is not someone living in this house playing two roles, as we had thought."

"Yes, I realized that, too. But Mr. Kindaichi, who could this man be? What part is he playing in this case?"

Kindaichi shook his head slightly. "I don't know. If I did, I might be able to solve this case. But, without a doubt, he must be someone intimately connected with the Inugami clan. He even gave the Inugamis' Tokyo address at the inn. Last night, too, he knew just where to find Tamayo's room."

Tachibana looked at Kindaichi's face with a start. "So that means he knows the layout of the villa quite well."

"Exactly. This villa, as you know, has such a strange and complex structure that I, for example, still can't understand how it is arranged even after visiting several times. If he came with the intent of ransacking Tamayo's room, he must be very familiar with the layout."

Tachibana remained in silent contemplation. After a while, though, breathing in deeply and audibly, he declared with determination, as if trying to convince himself, "We'll find all that out when we catch him. Yes, that's the solution—to catch him. There might have been some oversights in the investigation before, because we thought he might be someone in this house playing two roles, but now that we know that's not the case, we'll catch him soon for sure."

Things, however, did not work out quite as the chief had planned. Despite an all-out effort by the police, they could not ascertain where the repatriated soldier had gone. Where he had come from, however, became apparent soon enough.

A considerable number of people had seen a man matching the description getting off the train at Upper Nasu on the evening of November 15, that is, the day Také was killed. He had probably come from Tokyo, since that was where the train originated. Moreover, quite a few witnesses had also seen him trudging along the road from Upper Nasu to Lower Nasu.

These facts seemed to indicate that it was Upper Nasu, not Lower Nasu, where the man really had business. Lower Nasu had a station of its own, so if that had been his destination, he would have stayed on the train until then. Because he had walked from Upper Nasu to Lower Nasu and stayed at the Kashiwaya Inn, however, there must have been some reason he could not stay in Upper Nasu.

Several people also saw the man after he had left the inn, and since as many as three of them swore to seeing him in the mountains behind the town, the police searched there too but again came up empty-handed. Probably, after leaving the Kashiwaya Inn, the man had hidden himself all that day in the mountains and had returned to the Inugami villa after nightfall. There he had rummaged through Tamayo's room, rendered Kiyo unconscious, and escaped. His subsequent whereabouts, however, were a total mystery.

Thus, as the police grew increasingly impatient, five days passed, then seven—until it was November 25, exactly ten days after Také was murdered. On that day a second grisly killing occurred. The one who occasioned this incident was again the lovely Tamayo.

By November 25, the mountainous country around Lake Nasu already looked wintry. The peaks of the Northern Japan Alps, seen in the distance across the lake, whitened daily, and on some mornings the banks of the lake were covered with a thin layer of ice. Yet when the weather was fine, the days were sparkling and pleasant, making it probably the most refreshing season of the year. The wind could be a trifle chilly, but the warm sunshine reached the depths of one's soul.

That day, Tamayo, yearning for the sunshine, had rowed her boat onto the lake. She was alone, of course, and had not even told Monkey, for ever since the earlier incident with the boat, he had steadfastly refused to let her go out on the lake. Knowing that, she had secretly rowed out anyway, like a child sneaking out of the house to play.

Ever since that earlier incident, Tamayo had felt psychologically under siege. Day after day, she was barraged with questions by suspicious policemen, while the members of the Inugami clan showered her with looks of hatred, malice, and fiery jealousy. She was suffocating.

Even less endurable was the marriage offensive launched by Tomo and his family. Although in the past they would not so much as look at her, now they would shamelessly wag their tails, so to speak, and tag along after her. Tamayo shuddered with loathing.

Out on the lake for the first time in a long while, Tamayo felt her soul cleansed. She even thought about abandoning everything, forgetting everything, and rowing farther and farther away forever. The wind was a bit brisk, but the sun was warm and pleasant, and before long she had reached the middle of the lake. She supposed that the smelt-fishing season must be over, for she could not see any boats on the lake, just a single commercial fishing vessel in the distance casting nets near Lower Nasu. There was no one else about in the hushed stillness of the afternoon.

Tamayo placed the oars inside the boat and lay back, stretching out. It had been a long time since she had looked like this at the sky, so amazingly distant and high, and as she lay there gazing steadily, she felt herself being drawn up toward the heavens. Tamayo softly closed her eyes. Soon, fleeting tears were moistening her eyelashes.

How long she had lain there like that she did not know, but suddenly, she heard a motorboat engine in the distance. At first, Tamayo paid it no heed, but realizing that the noise was gradually approaching, she sat up and turned around. It was Tomo.

"Oh, there you are. I've been looking all over for you."

"Is anything wrong?"

"Chief Tachibana and that man Kindaichi are here, and they want us all to gather because they have something important to say."

"Oh, then I'll head back right away." Tamayo took up the oars in her hands again.

"No, the rowboat's too slow," said Tomo, drawing his motorboat nearer. "Get in. The chief seems to be in a big hurry. He says there's not a minute to lose."

"But the boat…"

"We'll have someone come for it later. Hurry, get in. We mustn't be late or who knows how angry the chief will be."

Neither Tomo's words nor actions were the least bit unnatural, and besides, what he had said seemed quite plausible. Tamayo was deceived in spite of herself.

"Alright, then. I'll do as you say."

Tamayo rowed up close to the motorboat.

"Put the oars in the boat," said Tomo. "It'd be a bother if they were carried away. Here, I'll hold the boat steady, so climb aboard. Careful…"

"Yes, I'm fine."

Tamayo thought she had transferred her weight onto the motorboat smoothly, but just then, one of the boats lurched wildly.

"Watch out!"

She staggered and fell against Tomo. He held out his arm as if to help her. But at that instant, his hand covered her nose with a handkerchief soaked with some sort of liquid.

"What are you doing?" Tamayo struggled furiously, but Tomo's arms clasped her tight, and the wet handkerchief was pressed harder and harder against her nose. She felt a sweet-sour smell race from her nose to her brain.

"No… no…" Tamayo's resistance grew gradually weaker, and soon she was slumped in a deep sleep in Tomo's arms. Tomo gently lifted her disheveled hair off her face, then lightly kissed her forehead and bared his teeth in a grin. His eyes glowing with desire, Tomo gulped and licked his lips like a hungry beast. Then, he laid Tamayo down and, hunched over, started up the motorboat, heading in the opposite direction from the Inugami villa.

Except for the lone kite that flew overhead in slow, lazy circles, not a soul had noticed what had occurred.

# The Man in the Shadows

About four kilometers from Nasu on the opposite shore of the lake is a lonely village called Toyohata. Although it had always been poor, it nevertheless prospered considerably for a while when there was a good demand for cocoons. Now that the export of silk was at an all-time low, however, the whole village seemed devoid of life. Of course it was not just Toyohata Village that was affected in this way; the entire region around Lake Nasu now faced this agonizing fate.

At the western edge of the village flowed a stream, and where it emptied into the lake, the earth and sand it deposited formed a delta that grew larger year by year, encroaching upon the lake. The delta was covered with dead reeds that swayed desolately in the wind.

It was among these reeds and into the mouth of the stream that Tomo's motorboat now glided. He slowed down, and with his darting eyes quickly took in the scene around him, but all he saw were the dead reeds waving forlornly. Not a soul was in the rice paddies or mulberry fields, now that the harvest was over. Only the same lone kite, drawing rings in the sky, observed him from above.

Chuckling to himself at his luck, Tomo began to maneuver the boat upstream between the reeds, hunched over as if hiding himself from sight. Soon, above the reeds before him there appeared a European-style building, a structure that was pitiably dilapidated now but that must have been quite grand in its day.

Why such a building in such a place? Everyone who first discovers it seems to wonder about this, but there is a good reason for its location. Toyohata Village was where the Inugami clan got its start, and this building now visible among the reeds was where Sahei first made his home. Because of the village's inconvenience, however, Sahei eventually moved his business headquarters to Upper Nasu. He also built a new villa there.

Since that time, this house in Toyohata Village had not been occupied, and was preserved only as a kind of family monument. With the war, however, less and less effort could be devoted to its upkeep, and when its caretaker was drafted, there was nothing else to do but let it go to ruin. Now, after Sahei's death, there remained no one with any affection for the old house, and it had been left to grow increasingly dilapidated. The villagers had taken to saying it was haunted. It was toward this house that Tomo now seemed to be heading.

No doubt in the old days, this building had looked out directly onto the lake. Now, however, the ever-growing delta separated it far from the water's edge, and it stood alone, as if forgotten, among the desolate reed beds.

Tomo navigated the boat up the stream and rammed it into a reed bed by the house. This far in, the water was shallow and the mud deep, so maneuvering was not easy. Finally, though, he managed to moor the motorboat between the thick clumps of reeds and leaped out, causing several alarmed birds to flap and fly out from the base of the reeds. "Damn! What the…!" Frightened, Tomo swore in vexation. He could not leave the boat where it might be seen, so he pulled on the mooring line, drawing the boat closer, and soon he managed to hide it among the clumps of reeds. Relaxing at last, he wiped the sweat from his brow and looked on Tamayo's face as she lay unconscious on the bottom of the boat. Tomo felt a thrill run through his body. How beautiful she was, lying sleeping so innocently! Traces of her short-lived struggle as she was being overcome by the drug still remained in her disheveled hair and knitted eyebrows, but even that did not detract from her beauty. Sunshine filtering through the reeds made golden spots of light dance on her cheeks, moist with perspiration. Her breathing was a bit rapid.

Tomo gulped in anticipation, then glanced quickly around, as if someone was looking over his shoulder at this delectable treat. He remained thus for some time crouched on the reed bed, gazing at Tamayo's sleeping figure in the boat. For one thing, it was a sight he could never tire of watching; and, for another, he still seemed to be having trouble making up his mind. Huddled among the reeds, Tomo continued biting his nails and watching Tamayo's sleeping face. He was like a child who had started a bit of mischief but who could not decide if he should carry it through to the end. The exquisite beauty of his target was unnerving him all the more.

"Oh, the hell with it. What does it matter? I'm going to have her sooner or later anyway." Muttering to himself, Tomo quickly extended his arms and lifted Tamayo. The motorboat lurched violently, and loaches splashed in the mud among the reeds.

The weight and warmth of Tamayo's body in his arms, her virginal fragrance like fresh-picked fruit, the pulsing of the blood beneath her silken skin—Tomo already felt overcome with excitement. Nostrils flaring and eyes bloodshot, he proceeded through the reeds carrying Tamayo. He was perspiring profusely, sweat pouring down his cheeks, even though the November air was biting cold.

Beyond the reed beds were the remains of a wooden fence, originally painted white but now lying mostly broken, rotted, and covered with mud and dirt. The sight inside the fence, too, was depressing, for the entire grounds were buried under dead leaves. Hastening past the fence with Tamayo in his arms, Tomo then stepped slowly through the dead leaves, edging closer and closer to the empty house, like a fox with its prey in its jaws. He did not want to be seen, could not afford to be seen, and had to watch the lake and the land constantly for any movements.

Suddenly, Tomo caught his breath and bent low among the reeds. For a long time he remained thus with Tamayo in his arms, as immobile as a rock, observing silently. He had been overcome by a powerful sensation—somewhere, someone was watching him.

A minute, two minutes. Tomo's heart was pounding wildly. Sticky, oily sweat oozed out onto his brow. But nothing happened. Everything was as hushed as ever, and the only sound he heard was the rustle of the reeds in the wind. Tomo lifted his face from between the reeds and looked at one of the windows of the house ahead. He was sure he had sensed something moving in that window.

There was a gust of wind, and as if in responding welcome, sooty curtains fluttered inside the paneless window. More miserably torn than any rag, they whipped the window frame with every breeze. No one had bothered to steal them, they were so tattered, and they remained untouched in this old abandoned house.

Seeing the fluttering curtains, Tomo clicked his tongue in irritation and lifted Tamayo's body again. Then, checking around, he leaped out from among the reeds with animal swiftness and dashed from the veranda into the living room of the old house.

The smell of mold stung his nose. Spider webs hung from the walls and ceiling like festive ornaments. Because the lake was home to countless flying insects, spiders had cast their webs everywhere in anticipation of a good catch, and the instant that Tomo had rushed in, all the captive creatures still alive started beating their wings in unison, causing the fringes of the hanging webs to shake violently, as if in a storm. He was hit by a pungent odor that made him think of rotting fish.

Averting his face, Tomo looked at the entrance hall and began climbing the stairs, when he saw something that stopped him cold. Someone must have climbed these stairs recently, for there in front of him was a muddy footprint.

Tomo stared hard at the footprint with bated breath as if it were something terrifying. Soon, however, realizing that in fact there were other fresh footprints of several different types all over the entrance and stairs, he relaxed and sighed deeply. He remembered that the police had searched this empty house looking for the repatriated soldier. These, then, must belong to them. Relieved, Tomo began climbing the stairs, endeavoring to make as little noise as possible, for stumbling even slightly produced a sound that echoed throughout the house and made his blood run cold.

The second floor looked as sorry as the first. Every pane of glass was broken, and hardly any of the door hinges remained.

Tomo must have cased the house beforehand, for he went straight to one of the doors, kicked it open, and entered the room carrying Tamayo. It was a dreary, empty room devoid of all ornament, with only a steel-framed bed and a sturdy-looking chair in one corner. The bed had a straw mattress whose stuffing was coming out, but of course there were no sheets or blankets. The entire room was a picture of desolation and ruin.

Tomo gently placed Tamayo's body on top of the straw mattress. Wiping off the sweat that poured down his face, he continued to glance around. Everything was going smoothly. No one knew he had brought Tamayo to this abandoned house. It would all be decided here and now, and when it was over, everything would proceed as he had planned, no matter how Tamayo cried or wailed. Then the woman, the money, and the power would all be his.

Tomo trembled with excitement, like a warrior going into battle, his mouth dry and his knees shaking. He removed his necktie with quivering hands, tore off his jacket and shirt, and threw them on the chair. The brightness of the room made him uncomfortable, but unfortunately there was no shutter or curtain to cover the window. Biting his nails, Tomo looked around the room for a while, trying to come up with a plan, but soon he muttered, "Hell, what does it matter? Nobody's looking. Besides, the lady herself is sleeping soundly."

Stooping over the bed, Tomo began removing Tamayo's clothes, piece by piece. As the gentle slope of her shoulders and the curves of her ample breasts revealed themselves to him, Tomo could no longer control his excitement. His fingers shook as if in fever, and his breath came in rapid gusts.

Just then, he heard it—a single, faint knocking sound followed by the creak of a floorboard. Tomo leaped away from the bed like a locust and braced himself, watching and listening, lying in wait for the attacking enemy. But he did not hear another sound.

Tomo, however, was still worried and decided to investigate. There was nothing amiss—just a nest in a corner of the kitchen full of newborn baby rats. "So that's all it was—squealing rats," he thought to himself. Clicking his tongue in disgust and climbing back up the stairs, Tomo began to open the door to the room. Suddenly, he caught his breath. When he had walked out of this room a minute ago, he had left the door open. How could it be that it was now shut? Had it shut by itself, perhaps blown by the wind?

Placing his hand on the doorknob, Tomo opened the door cautiously. The room seemed unchanged. Relaxing, he walked up to the bed when suddenly, he felt as if he had been struck by lightning. Someone had placed Tamayo's jacket over her bare breasts!

Tomo could not move; it seemed as if the soles of his shoes were stuck to the floor. He was not a daring man to begin with; in fact, he was exceedingly cowardly. Today's undertaking, therefore, had required tremendous determination on his part, and he had been continually jumpy even after setting his plan into motion.

Tomo was drenched with sweat, his mouth parched and the depths of his throat burning. He wanted to say something, but his tongue seemed tied in knots, and all he could finally manage was "Who... who's there?"

Then, as if in reply, he heard the floorboard creak on the other side of the door to the adjoining room. Yes, there was someone in the other room. Why hadn't he checked it out before? The eyes that had been watching him from the window had not been a product of his imagination. Whoever it was had been hiding in this house, in the very next room. Why hadn't he checked it out earlier?

"Who is it! Come out! Who's hiding there?"

Immediately the door started opening—slowly, little by little. Then, Tomo saw the figure of the man standing there— a man who appeared to be a repatriated soldier, with a field cap pulled low over his brow and his face hidden with a muffler.

About an hour later, Monkey received a strange phone call at the Inugami villa.

"Hello. Is this Monkey? I want to make sure I'm speaking to Monkey. Me? It doesn't matter who I am. I just want to let you know about Miss Tamayo. You'll find her in the abandoned house in Toyohata Village—you know, the one the Inugamis used to live in a long time ago. Go up the stairs and into the room immediately to the left. Please go for her right away. Don't sound an alarm, though, because it would be embarrassing for her if people found out about it. So it would be best if you did everything alone. Oh, and you'll probably find her still sound asleep, but you needn't worry about that. She'll wake up when the effects of the drug wear off. Alright? I'm counting on you. Remember, go as quickly as you can. Goodbye."

# The Koto String

The chirping of the birds Tamayo had been listening to in her dream slowly became reality, and she at last began to come out of her deep sleep. Trying to force away the suffocating pressure that lay over her, she had unconsciously extended her hands to raise herself when she finally woke up. Even then, she could not immediately comprehend her situation, and she stared blankly ahead for a while. She had a dull headache, and her joints were stiff. It was an effort just to get up, not like a normal morning at all. She thought that perhaps she was ill.

As her thoughts wandered thus, she suddenly remembered what had taken place in the middle of the lake. The careening motorboat, being caught in Tomo's arms, and then that wet handkerchief over her nose. After that, everything was a blank.

Tamayo sprang upright in her bed. She just barely kept herself from screaming. The scream she was able to stifle, but she could not stop her body from shaking. She felt her skin growing hot, then cold. She pulled her pajamas tight around her and, without moving a muscle, took stock of her condition. Weren't these proof—the headache, the stiffness? Weren't these proof that she had been violated? She quivered with violent rage. After the rage came an indescribable sorrow and despair that welled forth from within her. Tamayo sat immobile on her bed, staring straight ahead, feeling, in her despair, a sudden darkness descend around her.

Eventually, however, Tamayo noticed that she was in her own bedroom, had been lying in her own bed, and was wearing her own pajamas. How could that be? Had Tomo carried her into this room to disgrace her? No, that was unthinkable. Then, had he brought her back here after he had done his evil deed? Tamayo's heart was about to burst with fresh sorrow and wrath.

Just then, she heard a slight noise on the other side of the door. Tamayo hurriedly wrapped a blanket around her chest and asked sharply, "Who is it?" There was no immediate reply, so she asked once more, "Who's there?"

"Sorry, Missy. I was just worried about how you're feeling."

It was Monkey's voice. His tone was as naive and direct as ever but was filled with gentle concern. Tamayo could not answer him at once. Did Monkey know? Did he know that she might have been subjected by Tomo to the worst indignity a woman could endure?

"I'm alright. Everything's fine."

"That's good. By the way, Missy, there's something I really want you to see. Yeah, I think you should see it as soon as possible. The sooner you see it, the sooner it'll put your mind at ease."

"What is it?"

"A scrap of paper. A little bitty scrap of paper."

"And this scrap of paper will put my mind at ease?"

"That's right, Missy."

Tamayo thought for a while. "Then slide it in under the door," she said. She did not want to see anyone yet. She did not want anyone, not even Monkey, to see her face.

"Okay, I'll do that. Once you see it, you'll feel better. I'll talk to you about it when you've had a chance to settle down a bit, but you lie down and rest real quiet like for now, okay?"

He spoke almost like a nursemaid, in gentle, comforting tones. She felt tears rise to her eyes.

"Monkey, what time is it?"

"A little past ten."

"Yes, I know, but…"

As Tamayo murmured hesitantly gazing at the clock by her bedside, Monkey finally seemed to realize what she meant. "Oh, I'm sorry, Missy. Of course, you've got no idea when it is. It's the next day. It's been the night, and now it's past ten in the morning. Understand?"

"Yes, I understand."

"I'll slide this scrap of paper under the door, so you read it and rest some more, okay? I'll be leaving now 'cause the chief is calling for me."

After waiting for Monkey's footsteps to recede into the corridor and to grow gradually fainter, Tamayo slid out of bed. She could see a corner of the piece of paper sticking out from beneath the door. She took it and returned to her bed. It was a small scrap of paper that seemed to have been torn from a pocket notebook, and it had some writing on it that was difficult to decipher. She turned on the lamp by her bed.

The writer must have tried to disguise his hand, for the letters were strangely stiff and awkward. As she read the words, Tamayo felt her whole body grow cold, but then, the next instant, glowing hot:

Tomo did not succeed. I bear witness to the fact that Tamayo remains as pure and untouched as before.

THE MAN IN THE SHADOWS

Could it really be true? Who was this Man in the Shadows? More than that, why did Monkey have this scrap of paper?

"Monkey! Monkey!" Tamayo cried out at once, but by then he was no longer there to answer. After pondering the situation for a while, she slid out of bed and hurriedly changed into her clothes. She was still a little woozy but was not about to let that get in her way, for she had to be liberated from this doubt—this horrible doubt—without any delay.

Putting on her clothes and quickly making herself presentable, Tamayo stepped out into the corridor in search of Monkey, but he was nowhere to be seen.

That's right, she remembered, he said something about the chief calling him. As she made her way down the corridor toward the main part of the villa, she saw the door to the living room open and a crowd of people inside.

"Tamayo!" It was Sayoko who first spotted her and came rushing out of the room. "I heard you weren't feeling well. Are you alright? You look pale."

Sayoko looked ill herself.

"Yes, thank you, Sayoko." Tamayo peered into the living room and frowned. "Has something happened again?"

Inside she could see Chief Tachibana and Kindaichi, as well as the other members of the Inugami clan. Tomo's absence and the strangely stiff expression she saw on Monkey's face made her apprehensive.

"Well, yes, maybe…" Sayoko looked at Tamayo's face with questioning eyes. "Tomo hasn't been seen since last night."

Tamayo blushed. Could it be that Sayoko knew about yesterday and was trying to coax information out of her? "And?"

"And Aunt Umeko and Uncle Kokichi were very worried, so they phoned the chief, thinking that perhaps something…

something strange might have happened again." Poor Sayoko's face was contorted with anguish. It was probably not his parents but indeed Sayoko herself who was most concerned about Tomo's disappearance.

Just then, a smiling Chief Tachibana came out of the room.

"Miss Tamayo, I heard that you weren't feeling well. Are you alright?"

"Yes, thank you."

"If you feel up to it, won't you come in? There's something we need your help with."

Tamayo looked at the chief's face, and then turned her gaze toward Monkey inside the room. He was glaring at her angrily. Tamayo looked at Chief Tachibana and asked falteringly, "What... what's this all about?"

"Come in. Please come in."

Unable to refuse, Tamayo entered the room and seated herself on the chair indicated by the chief. As she did, Sayoko anxiously drew near and stood behind her. Tomo's parents, Takeko and Toranosuke, Matsuko, and Kiyo were all seated around the room, while Kindaichi stood a bit apart, nonchalantly observing everyone.

"Miss Tamayo, we need your help. As you've no doubt heard from Miss Sayoko, Mr. Tomo hasn't been seen since last night. It may be nothing to worry about, but things being as they are, his parents are extremely concerned and have asked us to find him as quickly as possible. And..." Tachibana stared at Tamayo's face with searching eyes. "And after making several inquiries, we have obtained information from the other servants that Monkey here might know where he is. So we've been questioning him, but he refuses to speak, saying that since it concerns you as well, he will not say anything unless he has your permission. And so, we'd like you to help by asking Monkey to tell us everything."

Tamayo felt her blood run cold, finally realizing what she had walked into. The chief did not know anything. It was because he did not know that he could make such a request so mercilessly, without any compunction. Tamayo closed her eyes in agony, but just then, she felt someone grasp her arm strongly. Lifting her eyes, she saw Sayoko, eyes brimming with tears, gazing at her in entreaty. Unconsciously, Tamayo squeezed the note from the Man in the Shadows more tightly in her hand.

"Yes, in fact, I wanted to ask Monkey about that, too. Before we hear Monkey's story, though, I'd like you to hear mine first. Unless you do, the facts may be out of sequence and difficult to understand."

Tamayo's cheeks were deathly pale, and the hands she had placed on her lap trembled slightly. Despite this, she related her previous day's experiences in the middle of the lake without faltering. Besides, there was not that much to tell.

When Tamayo had finished her tale, everyone looked at her, stunned. Umeko and Kokichi, Tomo's parents, exchanged glances. Chief Tachibana, having realized his mistake in forcing this cruel tale out of Tamayo, kept coughing awkwardly. Sayoko, meanwhile, grasped Tamayo's hand, her eyes wide with emotion. Tamayo squeezed her hand in return and went on, "So I don't know anything that happened after I got in the motorboat—where Tomo took me or what he did." She hesitated a moment but again gathered courage. "I have no recollection of anything, but when I woke up just now, I was lying on my own bed. Moreover, it seems that Monkey knows how I got there. So I, more than anyone else in this room, want to hear Monkey's story. I want to hear, I want to know what Tomo did to me."

Although she tried her best to calm herself, Tamayo felt an irrepressible rage burn forth within her like a blue-white flame, and her voice quavered and rose shrilly. Sayoko still held her hand sadly.

"Alright, Monkey, tell me. There's no reason to hesitate. I want you to tell me all you know. No matter how terrible it is, it's better that I know for sure, right now, rather than find out later, so I can be prepared."

"Missy, did you look at that scrap of paper?"

"Yes, I did. I'd like to hear about this piece of paper, too."

Monkey licked his lips nervously and began to talk in his muttering tone about the previous day. Unused to speaking much at all, he could not tell his tale smoothly. Chief Tachibana and Tamayo had to guide him on at times with helpful remarks.

According to Monkey, at around four o'clock the previous afternoon he had received an anonymous phone call telling him of Tamayo's whereabouts. Monkey did not really understand what the caller was talking about, but he said that Monkey should not make a big commotion, because that would embarrass Tamayo, and that he should go to her quietly, without telling anyone. After the caller had said what he wanted to say, he hung up.

"So you went to find Miss Tamayo."

"Yeah, he said not to tell anybody, so I went real quiet on the boat."

"And you found her in the empty house in Toyohata Village, just like the caller had said."

"Yeah."

182

"Can you be more specific about what you found there? Was Mr. Tomo no longer there?"

"Missy was lying on the bed. I thought for sure she was dead, she looked so pale. But I found out right away she wasn't dead, she had just breathed in some drug that made her sleep. I could smell it real strong around her nose and mouth."

"But Tomo, what happened to Tomo?" Umeko's hysterical voice pierced the quiet of the room.

At her question, Monkey whirled around and glared at her with blazing eyes. "Tomo? You mean that bastard? Oh, yeah, that bastard was there, too, in the same room. But he couldn't do anything. He'd been stripped half-naked and tied to a chair with a rope, over and over. What's more, he was gagged. Never seen such a pitiful sight."

"Did you tie him up, Monkey?" Kindaichi interjected calmly.

"Nope, not me. Not me. Probably that Man in the Shadows who telephoned me."

"The Man in the Shadows?" Tachibana frowned. "Who's that?"

"Missy, you got that scrap of paper?"

Tamayo handed the piece of paper to the chief without a word. Tachibana read it, raised his eyebrows in wonder, and handed it to Kindaichi. Kindaichi, too, contorted his face.

"Monkey, where did you find this piece of paper?"

"It was pinned to the front of Missy's jacket with a safety pin."

"I see. Chief, you'd better preserve this evidence carefully."

"Yes, I'll take it for now anyhow." Tucking away the piece of paper in his pocket, Tachibana continued, "So, what did you do after that, Monkey? Did you bring Miss Tamayo back home?"

"Yeah. Oh, yeah, I went by rowboat but came back by motorboat. I figured it'd serve the bastard right if I took his boat."

"And Tomo... what about Tomo?" Umeko screeched again.

"Tomo? He's probably still in that room. It wasn't my job to take him home," Monkey sneered.

"Still bound and gagged?" Umeko screamed.

"Oh, yeah. Bound and gagged. And stripped half-naked, too. I felt he was too filthy even to talk to, so I didn't pay him any attention, struggling and groaning like that. No, wait. That ain't exactly right. I did pay attention to him—I gave him a good whack right in the face as I was going out," he said with a peal of laughter.

Umeko jumped up and screamed in insane frenzy, "Somebody go, go and help him! My baby, he's going to freeze to death!"

Soon thereafter, a motorboat could be seen exiting the sluice gate of the Inugami estate onto Lake Nasu. Inside were Chief Tachibana, Kindaichi, Tomo's father Kokichi, and Monkey as guide. Sayoko, too, had insisted that she go along, and so she accompanied them.

When they arrived at the delta of Toyohata Village, they saw the rowboat Monkey had left the day before still floating among the reeds. From that, too, it seemed certain that Tomo was still in the empty house.

Yes, Tomo was indeed inside the empty house.

As the group, led by Monkey, entered the barren bedroom, they saw Tomo, naked from the waist up, head hanging down on his chest, still gagged and bound to the chair with his hands tied behind him.

"Ha! The bastard's fainted! I'm sure he's learned his lesson now," Monkey spat out hatefully. Kokichi ran up to Tomo, hurriedly removed his gag, and raised his son's face. At that moment, though, he released Tomo's head with a cry, so that it once again dropped forward as if the neck were broken. Then they saw it—something strange wound around Tomo's neck.

It was a koto string. The string had been wound around Tomo's neck three times and buried deep in the flesh, making horrible bruises. There was a jarring scream, and someone collapsed to the floor. It was Sayoko.

# The Unfortunate Sayoko

A koto string—yes, a koto string. The Nasu police had been summoned to the scene, and as Kindaichi blankly watched them taking photographs with great commotion, a terrifying idea began to whirl around in his head. When Také had been killed, his head severed from his body and substituted for that of a chrysanthemum doll, Kindaichi had agonized because he did not understand the significance of that act. Now, however, seeing a koto string wound around the neck of the second body, a terrible suspicion flashed through his mind like lightning.

*Yokikotokiku*—ax, zither, and chrysanthemum. With the koto string having been found around Tomo's neck, two of the three Inugami heirlooms were now seemingly connected with the murders. Was there really some connection? Of course there was—there had to be. Just the one murder with the chrysanthemum doll could be attributed to chance, but a koto being involved in a second murder was too much to be coincidence.

These murders must be intimately connected with the Inugami motto and heirlooms, and the culprit was deliberately flaunting that connection in their faces. As Kindaichi's thoughts wandered thus, his body grew as cold as ice with a fresh terror. Since the chrysanthemum and zither had already been used, would the ax be next? And if so, who would be the victim? He vividly saw the figure of the masked Kiyo in his mind's eye, for since the chrysanthemum, or *kiku*, had been used for Také, and the zither, or *koto*, for Tomo, then it seemed only natural that the ax, or *yoki*, was meant for the one remaining cousin. Reaching that conclusion, Kindaichi felt his flesh crawl, for he also remembered who would benefit most if all three men were dead.

Just as the police photographers, acting on Chief Tachibana's orders, had finished photographing Tomo's body from every angle, Kusuda, the medical examiner, came running into the room.

"Chief, another one?"

"Hello, Doctor. It's bad. I wish we didn't have to deal with cases like this. Shall I untie him?"

"No, hold on a minute." Kusuda carefully examined the body, still lashed to the chair, and when finished, turned to Tachibana. "You can untie him now. Have you taken photographs?"

"Yes, we have. Kawada, untie the rope," the chief called to one of his detectives.

"Wait. Just a moment, please." It was Kindaichi now who hastily stopped him. "Chief, could you call Monkey in here? I want to check something again before you untie him."

Summoned by one of the detectives, Monkey appeared. His face was rigid with tension.

"Monkey, I want to ask you one more time, just to make sure. Are you certain that when you came here yesterday, Tomo was bound to this chair?"

Monkey nodded grimly.

"And he was definitely alive at that time?"

"Oh, yeah."

"Did he say anything?"

"Yeah, he was trying to, but since he was gagged and all, he couldn't really talk."

"You didn't even take off the gag."

Monkey scowled angrily at Kindaichi but immediately averted his eyes, saying, "Of course, if I'd known that this was going to happen, I'd have taken off his gag and untied him, too. But back then, I was just fuming mad."

"So you hit him."

Monkey nodded grimly again, probably now regretting how he had acted.

"Okay, I understand. What time was it when you left this place with Miss Tamayo?"

"About half past four, or maybe closer to five. It was already dark outside."

"So between about half past four and five, Tomo was still alive. I don't suppose you killed him as a parting shot."

"Wh-what? No, of course not. I just gave him a good whack."

Monkey heatedly denied the accusation. Kindaichi calmed him down. "One last question. Was Tomo exactly in this position, in this state, on the chair when you left him? Look at the knot, for example."

"Can't really say. I didn't look at him from up close or anything, so I don't know about the knot, but I think he looked about the same."

"Okay, thank you. You can go now. We'll call you if we need you again."

Waiting until Monkey had left, Kindaichi turned toward Tachibana. "Chief, take a look. I want you to look at this closely before we untie the rope. See how there are abrasions all over Tomo's upper torso? They were clearly made by the rope. For there to be this many abrasions, the rope must have been quite loose, but look at this..." Kindaichi forced his finger in under the rope that bound Tomo. "The rope is biting into the flesh so tightly, so firmly, that it's difficult to even get a finger in. So, how could these abrasions have been made?"

Tachibana's eyes widened in wonder. "Mr. Kindaichi, what does this mean?"

"I don't know, Chief. I'm puzzled myself." Kindaichi scratched his head absentmindedly. "It's a very odd discrepancy, the abrasions covering his upper torso and the tightness of the rope, and I think we should keep it in mind. Anyway, I'm sorry to have kept you waiting. Please, go ahead and untie him."

The rope was untied, and Tomo's corpse was laid out on a cot. As Kusuda examined the body, a detective popped his head into the room. "Chief?"

"Yes, what is it?"

"There's something I'd like you to see."

"Alright. Kawada, you stay here and help the doctor if he needs anything. And, by the way, Doctor…"

"Yes?"

"There's a lady in the other room who's fainted. Could you see to her when you've finished over here? It's the Inugamis' Sayoko."

With Kindaichi tagging along after the chief, the detective led them into the dressing room adjoining the bathroom next to the kitchen. There, on the wooden floor, they were surprised to find a small clay cooking stove, a pan, a pot for cooking rice, a teapot, and a cardboard box half full of charcoal. Obviously someone had been cooking there recently.

"You know, Chief," said the detective, looking at the two men, "we checked this house right after Také's murder, to see if that repatriated soldier who was staying at the Kashiwaya Inn might be hiding here. I'm absolutely certain there was nothing like this here then. So if someone did sneak into this house, it had to be after we checked it."

"I see."

Happily scratching his head, Kindaichi said, "Perhaps he thought this would be the safest place to hide since the police had already searched it once."

"Yes, exactly. That's what I thought, too. But if so, that means this guy knew we had searched it. How could he have known that?"

"Y-y-yes, D-D-Detective, that's what I find extremely interesting. Perhaps information on everything you police are doing is somehow being passed on to him."

Kindaichi seemed to be enjoying himself tremendously, but Tachibana, in contrast, looked rather cross, and countered, "What do you mean, Mr. Kindaichi? You seem to be assuming that the person who was here is the man we're looking for, but that doesn't necessarily have to be the case, does it? It could have been some vagrant."

"But, Chief, there's more." The detective opened the door to the bathroom. "Look. Whoever was hiding here washed his food and cooking utensils in the bathroom. He could have done the cooking here, too, but he didn't because someone could have seen the fire from outside. Same with the kitchen. That's why he did the cooking in the dressing room, because it can't be seen from the outside. What's more, look here, in the bathroom."

There was no need for the detective to continue. On the white tile covered with scattered bits of greens was a large footprint—without question, the impression of a combat boot, so sharp and clear as to have been made with a stamp. Chief Tachibana uttered a low groan in spite of himself.

"Of course, it doesn't necessarily mean that because he's wearing combat boots, it's the man we're looking for, but judging from the circumstances…"

"We've certainly moved a step closer to that probability. Nishimoto, be sure and make an impression of this print."

Turning back toward Kindaichi, Chief Tachibana started talking forcefully, irate. "So, Mr. Kindaichi, what do we have— that Tomo brought Tamayo here without knowing this repatriated soldier was hiding here, that he and Tomo fought, and that Tomo ended up being bound to the chair. After tying Tomo up, the man who was hiding here phoned Monkey and told him Tamayo was in this house. Then, Monkey came, but he just took Tamayo home and left Tomo tied to the chair. So that's what we have up to now, but if that's so," said the chief with emphasis, "then who killed Tomo? Did the repatriated soldier return after Monkey had left and strangle him?"

Kindaichi scratched his head lightly all around. "Chief, I was just thinking the same thing. If that man was going to kill Tomo, why didn't he do so before calling Monkey? He would have known that once he'd told Monkey, this house was bound to become a focus of attention. Fortunately or unfortunately, Monkey being the way he is, he didn't tell anyone until this morning, but the man who was hiding here certainly couldn't be sure of that. In that case, it would have been extremely risky for him to return to this house after he had told Monkey about it. And besides… no, I shouldn't say anything rash without knowing the time of death."

Tachibana stood thinking in silence but soon turned to his detective and asked, "Nishimoto, was there anything else?"

"Yes, sir. Just one more thing. I'd like you to take a look at the shed."

The shed, which stood just outside the kitchen door, was a structure with a floor space of about seven square meters. In one corner of the earthen-floored room, filled high with various kinds of junk, was a large pile of fresh straw. Kindaichi and Tachibana grew wide-eyed at the sight. "He must have been sleeping here."

"Yes. It's just after the harvest, so there are strawstacks everywhere. Take a little from this one, a little from that one, and no one's the wiser. And besides," said the detective, stomping on the straw, "it's so deep and thick, it's bound to be a lot warmer than any cheap, thin quilt."

"I see." Tachibana looked abstractedly at the straw bed. "But I wonder if this really means unmistakably that someone was hiding here. I don't suppose this could all be a sham…"

"A sham?"

Hearing his detective retort in surprise, Tachibana began to speak in an angry tone of voice. "You know, Mr. Kindaichi, we really don't know anything certain about what happened here yesterday. Sure, we've heard stories from Tamayo and Monkey that sound plausible. But who's to say those stories are true? According to Tamayo, Tomo used something like chloroform on her and brought her to this house, but maybe, just maybe, couldn't it have been Tamayo who seduced Tomo and tricked him into coming here? Monkey says he got a call from an anonymous caller and then came here, but maybe that's a lie and in fact he was here first lying in wait for Tomo. Mr. Kindaichi, I'm sure you remember that Monkey has old koto strings for repairing his fishing nets."

Detective Nishimoto looked in astonishment at the chief's face. "Then, Chief, you think that all these pieces of evidence we've found were manufactured and that Tamayo and Monkey conspired to kill Tomo?"

"No, I'm not saying that. I'm just saying that it's not out of the question. And that footprint, too, it seems too clear and sharp, as if it were made with a stamp of some kind. But... well, never mind, you go ahead and investigate more fully based on your own line of thinking. Mr. Kindaichi, Dr. Kusuda should be about finished by now. Shall we go?"

When the two men returned to the room on the second floor, the doctor was gone, and only the detective was keeping watch over the corpse.

"Kawada, where's Dr. Kusuda?"

"He went to see about the lady in the other room."

"Oh, right. And what about the results of the post-mortem?"

"He said that he would present an in-depth report after the autopsy. But to give you the main points," said the detective, looking at his pocket notebook, "the time elapsed since death is approximately seventeen to eighteen hours. Therefore, counting back, that means the time of death was between eight and nine last night."

Between eight and nine last night. Chief Tachibana and Kindaichi instinctively exchanged glances. According to Monkey, he left this house sometime between half past four and five in the afternoon. If so, it appeared that Tomo had remained alive and tied to this chair for three or four hours after Monkey had left.

The detective continued, comparing the expressions on the two men's faces, "Yes, sir, between eight and nine last night. But there's something else that's strange. Dr. Kusuda says that the koto string wound around the victim's neck was placed there after he was dead and that he was actually strangled with something thicker, like a rope of some kind."

"What!" Chief Tachibana literally jumped in surprise, but just then, as if in response to his voice, there was a woman's shriek from another room.

Kindaichi and the chief looked at each other aghast. They knew it was Sayoko, but they were taken aback by the pathetic, heart-rending sound.

"Chief, let's go see. Something has happened."

Sayoko was being tended to by Monkey and Kokichi in a room three doors down the hallway. The instant Kindaichi and Chief Tachibana stepped inside the room, however, they saw a sight that stopped them dead in their tracks: Sayoko, restrained on both sides by Monkey and Kokichi, with a face that showed she was no longer sane. With eyes slanted sharply upward and the muscles of her cheeks twitching horribly, her mad strength was such that she would sometimes nearly hurl off even the powerful Monkey.

"Monkey, hold her tight. I'm going to give her another shot. I think one more should do the trick," the doctor said, as he gave her the last of several injections. They heard three more pathetic, gut-wrenching wails from Sayoko's lips, but then the drug must have taken effect, for she gradually became quiet until, finally, she lay sleeping like a baby against Monkey's chest.

"Poor girl," Kusuda muttered sadly as he put away his syringe. "Her nerves must have simply snapped. I just hope it's a transient episode."

The words alarmed Tachibana. "Doctor, then you mean there's a danger of insanity?"

"I can't say anything for sure. The shock was just too great." Kusuda looked back and forth at the chief and Kindaichi. "Chief," he said after a pause, his face grave, "she's pregnant. Three months pregnant."

# The Blood on the Forefinger

Tomo had been found murdered. The news from across the lake hit the Inugami villa like a jolt of electricity, throwing its occupants into a panic. Needless to say, the one who received the greatest shock was Tomo's mother, Umeko, whose usual hysteria, already aggravated by worry and anguish since the previous night, finally exploded in response to the dire news. Her grief and indignation made her say things to Detective Yoshii, who had brought the news to her, which were so shocking they could not be overlooked:

"Damn her! Damn her! Damn that Matsuko! That bitch killed him. That bitch killed my Tomo. Detective, you have to arrest her. You have to arrest her and put her to death. Not just the regular death penalty—that's not good enough for her. I want to hang her by her heels, rip her to shreds, burn her till she's black, and pull out her hair, strand by strand."

Like a raging demon, Umeko named various other horrible forms of punishment she would mete out to Matsuko. But after a while, she stopped and began to weep bitterly. Her tears seemed to calm her down a bit, for between her sobs she gave Detective Yoshii the following statement.

"Detective, you know about Father's will, don't you? If he hadn't left that will, Matsuko's son, Kiyo, would have been the legal heir to the Inugami estate. She had been counting on that and looked forward to wielding power like a queen regent. Thanks to the will, though, all her plans went up in a puff of smoke. The will gives the Inugami fortune to the man who becomes Tamayo's husband, but her Kiyo's face is a pulpy mass of flesh—a red pomegranate that's ripened and burst. God, how disgusting. It makes my flesh creep just thinking about it. I don't care how strange Tamayo's tastes are, she would never choose such a monster for a husband. So, from the first, it was inevitable that Kiyo would lose the contest for Tamayo's hand. Matsuko couldn't bear that, so first she killed Také and then our son, Tomo. With them dead, Tamayo would have to marry that monster whether she liked it or not, because she'd lose her right to inherit if she refused to do so. That would be the only way for Kiyo to lay his hands on the Inugami fortune. Oh that evil, evil bitch! Detective, you have to arrest her. You have to arrest Matsuko."

Umeko's own words had caused her to grow increasingly excited. But when Detective Yoshii informed her that the cause of death had been strangulation, and that the murderer, after strangling Tomo, had for some reason wound a koto string around his neck, Umeko stared at him in surprise. "A koto string?" Looking mystified, she asked back vacantly, "He was strangled with a koto string?"

"No, that's not right. He was strangled with something thicker, like a rope, and the murderer wound the koto string around his neck after he was dead. The chief, too, is puzzled as to why the culprit would do such a thing."

"A koto string," murmured Umeko slowly to herself. "A koto string… koto…" she kept repeating. Suddenly, she seemed to remember something, for her expression changed, and as her breath came in rapid bursts, she muttered, "Zither!… chrysanthemum!… Oh, God…" and fell silent.

After Umeko, the one who was the most shocked by the report from Toyohata Village was, needless to say, Sayoko's mother, Takeko. The news about Tomo did not particularly shake her; in fact she seemed to feel no emotion at all— except maybe satisfaction. She, after all, had had to endure her tragedy. However, when Detective Yoshii then told her about Sayoko's breakdown, and that she was pregnant, Takeko, like Umeko, was overcome by hysteria and blurted out some scandalous words. Incredibly, though, the content of her ravings paralleled Umeko's, for she accused her sister Matsuko of being the murderer and screamed that Matsuko had killed Také and Tomo so her son would be the heir to the Inugami fortune. What was also interesting, she had the same reaction as Umeko to Detective Yoshii's report about the koto string.

"A koto string... a koto string?" At first, Takeko, too, simply cocked her head in puzzlement, but soon she seemed to remember something and gasped with frightened eyes, "The zither! And the chrysanthemum last time!" With those words, she fell silent and refused to answer, no matter how much the detective or her husband, Toranosuke, pressed her to explain. After a while, she stood up, as pale as a ghost. "I'm going to go discuss this with Umeko. Although I don't see how it could be possible... it scares me. Perhaps, after I discuss it with her, I might be able to tell you about it," she said and staggered out of the room as if in a trance.

Least upset by the report from Toyohata Village was, of course, Kiyo's mother, Matsuko. When Detective Yoshii came finally to her room, she was in the middle of a koto lesson with her teacher, Kokin Miyakawa. Kokin had been staying in Nasu at the time of Také's murder, but thereafter had been making the rounds of her students' homes in Ina before returning the day before to her lodgings in Nasu.

When the detective entered, Kiyo joined them, seating himself wordlessly between his mother and Kokin. Realizing that Kokin would hear about it sooner or later anyway, the detective accepted her presence. He informed them all of Tomo's murder, as well as of Sayoko's madness. Matsuko, the very picture of meanness, did not so much as twitch an eyebrow at the news. She continued to play her koto.

Rather, it was Kokin, the koto teacher, who seemed the most affected by the detective's report. She had stopped playing the koto when the detective had walked into the room and had sat waiting politely. When she heard his account, she widened her almost sightless eyes in terror, shoulders shaking, and sighed deeply. Kiyo's reaction, on the other hand, was hidden behind his white mask, as ever expressionless and eerily mum.

For a moment, an awkward silence fell across the room, but Matsuko calmly continued to play her koto. No doubt she was well aware how her sisters felt about her and was acting nonchalant to dispel the damning image they had created. Yet her facade, too, began to crumble when the detective told of the koto string wound around Tomo's neck.

"The chief finds that very peculiar. It would be one thing if he had been strangled with the koto string, but he wasn't. Why would the murderer strangle him with some other rope and then wind a koto string around his neck afterwards, as if he had been strangled with it?"

Matsuko's koto playing gradually became faulty, clearly affected by the detective's words. Still she did not stop.

"So the murderer," continued the detective, "wanted for some reason to focus our attention on the koto string. That is the only possible explanation. A koto string, or perhaps a koto itself. By the way, when Mr. Také was killed, the murderer made use of a chrysanthemum doll—in other words, chrysanthemum. And now, a koto, that is, a zither. Zither and chrysanthemum. *Yokikotokiku*. Ax, zither, and chrysanthemum."

That instant, Matsuko's fingers made a terrible scraping sound, and one of the koto strings snapped in two.

"Oh!"

Matsuko and Kokin cried out almost in unison. The koto teacher half rose on her knees in alarm, while Matsuko hastily removed the plectra from the fingers of her right hand. Blood was dripping from her forefinger. Taking out a handkerchief from her kimono sleeve, she hurriedly wrapped it around her finger.

"Did you hurt yourself?" inquired the detective.

"Yes, when the koto string broke just now."

Kokin, the koto teacher, had remained frozen on her knees, breathing rapidly, but when she heard Matsuko's words, she knitted her eyebrows as if in confusion and muttered to herself, "When the koto string broke just now?"

It was at that moment that the detective saw a flash in Matsuko's eyes, an expression of vehement hatred. The flash was gone in an instant, however, and her eyes reverted immediately to their former coldness.

The nearly sightless Kokin of course had not noticed Matsuko's reaction and remained on her knees, with her hand to her breast as if to still the beating of her heart. Beside her, Kiyo waited awkwardly. For some reason, when

Kokin had cried out and half risen, Kiyo had rushed to her side and had moved as if to support her.

Matsuko regarded her son and her teacher with a puzzled expression but soon turned toward Detective Yoshii. "Was there really a koto string wound around Tomo's neck?"

"Excuse me, I'll be leaving now," Kokin announced abruptly, standing up nervously. She must have been frightened by the detective's story, for she was terribly pale and seemed unsteady on her feet.

"I'll see you out, then." Kiyo stood up after her.

Surprised, Kokin looked at him with her nearly blind eyes. "Oh, my, Mr. Kiyo, how kind of you. But I don't want to impose."

"It's quite alright. I don't want you to stumble, so please let me see you to the door."

Kokin could not refuse, for Kiyo had gently taken her hand. "Well, thank you very much, then. Goodbye, Mrs. Matsuko."

Matsuko, head cocked, stared curiously at the two of them leaving but soon turned toward the detective and asked again, "Detective, is it really true what you said just now, that there was a koto string wound around Tomo's neck?"

"Yes, it's true. Does that mean anything to you?"

Matsuko remained thinking silently for a while but then lifted up eyes that almost seemed possessed. "Well, yes… it might… uh, did my sisters say anything to you about it?"

"They also seem to know something, but they won't say what it is."

Just then, Kiyo returned. Instead of sitting down in the room with Matsuko and the detective, however, he simply acknowledged them with a nod and continued on to his room. As he walked past, Matsuko shuddered, as if she felt an icy draft from his body.

"Mrs. Matsuko, please tell me if you know anything about this. It's best that everything be out in the open."

"Yes, well…" Matsuko still gazed ahead with the eyes of one possessed. "I cannot tell you without discussing it first with my sisters. Besides, it's such a strange, unbelievable tale. I want to talk to them first and then perhaps I'll be able to tell you about it when Chief Tachibana returns."

Using a bell to call the maid, Matsuko told her to summon Furudate, the family lawyer, at once. Then she fell into silent meditation. It was two hours later that Chief Tachibana and Kindaichi returned to the villa from Toyohata Village.

# Atrocity

In the large tatami-mat room deep inside the Inugami villa, the photograph of the late Sahei Inugami—his refined features showing, even in old age, traces of his former attractiveness—still stood, covered with large chrysanthemum blossoms, on the plain wood altar at the head of the room. Today again, two more people—a man and a woman—were missing from the assembled members of the Inugami clan. One had to wonder what Sahei, looking out from the photograph on the altar, must have thought, seeing that key members of his family had disappeared, like the teeth of a comb falling out, every time they gathered in this room.

The other day it was Také. Now today it was Tomo and Sayoko. The latter, temporarily affected by the terrible shock she had received, might return to her normal condition some day, but the former, whose body at that moment was lying on a table in Nasu Hospital being autopsied by Dr. Kusuda, would never attend a family conference again.

Thus, except for the missing Shizuma Aonuma, the sole surviving male related by blood to Sahei Inugami was now Kiyo, who sat like a lifeless statue in his white, rubber mask, enveloped in otherworldly stillness—the stillness of a mysterious marsh deep in the mountains that had lain unknown to humans since ancient times.

Near Kiyo sat Matsuko; a bit apart from them Takeko and her husband, Toranosuke; and still further away Umeko, eyes red from weeping, and her husband, Kokichi—this now being all that was left of the Inugami clan. Along with them, needless to say, yet slightly apart from the group was Tamayo, her fatigue from the continuing series of shocks since the previous day visible, but her radiance undimmed nevertheless. Her sublime beauty was indeed as endless as an ever-flowing spring, becoming more entrancing each time one saw her. Monkey sat next to Tamayo.

At a slight distance from the family members were Chief Tachibana and Kindaichi, back from Toyohata Village, as well as the lawyer Furudate, who had been summoned by Matsuko. Also present was Detective Yoshii, who had returned from the village ahead of the others, bearing the bad news. Everyone looked like they were choking from the tension, waiting for the unveiling of a monumental secret.

It was so hushed they could hear the crackling of the fire in the brazier placed between them, and together with the keen scent of the chrysanthemums, a sinister aura suffused the room. Matsuko finally broke the suffocating silence.

"I will now answer your question. Takeko, Umeko, you do agree that I should tell them everything, don't you?" Matsuko spoke in her usual, insistent tone. Pressed thus again, Takeko and Umeko exchanged frightened glances but nodded gloomily in resignation.

"This is something we have kept a secret among ourselves and have never told anyone else before, something which the three of us made a firm pact never to reveal and, if possible, would have preferred to keep secret all our lives. But with all that has occurred, we cannot possibly keep it a secret any longer. Both Takeko and Umeko agree with me that if we must divulge this secret in order for you to avenge their sons' deaths, then so be it. It is no longer of consequence how you will feel about us after hearing this tale. We all have our reasons for what we do. Everyone has a right to protect his or her happiness, and a mother especially must fight not only for her own happiness but for that of her children as well, even if people criticize her."

Pausing, Matsuko glared around at the assembled group with the piercing eyes of a vulture. Soon, she began again.

"It was right around the time that Kiyo was born, so about thirty or so years ago. I think you all have probably heard that around that time our father, Sahei Inugami, became involved with a woman of lowly birth named Kikuno Aonuma. She used to work at the silk mill he owned and must have been eighteen or nineteen. She was not particularly attractive or bright, just an ordinary girl whose sole distinguishing quality was her meekness. How that creature managed to seduce our father I have no idea, but once he became involved with her, he was completely infatuated, so much so that it was embarrassing even to watch him. I suppose that's what happens when a man falls in love later in life—Father was past fifty at the time. The Inugami business finally stood on solid ground, and Sahei Inugami was counted among the top businessmen in the country, yet there he was, head over heels in love with a humble factory worker employed at his mill, a mere girl of eighteen or nineteen. So you can imagine what a scandal it caused."

Even now, Matsuko's voice quivered with renewed anger. "Maybe Father at least had some scruples when he thought of us, for he had the sense not to bring her to this villa. He purchased a house on the outskirts of town and had her live there. At first he would go there off and on, being careful not to be seen, but gradually he became more brazen, until finally he was there more or less all the time. I'm sure you can see how embarrassing it was for us."

Matsuko's tone became increasingly heated as she continued, "People were extremely critical. Just some ordinary rich old man, the type you find anywhere, acting like a young fool wouldn't have caused that much gossip. But here was this leader of the Shinshu business world, a renowned representative of Nagano Prefecture, a man whom people called the Father of Nasu, disgracing himself. The taller the tree, the more wind it catches, and the more famous and more important Father became, the more enemies he acquired—political enemies, business enemies, all kinds of enemies. Those people, seeing a chance to undermine him, seized the opportunity. They had scandalous articles about him published in the newspapers and outlandishly lewd jingles spread far and wide. Really, when I remember those times, I cringe at what we had to endure. If it had been only that, though, if it was just being made an object of people's ridicule, we could have endured it somehow. But then I heard a rumor that I just could not ignore."

The unforgiving Matsuko, probably still unable to forget the anger she had felt at the time, sounded like she was grinding her teeth. "People were saying that Kikuno was pregnant and that Father intended to bring her to this house as his legal wife and throw us out into the street. Imagine my anger when I heard that. No, the anger wasn't just mine; it was also the bitterness and anger my mother had passed on to me. And the same fire was burning in the hearts of Takeko and Umeko as well."

Matsuko turned around and glanced at Takeko and Umeko, who both nodded in agreement. As far as this one issue was concerned, these three half-sisters were always in perfect agreement.

"As you have no doubt heard, the three of us all have different mothers. None of our mothers was ever allowed to become Father's legal wife, all three having to remain his mistresses to the end. How they must have resented and regretted this. Our mothers had already passed away by the time the incident with Kikuno occurred, but as I remember, Father's treatment of them was totally inhuman. You must think it strange that this house has numerous annexes, but that is a reminder of the kind of bestial life our father led. Father kept each of his three women in one of these annexes, like chattel. Yes, that's the only way to describe it—they were kept like chattel. He had not an ounce of love for any of them and kept them merely to use whenever he needed to satisfy his filthy male lust. Not only did he feel no love for them, he even looked down on them with contempt. So they say he was extremely cross when each of the three women conceived and gave birth to us. He thought that our mothers should just meekly make themselves available to him and that they had no business doing such an unnecessary thing as conceiving children. You can imagine what a cold and unfeeling father he was to us his daughters."

Matsuko's voice quivered with anger, and her stubborn tone now burned with fiery emotion. Takeko and Umeko nodded, their expressions stiff. "The only reason our father raised us was because he couldn't very well abandon or kill us, like puppies or kittens. So he brought us up reluctantly, simply because he had to. He hadn't a trace of fatherly love for us. But then he became infatuated with this humble little thing from heaven knows where and was planning to throw us out and bring her into this house—and, what's more, as his legal wife. I don't think anyone can blame me for being angry about it."

Kindaichi could not stop the cold sweat that trickled down his arms, for the animosity and hatred he sensed between parent and child was inhuman. In any case, Kindaichi thought to himself, how could Sahei Inugami have been so cold to his three mistresses and the daughters they bore him? Could there have been some terrible defect in his personality? According to *The Life of Sahei Inugami*, Sahei was warm-hearted and kind to a degree unusual for such a successful man. Of course, the writer might have exaggerated or slanted the truth, but in fact, ever since arriving in Nasu, Kindaichi had often heard Sahei described in a similar manner and had been impressed that the people of Nasu even now adored him like a loving father. So why, then, had Sahei been so cruel and cold solely to his children and mistresses? Just then, Kindaichi remembered the scandalous rumor about the young Sahei he had heard from the priest of Nasu Shrine. Perhaps his youthful involvement with Daini Nonomiya, Tamayo's grandfather, had influenced Sahei's attitude toward them in some significant way. In other words, could the homosexual relationship he had experienced in his early years have affected his subsequent sex life, preventing him from having human feelings toward his mistresses and daughters? Yet that alone could not possibly explain Sahei's abnormal coldness toward them. There had to be more. There had to be some other, more significant reason, but what could it be?

Just then, however, Matsuko began her tale again, so Kindaichi's musings were interrupted. "There was another reason why I was so incensed. I was already married and had just given birth that spring to a son—Kiyo here. Father had absolutely refused to leave control of the family estate to my husband, but everyone said, and I happily believed as well, that since Kiyo was Father's direct grandson, he would eventually become the head of the Inugami clan. If, however, Kikuno became Father's legal wife and had a son, that baby would become the legal heir and would get the entire Inugami fortune. I burned with a doubled wrath, my body and soul consumed with both the bitter resentment bequeathed to me by my mother and anger for my own child's sake. Takeko and Umeko felt the same bitterness and anger as well. Takeko had already married Toranosuke by then and showed signs of being pregnant. Umeko was engaged to Kokichi and was to be married in the spring. We three had to fight for our children—the child who already was and those who were to be. So one day, the three of us went together to the house Father had bought for Kikuno and let him know, in no uncertain terms, how we felt."

Matsuko's lips became oddly contorted, and her words blazed with fiery fury. Kindaichi's arms grew wet again with sickly cold sweat, while Chief Tachibana and Furudate frowned and exchanged glances.

"I'm sure that hearing all this, you must think me a very shameless and vulgar woman, but I don't care. I did it because I'm a mother, and because of the years and years of accumulated hatred. So after all three of us had gone on cursing and reviling Father, I finally told him, 'If you absolutely insist on making this woman your legal wife, I have some plans of my own. I will kill you both before this woman has her child and then kill myself. Then, the Inugami fortune will remain as Kiyo's, even if he will also be burdened with the shame of having a murderess for a mother.'"

Matsuko raised the corners of her mouth in a grotesque smile and glared at the others in the room. Kindaichi, struck with terror, looked at Tachibana and Furudate. What unspeakable hatred between flesh and blood, what a terrifying picture of enmity between father and child. He felt uncomfortable just sitting there.

Matsuko continued. "Even Father seemed to have felt some fear at my threat. He knew I was a woman who would not hesitate to resort to such measures. So the issue of Kikuno becoming his legal wife never came up after that. Father wasn't the only one who was frightened; Kikuno, being a woman, was even more so. She was scared out of her wits, so that finally, probably unable to endure the fear any longer, she ran away from the house and disappeared, even though she had almost reached the final month of her pregnancy. When we heard this, the three of us sighed with relief and exulted in our victory. But little did we know that Father had outwitted us."

Again glancing sharply around the room, Matsuko went on. "You all know about the three heirlooms of the Inugami clan, the ax, zither, and chrysanthemum—*yokikotokiku*— and what significance they have for this family. Soon after Kikuno disappeared, we heard from one of the directors of the Inugami Foundation that the heirlooms were missing and that apparently Father had given them to Kikuno. I was livid. I nearly suffocated from anger. I decided at that time, alright, if that's how he's going to play it, I'll play dirty, too, and use any means I can, no matter how outrageous. The first thing we had to do was to find out Kikuno's whereabouts, even if we had to turn over every stone, and to retrieve the ax, zither, and chrysanthemum. So we hired an army of people to search for her. In these rural parts, it is difficult for anyone to disappear without a trace, and we were soon able to ascertain that Kikuno was hiding in a detached room of a farmer's house in Ina and, what was more, that she had safely given birth to a son two weeks before. We knew we didn't have a minute to lose. So one night, the three of us went together to the farmer's house in Ina to attack Kikuno."

Even Matsuko hesitated at this point. Takeko and Umeko, too, perhaps remembering their terrible deed, shuddered. Everybody was listening to Matsuko's story with bated breath.

"It was a night so cold even the moon seemed frozen. Frost covered the ground and glistened like snow. We first gave money to the farmer from whom Kikuno was renting her room and told him and his family to leave the house for a while. The authority of the Inugami clan extended even to Ina, so no one dared refuse us. Passing down the corridor into Kikuno's room, we found her lying on her futon in her robe, breast-feeding the baby. When she saw us, she stared at us for a moment, the very picture of terror, but the next instant, she reached for an earthen teapot that was near her and threw it at us. The teapot hit a pillar and smashed to pieces, raining scalding hot water down on us. This infuriated me. As Kikuno, with the baby in her arms, tried to flee from the veranda, I flung myself on her from behind and grabbed the sash around her waist. It became untied and slipped off, causing her robe to fall open, but she leaped, robe flapping, down from the veranda. I caught hold of her collar, however, while Umeko took the baby away from her, and as she struggled to get it back, the robe came off and

211

she was left standing there in her underwear. I seized her hair and pulled her down onto the frosty ground, grabbed a bamboo broom lying nearby, and beat her over and over. I could see countless welts rising on her pale skin. Blood started to flow. Takeko drew bucketfuls of freezing water from the well and poured them over her, again and again."

Despite the horrific scene she was describing, Matsuko showed almost no emotion whatsoever. Her face was without expression, like a Noh mask, and her voice droned on monotonously, as if she were reciting something from memory. Her very lack of emotion made the listeners feel even more vividly the horror of what had occurred. Kindaichi shuddered at the atmosphere of evil that her words evoked.

"Until then, none of us had said a word, but soon Kikuno cried out, screaming and gasping, 'What do you want with me?' So I told her, 'You know damn well what we want. We came for the ax, zither, and chrysanthemum. Hurry up and give them to us.' Kikuno, however, was surprisingly stubborn and would not give in easily. She kept saying that since Mr. Inugami had given them to the baby, she couldn't give them back to us. So I took up the broomstick again and I beat her over and over, while Takeko poured bucketfuls of water over her. Kikuno crawled around on the frost-covered ground screaming, but still she wouldn't say yes. Just then, however, Umeko, who was standing on the veranda holding the baby, said, 'Matsuko, there's no need to be so rough with her. There's a much easier way to make her do as we want.' So she said, and taking off the baby's diaper, she took a red-hot pair of tongs from the brazier and touched it to his bare bottom. The baby screamed as if he were on fire."

Kindaichi felt nauseous, the pit of his stomach turning as hard as stone with disgust. Oily perspiration covered the foreheads of Chief Tachibana, Furudate, and even Detective Yoshii. Monkey, too, looked frightened. Only Tamayo remained sitting as prim and coldly elegant as ever.

A faint smile rose to Matsuko's lips. "Umeko has always been the best strategist among us three. She is the most daring. With Umeko's one stroke, Kikuno, as stubborn as she had been, finally gave in. Weeping as if she had gone mad, she returned to us the ax, zither, and chrysanthemum, which she had hidden above the ceiling panel in the closet. I was satisfied and was ready to go home, when Takeko said, 'Kikuno, you may look so sweet but you certainly are a brazen thing. I know perfectly well that you had a lover back at the silk mill and that you've been seeing him ever since. That baby is his, but you lie and claim that it's Father's. What a shameless bitch you are! Alright, I want you to write a statement and sign it: "Sahei Inugami is not the father of my child. The father is another man."' Of course Kikuno denied the allegations desperately, but just then, Umeko touched the fiery tongs to the baby's bottom again, so Kikuno, sobbing, did as we wanted. After that, I said to her, 'If you want to report this to the police, go ahead. No doubt we'll be arrested and sent to prison. But you know they'd never give us life sentences or put us to death, so as soon as we get out of jail, we'll be back to pay our respects.' Takeko, too, said, 'Kikuno, for your own good, you had better never show your face around Father or write to him, ever again. We've hired a legion of private detectives, so no matter how you try to keep it secret, we'll know right away if you do. If we find out you've contacted him, we'll come to say hello again.' Finally, Umeko said with a laugh, 'You know, if something like this were to happen again, I don't think that poor child could survive.' We thought that having heard all that, Kikuno would never go back to Father again. Confident of our success, we were about to leave, when Kikuno, who had been crying hysterically with the baby in her arms, suddenly looked up and spoke."

Matsuko paused and looked around the room with her piercing eyes, and her voice suddenly became fervent. "You fiends! God won't ignore what you've done. No, even if he does, I'll avenge myself. Some day I'll get back at you for this. Ax, zither, chrysanthemum. *Yokikotokiku*—what did those words mean? To hear good tidings? No, don't think you will hear good tidings forever. One day, the ax, zither, and chrysanthemum will be your undoing. Remember it well. The ax is for you, the zither for you, and the chrysanthemum for you!' With her hair wild and a ghastly expression on her face, blood trickling from the corner of her mouth, Kikuno ground her teeth like a madwoman and pointed at us, one by one. I don't remember, however, which she said was meant for whom."

Matsuko, having come to the end of her tale, fell silent. Sitting close by her, the masked Kiyo was shivering violently, as if gripped by fever.

# Tamayo's Identity

Matsuko's story had come to an end, but for some time, no one said a word. Perhaps unsettled by the lingering aftertaste of her lurid tale, everyone kept fidgeting and looking at each other awkwardly. Eventually, Tachibana leaned forward and said, "So you're saying that the one who committed these recent murders is Kikuno."

"No, I don't remember saying anything of the kind," retorted Matsuko in her ever-ornery tone. "It's just that you said these murders might be connected in some way to the ax, zither, and chrysanthemum, and so I told you about the only incident I could think of with a possible connection. I don't know if my story will turn out to be of any help, but that's something for you police to decide, isn't it?"

At her catty words, Chief Tachibana turned to Furudate, the family lawyer, and asked, "Have you found out anything about the whereabouts of this Kikuno and her son?"

"Actually, I had been planning to come here today to report, even if I hadn't received the phone call from Mrs. Matsuko."

"You've found out something?"

"Well, yes and no. I've obtained some information, but nothing useful." Furudate took some papers out of his briefcase. "Since this woman Kikuno Aonuma was orphaned at a very young age and has no known kin, we had an extremely difficult time finding out anything about her. We did discover one rather interesting fact. It turns out that Kikuno

Aonuma is the daughter of the cousin of Haruyo Nonomiya, Miss Tamayo's grandmother and the wife of Mr. Inugami's benefactor Daini Nonomiya."

Everyone in the room looked at each other in surprise.

"I guess this explains why Mr. Inugami lavished his affections on Kikuno to such a degree," continued the lawyer. "As *The Life of Sahei Inugami* tells us, Mr. Inugami regarded Daini's wife, Haruyo, with great fondness, like a mother or sister, and revered her for her saintly kindness. Because Kikuno was her sole surviving blood relative, Mr. Inugami might have been trying to repay Haruyo for her past generosity by favoring Kikuno and trying to make the child she bore him his heir."

A sneer appeared on Matsuko's lips, no doubt a sign of her determination never to let such a thing happen. The three half-sisters exchanged glances full of malice.

"So, that said, let me return to Kikuno's subsequent movements. Kikuno must have been so terrified by the threats you three ladies made that night that she disappeared from Ina with Shizuma—as the baby was named by Mr. Inugami—and went to stay with distant relatives in Toyama City. She had made up her mind not to return to Mr. Inugami's side and seems to have never even written him. She lived there for a while with Shizuma, but when the boy turned three, she left him with the relatives and married. Whom she wed, however, we have not been able to determine. It was more than twenty years ago and these relatives of hers were all killed in the war during the bombing of Toyama. And since these people had no other kin, we lose track of Kikuno completely at this point. It seems nobody in that family had much luck at all."

Furudate heaved a sigh. "Now, as for Shizuma, one of his former neighbors remembered him. Shizuma was adopted by the relatives Kikuno left him with, so his last name became Tsuda, not Aonuma. The Tsudas were very poor folk but apparently very kind, and since they had no children, they brought up Shizuma as their own. And it seems that when Kikuno left Mr. Inugami, he gave her a considerable sum of money in addition to the ax, zither, and chrysanthemum. She left part of those funds to be applied toward Shizuma's upbringing, so that he could at least finish junior high school. After that, he seems to have been employed somewhere, but he was drafted when he was twenty-one. He was discharged and re-drafted several times, but then finally, in the spring or summer of 1944, he was called to serve again and was assigned to a unit in Kanazawa. His whereabouts after that are unknown. That's all we can ascertain about Shizuma. Anything else would be pure speculation."

"But…" At that point Kindaichi opened his mouth for the first time. "Surely you can find out where his unit was sent from Kanazawa, can't you?"

"No, we can't," answered Furudate with a grim expression. "You know how chaotic everything was at the end of the war. Documents, for example, have been lost or are in such a state of disorder that it's impossible to determine which unit was sent where. In addition, whereas men in other units are gradually coming home and providing information on those that haven't returned yet, it seems that not one soldier has been repatriated yet from Shizuma's unit. Considering what military transport was like at the time, it's possible that their ship was attacked while they were in transit and they're all sleeping at the bottom of the sea."

Kindaichi felt an indescribable gloom at Furudate's words. If what he said was true, what an unlucky star this young man Shizuma had been born under. Unable to declare his existence and insist on his rights at birth, he had even met an obscure end. Born into obscurity, perishing into obscurity—had Shizuma's life been literally just a fleeting dream? Kindaichi could not help but be moved to pity.

"We will continue to investigate, but it is our opinion that while Kikuno's fate remains uncertain, Shizuma's seems quite hopeless—although I pray that's not the case." Thus said Furudate in closing. He replaced the documents in his briefcase.

A hushed stillness pervaded the room, and no one said a word. Perhaps mulling over what Furudate had said, they all sat staring vacantly ahead. It was Chief Tachibana who at last broke the silence, clearing his throat awkwardly. "Well, then," he said, turning to the members of the Inugami clan, "now that Mrs. Matsuko's explanation has given us a general understanding of the connection between the ax, zither, and chrysanthemum and the recent murders, let us return to last night. As I'm sure you all have heard, Mr. Tomo was found strangled to death inside the abandoned house in Toyohata Village. The time of death is estimated to have been around eight or nine last night." The chief glanced around at the faces of the people in the room. "Therefore, I am afraid I must ask each one of you to tell me what you were doing then. Mrs. Matsuko, will you start us off?"

Matsuko looked indignant and glared at the chief, but soon, turning toward Kiyo, she said with perfect composure, "Kiyo, what time was it when my koto teacher left? Was it past ten?"

Kiyo nodded without a word. Matsuko turned again to Chief Tachibana. "There you have it. Last night my koto teacher Kokin Miyakawa arrived early in the evening, had dinner with me, and then gave me a lesson until about ten at night. I believe these two are aware of that, too, for they must have heard the sound of the koto," she said, indicating Takeko and Umeko with her chin.

"About what time did you have dinner?"

"About seven. After that, we rested for a while and then I brought out the koto. You can confirm it with her, if you like."

"During that time, you never once left your room?"

A sardonic smile rose to Matsuko's lips. "Well, it was rather a long time, so I did go to the bathroom two or three times, and oh yes, I went once to the main part of the house to get some koto string. I don't know if you're aware of it or not, but I've only moved to this annex because these people are staying here, and I usually live in the main part of the building. But even so, that must have taken only five or ten minutes."

"Some koto string?" The chief knitted his eyebrows slightly but immediately thought the better of pursuing that line and said, "And Mr. Kiyo?"

"He stayed with us the whole time listening to our music and helping with things like serving tea. I think he also left the room a few times, but never long enough to be able to go to Toyohata Village." Matsuko smiled sardonically again and said, "I think you'll be quite satisfied if you ask Mrs. Miyakawa. She has trouble with her eyes, but she's not blind, and she seems to have a sixth sense."

Thus Matsuko and Kiyo had alibis.

As Chief Tachibana then began to turn toward Takeko, Umeko interrupted from the side, "My husband and I can vouch for Takeko and Toranosuke's whereabouts. When we couldn't find Tomo anywhere from early in the evening, we became worried and went to Takeko's room for advice. Takeko and Toranosuke, and Sayoko as well, also were worried and helped us phone around—restaurants, cabarets, and the like. Tomo had been acting rather recklessly recently and sometimes went to places like that to amuse himself."

Umeko continued, glaring at Tamayo with hate, "So from around eight to eleven last night, we were desperately trying to locate Tomo. The maids will be able to confirm that, too. Besides, Chief, it's obvious that the person who killed Tomo is the same person who killed Také, and there's no way either Takeko or Toranosuke would kill their own son." Umeko's voice had grown gradually shrill and hysterical, and after a while she burst into tears.

Finally, it was Tamayo's and Monkey's turn, but when the chief directed his questions at them, Monkey bared his teeth angrily and growled, "Like I told you just now, Missy here was sleeping off that drug she'd been given, so she didn't know anything that was going on. As for me, I stayed up guarding her in the next room from the early evening all through the night 'cause I figured who knows what rascal might come again and try and do something bad."

"Can anyone else attest to that?"

"I don't know. I told everybody at dinner that Missy wasn't feeling well so I was going to stay with her all night."

"What time was that?"

"All the servants in this house eat dinner at about half past seven every night."

"Monkey, they tell me you have some pieces of old koto string."

Monkey's eyes glinted, but he simply nodded angrily without saying a word.

"Alright, then, I'd like to see them later," said Tachibana.

Ultimately, Monkey and Tamayo had the weakest alibis. But if Monkey had wanted to kill Tomo, he certainly could have done so when he went to the abandoned house for Tamayo. Or could he have returned once to the villa, suddenly felt a murderous urge, and returned anew to the abandoned house?

Kindaichi remembered what Furudate the lawyer had told him a while ago about Monkey. "Mr. Kindaichi, you wondered once whether Monkey might be Shizuma. I've checked out his background since then and have found out that's impossible. Monkey was born in Toyohata Village, and when he lost his parents at the age of five, Tamayo's mother felt sorry for him and took him in. The midwife who was there when he was born is still alive and swears to it, and besides there are many other witnesses in Toyohata Village who can attest to his identity."

Whether Monkey was or was not Shizuma, however, it was also undeniable that his actions raised many questions. Of course, it could all simply be coincidence, but—

Just then, Matsuko interjected in a sharp, aggressive tone, "Chief, they say you found a soldier's footprints in that abandoned house in Toyohata Village. Is that repatriated soldier who stayed at the Kashiwaya Inn in Lower Nasu the night that Také was killed still wandering around in these parts? Why don't you hurry up and catch him? Who is this man anyhow?"

Pressed sharply by Matsuko in this way, Chief Tachibana seemed at a loss for an answer. "Yes, well… the trap has been laid to capture him, but he's turning out to be a slippery one. As for who he is, we made an inquiry to the Bureau for the Support of Returning Veterans in Hakata right after Také's murder and received an answer from them a few days ago. They say that on November 12, that is, three days before Také's murder, a ship arrived in Hakata carrying repatriates from Burma. There was definitely a man aboard who called himself Sanpei Yamada and who moreover gave his eventual address as 3-21 Kojimachi, Tokyo, that is, the address of your home in Tokyo. After staying a night in Hakata, he left for Tokyo on the 13th. So, it seems unmistakable that he was the one who stayed at the Kashiwaya Inn in Lower Nasu the night of the 15th. I know I have asked you this before, Mrs. Matsuko and Mr. Kiyo, but do you have any idea who this individual might be?"

The masked Kiyo shook his head in silence. Matsuko, on the other hand, stared steadily at Chief Tachibana's face with a puzzled expression. Smiling wryly, she said, "If you know all that, I would have thought you would have accomplished more. So there was nothing else, no other evidence besides the footprints at the scene of the crime?"

"Well, yes… of course, there were various things."

As the chief began to speak, Kindaichi suddenly interjected, "We actually found something odd."

"Odd?"

"I'm sure you've all heard that Tomo was tied to a chair naked from the waist up. Well, he had rope burns all over his chest and arms—in other words, the traces of his struggle to free himself. For a rope to cause so many abrasions, it would have to be quite loose, but when we found him, the rope was wound around him very tightly, biting into his flesh without any slack at all."

Matsuko stared steadily at Kindaichi's face but then said in a calm, composed voice, "And? So what does that mean?"

"Oh, it doesn't mean anything. It's just an observation, but one I find extremely odd. And another thing... Chief?"

Chief Tachibana took out a man's shirt from his bag. "Mrs. Umeko, is this Mr. Tomo's shirt?"

Umeko examined the shirt, eyes brimming with tears, and nodded silently. The shirt was distinctive—a luxury item with five gold buttons shaped like chrysanthemums and sprinkled with diamonds. The top button, however, was missing.

"Do you have any idea when he lost this button?"

Umeko shook her head. "No, I don't, but it must have been after he left the house. Tomo was very fastidious about his appearance, so he would never go out in a shirt that was missing a button. Didn't you find the button in the abandoned house?"

"No, we didn't. We looked all over but couldn't find it. We thought it might have fallen off in the motorboat when he was... uh... struggling with Miss Tamayo, and so we searched there, too, but we didn't find it. If it fell into the lake, of course, it's gone."

Thus speaking, Chief Tachibana pushed the shirt toward Kindaichi. As he did so, who should come rushing into the room like a whirlwind but Oyama, the priest of Nasu Shrine—to reveal to the world a horrible secret.

What an indelicate man this Oyama was. He was no doubt excited, enthralled, and ecstatic over his discovery, but how could he expose someone else's secret, a secret of such tremendous ramifications, so triumphantly? Oyama glanced around the room, and abruptly throwing a cloth-wrapped bundle on the floor, he began to speak with an air of exultation.

"I've found it. I've found it, everyone. I've found out the secret of Mr. Inugami's will. Mr. Inugami treated Miss Tamayo so generously in his will not because she's the granddaughter of his great benefactor but because in fact she is his own granddaughter. Miss Tamayo's mother was the daughter of Sahei and Haruyo, Daini Nonomiya's wife. Daini himself knew about the relationship and permitted it."

At first everyone stared blankly at Oyama, red-faced in his excitement, as if they did not understand what he meant, but when they finally began to realize the terrible import of his disclosure, a great wave of agitation overtook them. Tamayo turned as white as a sheet and looked like she would faint at any minute, while the masked Kiyo's shoulders shook violently. For Matsuko, Takeko, and Umeko, too, it must have been a fresh revelation, for they glared at Tamayo's profile hatefully, eyes glittering with menacing light.

Suddenly Kindaichi began scratching his tousle-haired head, this way, that way, with wild abandon.

# A Monstrous Riddle

By the time mid-December has come and gone, Lake Nasu begins to freeze from its edges. Generally, skating on the lake is safe only after New Year's, sometime in mid-January, but occasionally, once every five or six years, when the winter is especially cold, it is possible to skate even in December.

This was such a year. By mid-December, one could see the ice along the edge of the lake behind the Nasu Inn growing visibly thicker every day, and on December 13, this recently formed ice set the scene for the discovery of a most bizarre corpse—the corpse of the last victim in the case of the Inugami clan. Before turning to the events of that day, however, let us first review the facts of the case.

These days, Kindaichi had been growing increasingly depressed as he watched the desolate landscape around the lake. It had already been nearly two months since he had made his way to Nasu in response to a letter from Toyoichiro Wakabayashi, and although three men had been murdered during that time, the case was still obscure, as if in a haze of smoke. The murderer was somewhere close by, right in front of him—he sensed that, he knew that, yet something was preventing him from seeing the killer clearly. Affected by his impatience, which was intensifying daily, Kindaichi had lately begun to lose all composure. He was so irritated he wanted to tear his hair out.

Thinking that perhaps by reviewing the case from its beginning he might be able to find some clue, he had perused his diary several times, taking note of important points. All he could see there, however, were facts already known to all; he remained just short of focusing on the mysterious figure that flickered behind a screen of smoke. How often Kindaichi had cursed himself for his ineffectiveness, violently scratching his head.

Let us itemize the important points Kindaichi excerpted from his diary, for although he had yet to recognize it clearly, the key to learning the truth behind the horrible Inugami murders was hidden in this list.

1. October 18. Summoned by Toyoichiro Wakabayashi, Kindaichi arrives in Nasu. The same day, Tamayo has a boating accident, and Wakabayashi is poisoned.

2. November 1. Kiyo returns from the war wearing a mask, and the late Sahei Inugami's will is read before the entire Inugami clan.

3. November 15. Suspecting the masked Kiyo of being an imposter, Také and Tomo go to Nasu Shrine to retrieve Kiyo's votive hand print. (Instigated by Tamayo.)

4. November 15, night. Asked by the family for a new hand print from Kiyo, Matsuko and Kiyo refuse, and the family conference ends in a quarrel at around 10 p.m.

5. November 15, around 11 p.m. Tamayo asks Také to meet her on the observation deck and gives him a pocket watch with the fingerprint of the masked Kiyo. (Watch still missing; might be at the bottom of the lake.)

6. November 15, night. Také is murdered. Estimated time of the murder is between 11 p.m. and 12 midnight.

7. November 15, around 8 p.m. A man calling himself Sanpei Yamada, dressed in the manner of a repatriated

soldier and hiding his face, checks into the Kashiwaya Inn in Lower Nasu. Around 10 p.m., he leaves the inn to go somewhere and returns around midnight, looking very agitated.

8. November 16, morning. Také's severed head is discovered on a chrysanthemum doll. The scene of the crime is determined to be the observation deck.

9. November 16. Matsuko and the masked Kiyo offer to comply with the family's request, and Kiyo makes a new hand print. Official comparison of this and the one from Nasu Shrine confirms they are identical and therefore that the masked Kiyo is in fact the true Kiyo Inugami. (Question: When the results were announced, Tamayo twice began to say something, but stopped. What was she going to say?)

10. November 16. Také's headless corpse is recovered from the middle of the lake.

11. November 16. A bloody boat, probably used to transport Také's body, is found on the shores of the lake in Lower Nasu.

12. November 16, around 5 a.m. The supposed repatriated soldier calling himself Sanpei Yamada leaves the Kashiwaya Inn, never having shown his face to anyone.

13. November 16, night. Také's wake ends about 10 p.m.

14. November 16, night. A man dressed in the manner of a repatriated soldier, with his face hidden, sneaks into Tamayo's room searching for something. (Question: What was he looking for and did he find it?)

15. November 16, around 10:30 p.m. Tamayo discovers the repatriated soldier in her room and screams. Her scream causes an uproar in the Inugami household.

16. November 16, same time. Sayoko witnesses Monkey fighting with the repatriated soldier (proving that Monkey and the repatriated soldier are not one and the same).

17. November 16, same time. The masked Kiyo, who upon hearing Tamayo's scream had run out of the house, is punched by someone at the base of the observation deck and falls there unconscious. (His mask comes off, and his hideous face is exposed for all to see.)

18. November 25. Tomo, planning to rape Tamayo, renders her unconscious with an inhaled anesthetic and takes her by motorboat to the abandoned house in Toyohata Village. (Unsubstantiated—only according to Tamayo's statement.)

19. November 25, around 4 p.m. Someone phones Monkey informing him that Tamayo is in the abandoned house in Toyohata Village. Monkey goes there immediately by boat and finds Tamayo unconscious on a bed, a memo signed by "The Man in the Shadows" pinned to her chest, and Tomo tied to a chair nearby, half-naked and gagged. Monkey leaves Tomo as he is and takes only Tamayo back to the villa by motorboat sometime between 4:30 p.m. and 5:30 p.m. (All unsubstantiated—only according to Monkey's statement.)

20. November 25, sometime between 8 p.m. and 9 p.m. Tomo is strangled to death. Alibis of all the members of the Inugami household during this time confirmed. In other words, there is no evidence of any of them having left the villa during this time.

21. November 26. After hearing Tamayo's and Monkey's statements, a group hastens to Toyohata Village to

rescue Tomo. They discover him tied to a chair half-naked and strangled to death, a koto string wound tightly around his neck. (Questions: Why were there extensive rope burns on Tomo's skin although the rope was wound around him so tightly there was no slack? Where is the missing diamond-studded button from Tomo's shirt?)

22. November 26. Sayoko goes insane.
23. November 26. The group at the abandoned house in Toyohata Village discovers various pieces of evidence indicating that the repatriated soldier had been hiding there.
24. November 26. Matsuko tells of Kikuno Aonuma's curse in connection with the ax, zither, and chrysanthemum.
25. November 26. There is an amazing revelation about Tamayo's identity.

Actually, Kindaichi's notations went into much more detail, but because that would be too tedious for the reader and, in addition, because an itemized list cannot do justice to some issues that will be explained at greater length later on, I have reproduced here only the most important portions.

Perusing this list repeatedly, Kindaichi always felt overwhelmed by the darkest gloom each time he reached the last item regarding Tamayo's identity. After the case had come to an end and all its secrets had been brought out into the open, it would be found that this indiscreet revelation by Oyama, the priest of Nasu Shrine, was indeed the climax of the case of the Inugami Clan.

It was when Také had been killed that Oyama had first told Kindaichi of the secret Chinese chest he had found in the treasure hall of Nasu Shrine. According to him, the chest had been sealed with a strip of paper cosigned by Sahei and his benefactor Daini Nonomiya, and it contained various papers, including old love letters that the two men had exchanged in their younger days. Kindaichi remembered the priest's words as he exulted in his discovery: that he intended to examine the contents of the Chinese chest thoroughly because he might find some previously unknown, valuable document about Sahei; that he didn't want to give the impression of delving into someone's secret out of vulgar curiosity; but that because Sahei Inugami was a benefactor to all the people of Nasu, he wanted to know what this great man was really like and then to write his biography.

There is nothing so terrible as a determined mind. Oyama had achieved his goal at last. By painstakingly organizing and carefully scrutinizing the contents of the Chinese chest, he had finally discovered Sahei's secret—and what an astounding secret it was.

Reading over the documents that Oyama had arranged in order, Kindaichi had found a record of the most singular and abnormal carnal drama played out by the young Sahei, Daini Nonomiya, and Haruyo, Daini's wife, a wretched account of their torturous passions and anguish. I cannot find it within me to publish those documents here, as the picture they paint is so immoral and deviant. I will limit myself to reporting the facts as simply as possible.

It was clear that there had indeed been a homosexual relationship between Daini Nonomiya and the young Sahei Inugami, but the liaison apparently ended after the first two or three years. Perhaps Daini became more reticent as Sahei grew older, but judging from what could be read between the lines, it seems that Daini Nonomiya, while not impotent, was not a sexually robust man. Unfortunately, moreover, the passion that he had felt, even if only slightly, toward the young Sahei seems not to have been aroused at all by his wife, Haruyo. In other words, while Daini was able to feel some sexual desire toward men, he was totally impotent with women. Because of that, when Sahei first became the object of Daini's attentions, the couple—Daini was forty-two and Haruyo twenty-two at the time—had been married for three years, but Haruyo still remained a virgin.

While the homosexual liaison between Daini and Sahei apparently ended after only a few years, Sahei continued thereafter to be a constant visitor and friend, and eventually he became intimate with his benefactor's wife. What stormy impulse pushed them into this relationship the documents in the Chinese chest did not reveal, but it greatly affected Sahei's subsequent character and became the major factor in his wretched sexual history.

At the time, Sahei was twenty and Haruyo five years older. As it was for both the first intimate encounter with a member of the opposite sex, the flames of passion burned intensely. Just as intense, however, were their feelings of guilt. Neither Sahei nor Haruyo were such damnable souls as to be able to hide their transgression brazen-faced. So after suffering through gut-wrenching anguish, they tried to kill themselves by drinking poison.

Luckily or not, this suicide attempt was quickly discovered and averted by Daini, but as a result, the whole of their secret became known to him as well. His response, however, was extraordinary. Apparently Daini not only forgave Sahei and Haruyo but in fact urged them to continue their immoral relationship. No doubt his attitude stemmed partly from his wish to atone for his treatment of his wife, whom he had long left a virgin, untouched since their marriage, yet he was also too concerned about appearances to divorce her and to give her openly to Sahei. For the same reason, Haruyo, too, did not wish a divorce. And so the strange relationship among the three took a new direction.

Haruyo, while legally Daini's wife, was in reality Sahei's wife and lover. Daini not only made it as convenient as possible for them to meet but also took steps to ensure that their secret would not become known. The two lovers always met in a room in Nasu Shrine, and when they did, Daini would leave the room but never the house. He would keep guard in another room like a faithful dog, to prevent the truth about his wife and her lover from leaking to the outside world. The three managed to keep their secret hidden to all, and their strange, unnatural relationship continued long thereafter. Eventually, Haruyo gave birth to a girl, Noriko, whom Daini recognized as his legal daughter without any hesitation whatsoever.

Thus passed these unnatural but tranquil days of passion, with no trouble arising among the three, at least superficially. Yet below the surface, what agony they must have suffered, each in his or her own way. As a woman of that era, Haruyo in particular must have been tormented by a guilty conscience. Novels like *Lady Chatterley's Lover* were not as yet widely known in Japan, and none of her countrymen had the generosity of heart to think that because her husband was impotent, a woman should be permitted to take a lover. The common attitude and accepted moral principle was that even if her husband refused to so much as touch her, a wife should simply endure in silence. And especially because Haruyo had received an old-fashioned upbringing, such notions had been strongly ingrained in her, and she was tormented by guilt over her relationship with Sahei. Yet, at the same time, she could not restrain the feelings that bound her to her hand-some, younger lover. Struggling with remorse and anguish, she nevertheless was consumed body and soul each time she met with him. Sahei, for his part, loved Haruyo even more as he realized the agony she was suffering, and as he succeeded in business and became a prominent entrepreneur, his pity and affection for this unfortunate woman deepened—this woman who was in fact his wife, who had even given him a child, but who could not openly declare herself as his. This indeed was the reason Sahei never legally married anyone: to demonstrate his lifelong devotion to Haruyo.

No doubt it was also to prevent his affections from pass-ing to another woman that Sahei made for himself such an accursed life: having three mistresses at once, all living in the same villa. As Sahei became more famous and distinguished, it probably became harder for him to meet with Haruyo, and he needed other women in order to vent his sexual ener-gies. If he had only one mistress, however, he feared that some day he might come to love her instead. Therefore, by having three at once, he could observe first-hand their base jealousies and petty feuds and thus continue to regard them with contempt. According to Matsuko, Sahei kept the three women only as tools to satisfy his carnal desires and had not an ounce of love for any of them. In fact, he feared love and guarded against it.

Sahei's inability to love his three daughters stemmed from the same source. Haruyo had already given him a daughter named Noriko—his eldest daughter and the child of the only woman he had ever loved. How Sahei must have adored her, but he could not call her his own, and while the Inugami clan gradually prospered, Noriko had to forever remain poor— the child of the humble priest of Nasu Shrine. Because of this secret indignation at the unfair hand life had dealt his beloved child, he remained throughout his life a cold father to Matsuko, Takeko, and Umeko.

The ultimate result of all of Sahei's rancor, indignation, and pity was his last will and testament. Haruyo had spent her life unable to proclaim herself the wife of Sahei Inugami, and Noriko, while born as the eldest daughter of Sahei Inugami, had died the wife of a penniless priest. And so Sahei's pity for this mother and daughter had grown and grown, until he decided to present Tamayo with such an extraordinary gift. Thinking of the turmoil within Sahei's heart, Kindaichi could not help but feel some compassion, but considering how the old man's will had become the cause of a series of terrible tragedies, he had to sigh and wonder if there could not have been some other way.

Thus the days passed, and it was the morning of December 13—already twenty days since Tomo's death—when another unearthly murder was discovered.

Mulling over the case the night before, Kindaichi had been unable to fall asleep. Thus he was sleeping in later than usual when, at about seven in the morning, the phone by his pillow rang, jerking him awake. Picking up the phone, he was immediately connected to an outside line, and he could hear the voice of Chief Tachibana.

"Mr. Kindaichi? Mr. Kindaichi?" Kindaichi did not think it was from the morning cold that the chief's voice was shaking.

"Mr. Kindaichi, please come right away. It's finally happened. A third Inugami has been murdered."

"Murdered? Who?" Kindaichi gripped the icy receiver more tightly.

"Just come right away. No, before that, go to your window facing the lake and look toward the back of the Inugami villa, and you'll understand. I'll be waiting, so please come quickly. Damn! I hate this case."

Hanging up, Kindaichi sprang up from his futon and opened one of the shutters. The freezing wind gusting over the ice stung his skin like needles. Sneezing a few times, Kindaichi nevertheless managed to extract a pair of binoculars from his traveling bag and hurriedly focused on the area behind the Inugami villa. The image that jumped into his eyes made him forget the cold completely, and he stood there frozen in horror.

Just below the observation deck where Také had been killed, something strange was sticking out of the ice by the water's edge. It was a man's body—or, considering the monstrous riddle that was to come to light later on, perhaps more accurately it was a "dy-bo," for it was sticking straight up in the air, feet up, thrust in the ice from the head to the waist, and its two legs in their flannel pajama pants spread in a V. It was a horrible, yet inexpressibly comical sight.

With this bizarre upside-down corpse directly before them, the various members of the Inugami clan, with rigid expressions, stood here and there on the berm and the observation deck of the boathouse. Kindaichi swept over their faces with his binoculars but caught his breath when he realized that there was one man he did not see. He closed his eyes. The masked Kiyo was missing.

# The Blood-Spattered Button

The news of the final Inugami murder was disseminated to newspapers throughout the country by the news agencies and was featured in all the evening papers that day. The continuing series of tragedies that had begun with the extraordinary will of the late Sahei Inugami was no longer just a local story but instead the focus of nationwide attention. While the simple fact of a third murdered Inugami (the fourth victim in the case, if we count Toyoichiro Wakabayashi) easily made the articles sensational enough, readers were additionally stunned by the monstrous riddle posed by the victim's body. Needless to say, the one who solved the riddle was Kindaichi.

"Ch-Chief, w-w-what's going on? W-why is that c-c-corpse sticking up in the air upside down?" Having rushed to the observation deck of the boathouse, Kindaichi could hardly speak in his excitement, for a weird, almost farcically comical idea had popped into his head as he had been hastening to the scene. It was almost driving him mad.

"How should I know, Mr. Kindaichi? I'm completely flabbergasted myself. Why the hell did the murderer stick Kiyo's body upside down in a place like that? Damn it! I hate this. It gives me the creeps." Chief Tachibana scowled and spat out his words, gazing bitterly at the accursed corpse sticking feet up out of the ice below. His men were having a difficult time trying to dig out the body—a task that seemed simple but in fact was not, for with the ice formed but not yet very thick, anyone stepping onto it risked the danger of having it break and being plunged into the water; but reaching the corpse by boat also presented difficulties. The detectives were having to cut away the ice bit by bit and to gradually maneuver the boat toward the corpse. Overhead, the leaden color of the sky portended snow.

"S-so you're certain that body is Kiyo's," muttered Kindaichi, his teeth chattering. It was by no means the morning cold, but an extraordinary thought, that was making him shiver body and soul.

"Yes, there's no mistake. Matsuko says those pajamas are definitely his, and besides, he's nowhere to be found."

"And Matsuko?" Kindaichi glanced around, for he did not see her anywhere either.

"I tell you, that woman's something else. She didn't cry or bawl like her sisters even when she saw Kiyo like that. She simply said, 'It's her. She's put the finishing touches on her revenge,' and then shut herself up in her room. But maybe that just goes to show how deep her feelings of hatred are."

Kindaichi noticed Tamayo standing motionless at the edge of the observation deck, with the collar of her coat turned up high around her neck, staring down at the wretched corpse. What she might be thinking, he could not tell, for her elegant profile remained as expressionless as ever, sphinx-like in its inscrutability.

"So, Chief, who first discovered the corpse?"

"Monkey—who else?" Tachibana still spat out his words bitterly.

"Monkey?" Kindaichi glanced at Tamayo and sighed. Whether she could hear their conversation or not, she remained as still as a statue.

237

"And what was the cause of death? Surely he wasn't plunged in there alive, was he?"

"We won't know until we dig out the corpse, but I wonder if maybe someone split his head open with an ax."

Kindaichi caught his breath. "I see. If Kiyo was the one killed, that means it has to be the ax this time. But if that's the case, Chief, how come we don't see blood anywhere?" There was not a spot of blood anywhere on the milky-white, frozen surface of the lake.

"I know. I thought that was strange, too. Also, if the murderer did use an ax, he must have brought it from somewhere else because there isn't an ax or comparable weapon anywhere in this house. After Matsuko's confession of the other day, I had them get rid of anything that even remotely resembled an ax."

By this time, the team of detectives had finally managed to steer the boat close to the body, and two of them took hold of its legs.

"Hey, be careful. Try not to damage the corpse," called down Chief Tachibana from the observation deck.

"Yes, sir. We know."

The third detective began breaking the ice around the corpse, which was submerged from head to waist. Soon, the ice had been broken into small pieces, and when the detectives shook the legs, the rest of the body shook as well.

"Good, it should be okay now. Pull it up gently."

As the two detectives, each holding a leg, pulled the corpse straight up out of the water and ice, the people standing on the observation deck could not help but catch their breaths and clench their fists at the sight. Kiyo's mask was gone, and emerging upside down from the ice was a most nightmarish face—a formless mass of flesh like an overripe pomegranate. Once, at the reading of Sahei's will, Kindaichi had seen the just repatriated Kiyo pull his mask up to around his nose, but this was the first time he had looked squarely at that hideous countenance. Moreover, having been buried in ice overnight, it had deteriorated to a purplish color, so that its ghoulishness was amplified. Strangely, however, he could not see any head wound such as Chief Tachibana had predicted.

After studying this gruesome face for some time, Kindaichi finally looked away, but as he did, his eyes were caught by the sight of Tamayo: she was staring intently at the face that even Kindaichi found too shocking to behold. What thoughts, he wondered, could be passing through her mind?

As the detectives were making their way back to shore with the frozen body in their boat, Dr. Kusuda, the medical examiner, came running up to the observation deck. Seeming tired and disgusted by the continuing series of incidents, he hardly even bothered to greet Chief Tachibana.

"Doctor, we need your help again. I know you can't ascertain any details until you conduct the autopsy, but if you could just give us the cause of death and the time elapsed since death."

Kusuda nodded without a word and began descending from the observation deck, when suddenly Tamayo called, "Excuse me, Doctor."

Kusuda, his foot already on the first step down, stopped and looked back at her in surprise. "Yes? Did you want something, Miss?"

"Yes, actually…" Tamayo hesitated momentarily, glancing back and forth between Kusuda and Chief Tachibana, but before long, she seemed to make up her mind. "If you're going to conduct an autopsy on that corpse, before you do, please get a hand print… the fingerprints of the right hand."

Her words hit Kindaichi like a bolt of lightning. "What, w-what did you say, Miss Tamayo?" He took a step forward, his breath coming in rapid bursts. "Are you questioning the identity of that corpse?"

Tamayo did not answer but turned her gaze toward the lake and stood waiting silently. This was a woman who spoke if and when she wanted to and could not easily be made to talk by others. Her solitary life had given her a steely will.

"But Miss Tamayo," said Kindaichi, licking his lips again and again, overpowered by a feeling he could not pinpoint, "we got a hand print from Kiyo before, remember, and it was found to be identical to the votive hand print." Kindaichi abruptly fell silent, for he had noticed a hint of scorn in Tamayo's eyes.

Tamayo, however, managed to extinguish the look immediately and said in a low, quiet tone, "Yes, but there's no harm in making sure. Besides, taking a hand print is not that much trouble, is it?"

Chief Tachibana, too, was staring at Tamayo's face with a frown, but soon he nodded toward Kusuda. "Doctor, I'll send a detective over later, then. Please plan to take fingerprints before you start the autopsy."

Kusuda nodded without a word and descended the stairs, while Tamayo, acknowledging the chief and Kindaichi with a nod, hurried down as well. Kindaichi left the observation deck with Chief Tachibana soon thereafter, but his gait betrayed his emotion: he staggered down the stairs as if intoxicated, for a storm had begun to rage in his mind.

Why was Tamayo dwelling on Kiyo's fingerprints? They had taken them once, and his identity had been proven beyond the shadow of a doubt. But… but… that confident air she had had just now… what thoughts lay hidden in her mind? Perhaps, just perhaps, thought Kindaichi, he had overlooked something very important. Suddenly Kindaichi stood frozen in mid-step, for the scene he had witnessed when Kiyo's hand print was compared with the one on the votive scroll had flashed before his mind's eye. The instant the forensics officer Fujisaki had announced that the hand prints were identical, Tamayo had begun to say something, not just once, but twice. She must know something. She must be aware of something he had overlooked. What could it be?

At the foot of the stairs, the two men parted company, Tachibana following Dr. Kusuda into the boathouse and Kindaichi trudging brooding toward the villa. There, Takeko, Umeko, and their husbands were gathered in a room in whispered conversation. When they saw Kindaichi passing by outside, Takeko opened the glass door to the veranda and called, "Mr. Kindaichi, may we speak with you?"

Kindaichi approached the veranda. "Yes?"

"I believe this is the button you were talking about." Takeko gently opened a folded piece of tissue paper she held in her hand. Kindaichi grew wide-eyed, for indeed, there before him was the missing button from Tomo's shirt.

"Mrs. Takeko, where did you find this?"

"I found Sayoko holding it this morning, but you know what condition she's in right now—she couldn't tell me anything, so I have no idea where she found it."

"Is she still… ill?"

Takeko nodded grimly. "She doesn't get agitated like before, but she's still totally incoherent."

"Mr. Kindaichi." Umeko spoke to him from inside the room. "That day, the day Tomo's body was found, Sayoko went with you to the abandoned house in Toyohata Village. Could she possibly have found it then?"

"No, absolutely not. Miss Sayoko fainted as soon as she saw Mr. Tomo's body, so she couldn't possibly have had the time. I believe Mrs. Umeko's husband is aware of that, too."

Kokichi nodded grimly.

"How odd, then," said Takeko, with hesitant eyes. "Sayoko hasn't left the estate at all since you people brought her back here that day. Where on earth could she have found it?"

"May I take a look?" Kindaichi took the packet from Takeko's hand and studied the button closely. It was a gold, chrysanthemum-shaped button sprinkled with diamonds, but Kindaichi could see a tiny black stain, probably blood, on the chrysanthemum base. "Mrs. Umeko, are you certain that this button is from Mr. Tomo's shirt?"

Umeko nodded silently.

"But perhaps there were some extra buttons lying around."

"No, that's impossible. There were only those five buttons in that set, with no extras."

"Then it has to be the button that came off Mr. Tomo's shirt that day. Mrs. Takeko, I wonder if you would let me borrow this button for a while. There's something I'd like to ask the chief to check."

"Of course."

As Kindaichi was carefully rewrapping the button in the tissue paper, Chief Tachibana came rushing into the room.

"Oh, Mr. Kindaichi, here you are." The chief strode up to him. "This one's rather odd. We thought that if there was another murder, naturally an ax would be used, but the culprit has outwitted us. Kiyo was strangled with a thin rope of some kind, like Tomo. The murderer seems to have then thrown the body into the ice upside down from the observation deck."

Kindaichi had been listening to the chief with an uninterested expression, and waiting for him to come to an end, he shook his head wanly.

"No, Chief. It's as it should be. There is an ax involved."

Chief Tachibana frowned. "But Mr. Kindaichi, we would know if there were an ax wound."

Kindaichi took out a notebook and fountain pen from his bosom. "Chief, that corpse is Kiyo, right? And since Kiyo was found upside down…" On a page of the notebook, Kindaichi wrote in large letters

KI YO

YO KI

Chief Tachibana's eyes looked like they might pop out. "Mr. Kindaichi!" He gasped loudly, opening and closing his fists.

"Yes, Chief. It's a childish riddle. The murderer has tried to use the victim's body to suggest an ax, the *yoki* of *yokikotokiku.*"

Kindaichi began to laugh in a high-pitched voice—a hollow laugh that sounded even hysterical. True to expectations, snowflakes started dancing down from the leaden sky.

# The Ill-Fated Mother and Son

Night. Half past nine. The area around Lake Nasu looked swollen with the snow that had fallen since morning, as if the ground had dressed itself in padded winter clothes. The lake, the towns and villages along the shore, and the mountain ranges behind them, all sighed under the large, wet snowflakes that fell with dizzying intensity. There was no wind, only the soft, white flowers of winter flickering down ceaselessly from the dark sky. The stillness of the night penetrated the soul.

As if that stillness had been gathered within the Inugami villa, Kindaichi, Chief Tachibana, and Furudate the lawyer sat in the drawing room, each lost in silence before the English-style fireplace. For a long time they had sat like that, without saying a word, staring at the blazing fireplace, from which they occasionally heard the thud of a piece of coal falling.

The three men were waiting for the autopsy report and the results of Fujisaki's comparison of the new hand print from Kiyo's corpse with the votive hand print. Kindaichi sat buried in a big easy chair, his eyes quietly closed. Ideas were swirling in his mind and beginning to solidify into definite shape, a process until now prevented by a blind spot that had hindered his thought processes. Today, however, he had finally seen where that blind spot lay, and he had Tamayo to thank for it. Kindaichi shuddered slightly, opened his eyes, and looked around him as if he had awakened from a dream.

The snow was falling faster. Soft, white flakes crossed the window pane without pause.

Just then, the three men heard the faint sound of wheels on snow stopping outside the front entrance, followed by the loud peal of the doorbell. They looked at one another, and Tachibana began to rise, but before he could, footsteps from somewhere inside the house pattered toward the entrance. Insistent words were exchanged. Soon the same footsteps approached the drawing room, and the door opened. It was the maid.

"Chief, there's someone here who wants see you," she said, an uncertain expression on her face.

"Someone for me? Who?"

"A woman. She says her name is Kikuno Aonuma."

The three men sprang out of their chairs.

"Kikuno Aonuma!" Chief Tachibana swallowed hard, his Adam's apple bobbing up and down. "Please, please show her in here immediately."

Soon after the maid left, there appeared at the door a diminutive woman wearing a dark overcoat, her head and face partly covered by an old-fashioned, reddish-brown veil. She must have come in a pedicab, for neither her coat nor veil was wet.

Nodding slightly to the three men, she turned away to take off her coat and veil and hand them to the maid, turned around again, and bowed politely. The sight of her face made them all stagger and gasp, fists clenched, as if the rug had been pulled out from under them.

"You… you're Kikuno Aonuma?"

"Yes, I am." The woman who answered quietly and raised her face was Kokin Miyakawa, the koto teacher.

Kindaichi, who had been standing bolt upright without moving a muscle, suddenly began violently scratching his head. Furudate, on the other hand, began wiping his palms with a handkerchief.

Kokin Miyakawa—the woman who had stepped forward to reveal her identity as Kikuno Aonuma—squinted her nearly blind eyes and quietly looked around at the faces of the three men. "I was in Tokyo today, when a student of mine told me about the article in the evening newspaper—the article about Mr. Kiyo. So I rushed here as soon as I could, because I felt I should no longer hide my identity."

The three men could not keep from exchanging glances. Indeed, if she had seen the early edition of the evening paper in Tokyo and had jumped on a train right away, it would be possible for her to arrive in Upper Nasu by this hour. However, could it not also be that by this statement, Kikuno Aonuma was trying to give herself an alibi? Suspicion flashed in Chief Tachibana's eyes.

"Then, you've just arrived?"

"Yes." Her face was flushed from having come suddenly into the warm room from the cold outdoors. She took out a handkerchief and quietly wiped the perspiration from her forehead.

"Alone?"

"No, one of my students was kind enough to accompany me, but I sent her on ahead to the inn. I myself went directly from the train station to the police station, but they told me you were here, Chief."

Chief Tachibana sighed lightly, as if disappointed. If a student had accompanied her, then Kikuno could not be lying.

"Yes, well… please, come sit down here." The chief pushed a chair toward her, while Kindaichi approached her and gently took her hand.

"Oh, that's alright, you don't need to… well, thank you, then."

Guided to the chair by Kindaichi, Kikuno bowed politely and sat down. Kindaichi then went to the door, opened it and glanced around outside, and closed it tightly.

"I had no idea you were Kikuno Aonuma," said the chief. "Right under my nose, too. Mr. Furudate, didn't you know?"

"Not at all, what with all those records destroyed and people killed during the war. If we hadn't had the war, I'm sure my investigations would have been more successful."

Kikuno smiled slightly and said, "It's no wonder you didn't find out. I made every effort to hide my former identity. Probably the only people who knew were my husband, who passed away seven years ago, and my relatives in Toyama, and those three are gone now, too."

"Who was your husband?" asked Kindaichi.

"His name was Shofu Miyakawa, and he, too, was a koto teacher. I visited his house once while I was living with my relatives in Toyama, and we became close."

"And so you married."

"Well, actually…" Kikuno hesitated. "We were never legally married. At the time, his wife was still living."

Kikuno flushed and looked down, while Kindaichi's sensitivity made him avert his eyes. Having started her young adult life as someone's mistress, this woman had been fated to live again as a kept woman, unable to become a legal wife. Thinking of the unfortunate circumstances she had endured, Kindaichi could not help but feel compassion for her.

247

Kikuno continued, still hesitantly, "Actually, his wife passed away three years after I placed myself in his care, and he proposed then that we wed, but I declined his offer. It would have been one thing if we had had children, but we didn't, and I was afraid that if I applied to change my family register, my whereabouts would become known in my home town, and that the people in this house might find out about the child I had left in Toyama."

Kikuno gently held her handkerchief to her eyes. Kindaichi, Tachibana, and Furudate exchanged looks of sympathy. For this poor woman, the horrific memories of that frosty night could never be wiped away. Because the threats made by the three half-sisters had penetrated the very core of her being, she had tried to hide her child from them, even if it meant subjecting herself to a life forever in the shadows. No wonder Furudate's investigations had been unsuccessful.

"So it is actually inaccurate for me to use the name of Miyakawa, but since all my students thought I was Shofu Miyakawa's legal wife, people were calling me Kokin Miyakawa before I realized it."

"Did your husband teach you the koto?"

"I knew how to play before I met him. In fact, that's how we got to know each other in the first place." Kikuno reddened slightly again.

Just then, Chief Tachibana shifted in his chair and coughed awkwardly. "About the son you left in Toyama—I believe his name is Shizuma. Did you ever see him after that?"

"Yes, occasionally. Once every three years or so."

"Then Shizuma knew you were his real mother."

"Not as a child. He had been legally adopted by the Tsudas, and they treated him just like their real son. I think he thought of me simply as a kindly aunt. But someone must have told him by the time he was in junior high school, for he seemed to be vaguely aware then of who I really was."

"Did he know about his father as well?"

"No, I'm certain he didn't. After all, I didn't even tell the Tsudas very much about his father, though of course they probably guessed."

"So Shizuma never found out about his father?"

"Well, to tell the truth…" Kikuno took out her handkerchief and quietly wiped her mouth. "I don't know if you're aware of it or not, but Shizuma was drafted and discharged repeatedly during the war, and each time he went into the service I traveled to Toyama to see him off. When a draft notice came for the last time in the spring of 1944, I had a premonition that I would never see him again, so I couldn't restrain myself and told him I was his mother. At that time, he asked me about his father."

"And you told him."

"Yes." A clear, pearl-like tear welled from Kikuno's eye and glided down her cheeks, as Kindaichi, gripped by pity, averted his eyes. Chief Tachibana, too, cleared his throat awkwardly. "I see. So then, I suppose you also told him the circumstances that led to your leaving his father, that is, Sahei Inugami."

"Yes. I had to, so he'd understand."

"And about the curse of the ax, zither, and chrysanthemum?"

The chief had tried to say those words as nonchalantly as possible, but even so, Kikuno raised her face with a start, glancing at the three men with a frightened expression, before immediately hanging her head again.

"Yes. I wanted him to know what I had suffered." Kikuno, shoulders quivering, held her handkerchief to her eyes.

Kindaichi asked her quietly from the side, "How did Shizuma react? I imagine he must have been very upset."

"Yes, he's a very gentle boy, but he tends to be rather emotional. When I told him, he didn't say a word, but his eyes were brimming with tears and he was shaking all over, the color drained from his face."

"Then, after that, he went into the service and left to fight in the war somewhere, far away from his home and country."

With gloomy eyes, Kindaichi stood up from his chair, walked to the window, and looked outside. The snow showed no signs of abating, and the wind had intensified. White whirls were dancing insanely outside. Gazing blankly at this scene, Kindaichi sighed heavily.

What an unfortunate young man this Shizuma was. The moment he learned the identity of his true father was the moment he started his fateful voyage toward his destiny. As he set out with the father's name he had heard for the first time etched in his mind, what was it that awaited him? A torpedo? A bomber? Or could he have skillfully evaded those attacks and still be alive somewhere?

Kindaichi spun around and strode back to Kikuno. Placing his hands on her shoulders, he looked down into her face from above. "There's one more thing I want to ask you about Shizuma."

"Yes?"

"You've seen that rubber mask Kiyo was wearing, haven't you?"

"Yes, I have."

"That mask was made identical to Kiyo's real face. Tell me, didn't Shizuma and Kiyo resemble each other?"

Kindaichi's question had an explosive effect. Kikuno grew rigid in her seat, while Chief Tachibana and Furudate both grasped the arms of their chairs, as if about to spring to their feet.

A piece of coal fell with a thud in the fireplace.

# The Three Hand Prints

"How did you know that?" It was a long time afterwards that Kikuno finally opened her mouth to speak. She was slumped deep in her chair, nervously wiping the perspiration from her forehead, fear written on her almost sightless eyes.

"Th-then, they do l-look alike?"

Kikuno nodded slightly, then said in a parched voice, "When I first met Mr. Kiyo, I was astounded. Of course, what I was seeing was a rubber mask and not his real face, but as you know, I have trouble with my eyes, so I couldn't tell that at first, and I was stunned because he looked so much like him—like Shizuma. They didn't just resemble each other; they were like twins. I thought for sure that Shizuma had come back from the war and was sitting there in front of me. But as I looked at him more carefully, I realized that he wasn't Shizuma, that the areas from the eyebrows to the eyes and around the sides of the nose were different. But you could tell the same blood was running through their veins. Since Mr. Kiyo was Mr. Inugami's grandson and Shizuma his son—so that they're nephew and uncle although of similar age—they both must resemble Mr. Inugami."

Kikuno ended quietly and wiped her flowing tears with her handkerchief. No doubt her heart was aching for her child, who, although the only son of Sahei Inugami, had been compelled to live in the shadows and was now missing at war.

Suddenly, Chief Tachibana turned toward Kindaichi. "Mr. Kindaichi, how did you know they looked alike?"

"No, no," said Kindaichi, looking away as if avoiding Tachibana's gaze. "I didn't know. But as Mrs. Kikuno said just now, they are uncle and nephew and moreover of similar age, so I thought perhaps there might be some resemblance. I had no idea they looked so much alike." Kindaichi was standing behind Kikuno, lightly scratching his tousle-haired head with a strange glimmer in his eyes.

Tachibana stared at Kindaichi's profile incredulously, but finally, realizing the futility of waiting for more of an explanation, turned to Kikuno once again. "Mrs. Kikuno, do you know where Shizuma is?"

"No, I don't," she answered without hesitation. "If only I did." She held her handkerchief to her eyes, choking with tears.

"But Shizuma knows your address, doesn't he?"

"Yes."

"Then if he's safe, he would try to contact you there."

"Yes, so I've been waiting, day after day, for word from him."

Tachibana, with compassionate yet still-suspicious eyes, continued to watch the weeping woman. He quietly placed his hand on her shoulder. "Mrs. Kikuno, when did you start coming to this house? And did you have any particular purpose in mind?"

Kikuno wiped away her tears and lifted her face quietly. "Chief, that is why I came to see you tonight, to explain. It was simply coincidence, not for any evil purpose, that I started coming to this villa. I don't know if you're aware of it or not, but a koto master named Shou Furuya used to come and give lessons in this region. Two years ago, however, she fell ill with palsy, and I began substituting for her. When Mrs. Furuya first proposed that I do this, I shuddered and refused, for I never wanted to set foot in Nasu or Ina again. Moreover,

253

when I heard that Mrs. Matsuko was one of the students, I was terrified. Various circumstances, however, forced me to take the job. I thought to myself at the time, though, thirty years have passed, my name, status and appearance have all changed completely," said Kikuno, sadly putting her hand on her cheek. "I thought that maybe Mrs. Matsuko wouldn't even recognize who I was. With that thought, and also because I was curious, I decided to be daring and come here. I had no ulterior motive whatsoever."

"And Mrs. Matsuko did not recognize you."

"Apparently not. After all, I look so hideous now, as you see."

True, it was probably impossible to find traces of Kikuno's former face in Kokin Miyakawa today. Kikuno must have been quite lovely when she had been the object of Sahei's affection, but Kokin today had one eye protruding, the other sunken and blind, and even a large scar on her forehead. How could one guess she had been a beauty? Besides, even Matsuko could not have imagined that an erstwhile factory worker at her father's silk mill might become a celebrated koto teacher from Tokyo. Thirty years can weave strange patterns in the tapestry of fate.

"If you started coming here two years ago, that means Mr. Inugami was still alive. Did you see him?"

"No, never. He was already bedridden by then. Besides, I couldn't see him now, looking like this. I was hoping I might at least get a peek at him, but…" Kikuno sighed. "But I'm glad I started coming here to give lessons, because, thanks to that, I got to attend his funeral and make an offering at the altar." Kikuno pressed her handkerchief to her eyes and began to sob again.

How brief their life together had been. Although their souls had been drawn so strongly to each other, they had been torn apart by his three rabid daughters. And even when Sahei lay dying, Kikuno had been able neither to see him nor to identify herself to him, even though she had been so near. The thought of Kikuno making an offering at Sahei's altar, weeping, hidden from the sight of others, brought a lump to Kindaichi's throat.

Tachibana coughed awkwardly. "I understand. Now, let's turn to the present case. Did you know from the first that there was a connection with the ax, zither, and chrysanthemum?"

Kikuno shuddered slightly and said, "Oh, no. Not at all. I didn't realize anything when Mr. Také was murdered. But the second time, when Mr. Tomo was killed, I was playing the koto with Mrs. Matsuko when the detective came in…"

"Oh, yes, that's right," Kindaichi suddenly interjected. "When Detective Yoshii came back from Toyohata Village to report on the murder, you were playing the koto with Mrs. Matsuko. I wanted to ask you something about that."

"Yes?"

"I heard this from Detective Yoshii. When he said that this case might have some connection with the ax, zither, and chrysanthemum, Mrs. Matsuko inadvertently plucked a string too hard and broke it. Is that right?"

"Yes." Kikuno stared questioningly with her nearly blind eyes. "Is that important in some way?"

"What I want to ask you is not about that, but about something that happened right after that. Mrs. Matsuko must have injured herself when the string broke, for blood covered her right forefinger. Then Detective Yoshii said, 'Did you hurt yourself?' Do you remember?"

"Yes, very well."

"In response, Mrs. Matsuko said, 'Yes, when the koto string broke just now.' I want to know about what happened right after that. Detective Yoshii told me that when you heard Mrs. Matsuko's words, you frowned as if you were puzzled and said, 'When the koto string broke just now?' Do you remember?"

Kikuno cocked her head slightly. "I don't remember for sure, but I might have said something like that."

"But it seems that when Mrs. Matsuko heard you say that, a threatening look appeared on her face, just for an instant. According to Detective Yoshii, an expression of the most menacing hatred flickered in her eyes. Did you not notice that?"

"Goodness!" gasped Kikuno. "No, I didn't notice that. I can't see too well."

"It's probably just as well that you didn't notice, because Detective Yoshii said the look on her face was terrible, and for that very reason it puzzled him and stuck in his mind. Now, what I want to know is, when Mrs. Matsuko said, 'When the koto string broke just now,' why did you look puzzled and repeat it questioningly and why did Mrs. Matsuko get such a dangerous look on her face when you questioned her? Do you have any ideas?"

Staring ahead, Kikuno remained thinking for a while without moving a muscle, but soon, shuddering slightly, she said, "I have no idea why Mrs. Matsuko had such a horrible expression on her face, but I do know why I questioned what she had said. I don't actually remember saying those words, but I suppose they must have slipped out because I was confused."

"Confused?"

"Mrs. Matsuko spoke as if she had hurt her finger just then, when the koto string broke, but that was a lie. The broken string might have caused the wound to reopen and bleed, but it wasn't then that she originally hurt her finger."

"When did she hurt it, then?"

"It was the previous night. As you know, I gave Mrs. Matsuko a koto lesson the night before as well."

"The night before?" Chief Tachibana turned and looked at Kindaichi's face with a start.

Kindaichi, however, did not seem particularly surprised and asked, "The night before. That was the night Tomo was killed, wasn't it?"

"Yes."

"How was Mrs. Matsuko injured? Can you tell us more about what happened?"

"Yes, well…" Kikuno seemed rather anxious and kneaded her handkerchief in her hands. "I thought it curious when that happened, too. I believe Mrs. Matsuko told you that she left the room several times during our lesson, and I confirmed that as well when you questioned me. Each time, she was gone only briefly, about five or ten minutes. But once when she left the room—I don't remember clearly which time it was—she returned promptly and began playing the koto again, but I noticed something curious. As I said, I have trouble with my eyes. It is not that I cannot see at all, but I have trouble with details. However, I have my ears. It might sound presumptuous for me to say this, but from my many years of training, I can easily distinguish the tones of a koto. So I noticed right away that she had hurt her finger, her forefinger, but was playing the koto despite the pain, trying to hide it."

Kindaichi seemed to be growing increasingly excited listening to Kikuno's account. He had been scratching his head, with its mess of hair, very slowly at first, then more energetically, until finally he was scratching it fiercely all over, this way and that.

"And M-M-Mrs. Matsuko said n-nothing about being hurt?"

"Not a word."

"D-did you say anything?"

"No, nothing. I thought if she was trying to conceal it, it would be best not to mention it, and so I pretended not to notice."

"Y-yes, yes, I see." Kindaichi swallowed hard, seeming to regain his composure somewhat. "Then, the following day, when Mrs. Matsuko spoke as if she had injured herself just then, you automatically questioned what you had heard."

"Yes."

"And as for why there was such a menacing expression on Mrs. Matsuko's face?"

Kikuno kneaded her handkerchief even more strongly. "That I do not know. But perhaps she realized that I had known about her injured finger and that upset her."

"In other words, Mrs. Matsuko didn't want anyone to know that she had hurt her finger the night before. Well, thank you very much, Mrs. Kikuno." Kindaichi's scratching movements came abruptly to an end. Turning to Chief Tachibana, he said, "Chief, please. If you have any questions…"

Chief Tachibana stared at Kindaichi with a dubious look. "Mr. Kindaichi, what was that all about? Are you saying Matsuko is involved in some way in Tomo's murder? But Tomo was killed in Toyohata Village, remember? Matsuko

258

was here in this villa and never left the room for more than ten minutes at a time."

"Let's look into that later, Chief. But right now, if you have any further questions for Mrs. Kikuno…"

Disgruntled, the chief stared at Kindaichi's profile, but eventually he realized he would get no further explanation and turned again to Kikuno. "One last question, then. What are your thoughts on this case, Mrs. Kikuno? The murderer has to be someone who knows what happened between the three ladies of this family and yourself. Who do you think it might be—that is, if you yourself are not the one?"

Kikuno jerked, and with a sharp intake of breath, she stared at Chief Tachibana's face for a while. Gradually, though, she hung her head and said, "Yes, that's what I was afraid of. I came here tonight because I thought if I kept my identity secret any longer and was eventually found out, suspicion was sure to fall upon me. That's why I decided to reveal my identity. I am not the murderer, nor do I have any idea who the murderer is," Kikuno said flatly.

As Chief Tachibana asked Kikuno a few more questions of little importance, a group arrived noisily from the police station. Kikuno, therefore, was asked to retire for the time being to the inn where her student was waiting. The group had brought the autopsy report and the results of the comparison of the hand prints.

"Chief," Fujisaki, the forensics officer, called to Tachibana. His face was flushed with excitement.

"Wait. Just a moment, please." Kindaichi interrupted him and summoned the maid with a bell. When she appeared, he said to her, "Could you ask Miss Tamayo to please come here?"

Soon Tamayo entered the room. She quietly acknowledged the assembled group with a nod and seated herself on a chair in a corner of the room, as veiled as always in elegant, sphinx-like inscrutability.

"Alright. Let's hear the results in order. What about the results of the autopsy?"

"Yes, sir." One of the detectives stepped forward. "I'll just summarize the main facts. The cause of death was strangulation, the weapon a thin rope of some kind, the time of death between ten and eleven last night. But the report says it was probably an hour or so after the death occurred that the body was plunged upside down into the lake."

"Thank you. Detective Yoshii, I believe you came to report on the stain on the button. What were the results?"

"Yes, it's definitely human blood. Type O."

"Alright. Thank you very much."

Kindaichi finally turned to Fujisaki. "Mr. Fujisaki, please. Your turn. What can you tell us?"

Fujisaki, who had been sitting by impatiently, took out of his portfolio a scroll and two sheets of paper, hands trembling with excitement.

"Chief, something's strange. As you know, we took a hand print from Kiyo Inugami previously. Here it is. See? It says November 16 here. This hand print is identical with the one on the scroll I got from Mr. Furudate. But this, the hand print we took from the corpse today… it's completely different from the other two."

A sound like the rustling of reeds in the wind arose from the group assembled in the room. Chief Tachibana jumped out of his chair, while Furudate the lawyer caught his breath and stared wide-eyed.

"That's impossible! How could that be! Are you saying the man who was killed last night wasn't Kiyo?"

"That's right. According to these hand prints."

"But when we took the hand print the other day…"

At that moment, Kindaichi quietly interrupted him. "Chief, the one who made the hand print that day was the real Kiyo. That's the big blind spot that was preventing me from seeing the truth. What better proof of identity than having identical fingerprints? It never occurred to me that the real Kiyo and his imposter had cleverly taken advantage of that mask and switched places."

Kindaichi then strode up to Tamayo. "But you knew, didn't you, Miss Tamayo?"

Tamayo returned Kindaichi's gaze in silence, but soon, a faint color rising to her cheeks, she rose, bowed slightly, and quietly left the room.

# The Yukigamine Mountains

December 14. On this memorable day, when light first began to illuminate the path to resolving the extremely convoluted case of the Inugami clan, Kindaichi awoke in splendid condition. With the blind spot that had been hindering his thought processes finally removed, everything had fallen into place for him with great speed. All day yesterday, he had been stacking building blocks of deductive reasoning in his mind, with the result that now he had reproduced the entire complex structure of the mystery. All that was left was to find the real Kiyo, something which the police would surely succeed in doing this time because they now knew the man they were looking for, and they were even armed with his photograph.

The previous night, for the first time in many days, Kindaichi had slept soundly. This morning, he had risen at around eight, enjoyed a leisurely soak in the hot spring, eaten breakfast, and was relaxing in his room when the phone rang. It was Chief Tachibana.

"Mr. Kindaichi? Mr. Kindaichi?" The chief's voice, a bit shrill with excitement, made Kindaichi knit his eyebrows. What could have happened now, he thought, when there was nothing more to happen?

"Yes, it's me, Chief. Is s-something wrong?"

"Mr. Kindaichi, it's Kiyo. He showed up last night at the Inugami villa."

"W-what? Kiyo? And did he do something?"

"Yes, but fortunately he failed. Mr. Kindaichi, could you please come to the station right away? We're going to go after him."

"Yes, I'll be right there."

Kindaichi asked the front desk to call a pedicab for him; then he pulled an Inverness cape over his kimono and half-coat and rushed from the inn at top speed.

The snow had stopped during the night, and it was a sparkling bright day. The ice on the lake, the lakeside towns, and even the surrounding mountains were covered with a soft, white blanket. The snow, being wet and heavy, was quick to melt, and one could hear the continual dripping from the eaves of the houses along the road.

Kindaichi climbed out of the pedicab in front of the police station, where he saw three cars with ski equipment tied to their rear bumpers and several armed policemen milling about. When he hastened into Chief Tachibana's office, the chief and Furudate were standing talking, wearing ski clothes and caps.

Chief Tachibana looked at Kindaichi's kimono and frowned. "Mr. Kindaichi, that kimono's going to be difficult. Don't you have any Western clothing?"

"Chief, what's going on? You're not planning to abandon the case and go play in the snow, are you?"

"Don't be ridiculous. We got a report that Kiyo escaped into the Yukigamine Mountains, so we're going to go hunt him down."

"Kiyo's gone into the Yukigamine Mountains…?" Kindaichi fixed his eyes on Tachibana with a start. "Chief, you don't suppose he intends to kill himself."

"There's a good possibility of that, so we have to capture

him as soon as possible, but there's no way you'll be able to join us dressed like that."

Kindaichi grinned. "Chief, don't write me off just yet. I'm from the northern part of the country, you know. I'm more used to skis than sandals, and all I have to do is tuck up my kimono so it doesn't get in the way. But I do need ski equipment."

"We have skis for you. Shall we go, then?"

Just then, a policeman came bustling into the room and whispered something to Chief Tachibana. Nodding with determination, the chief said, "Okay, let's get started."

Uniformed policemen and plain-clothes detectives were hanging onto the outsides of the first two cars. In the last car sat Chief Tachibana, Kindaichi, and Furudate, with an inspector in the driver's seat. Soon they were speeding through the town on roads muddy with melting snow.

"Sugiyama, how far up can we go by car?" the chief asked the inspector who was driving.

"This snow's not so bad, so we should be able to reach the eighth station. We might slip and slide a bit, though."

"The rest should be easy if we can get that far. I never thought I'd have to take up skiing again at my age, though. And I've never been good at mountain-climbing, either." With the pounds and paunch produced by liquor, it was not surprising that Chief Tachibana would find it hard to climb a snowy mountain.

"Chief, so what happened at the Inugami villa? What did Kiyo do?" asked Kindaichi.

"That's right, I haven't told you yet. Last night, Kiyo showed up at the villa and tried to kill Tamayo."

"Tamayo?" Kindaichi stared in surprise.

"Yes, Tamayo."

According to Chief Tachibana, Kiyo apparently sneaked into Tamayo's annex and hid in her bedroom closet while she was in the drawing room at Kindaichi's request. Around eleven, Tamayo retired to her bedroom, turned off the lights, and got into bed, but perhaps because of her excitement, she had trouble falling asleep, and tossed and turned for about an hour. She began to be bothered by a feeling of something not right in the closet. She thought she sensed someone inside it, moving and breathing.

Tamayo is a brave woman. Turning on the lights, she put on her slippers, strode up to the closet, and opened the door. A man jumped out—a man hiding his face with a muffler—who pounced on her, pushed her down on the bed, and began choking her with both hands. Hearing the commotion, Monkey came dashing into the adjacent sitting room from the corridor. The bedroom door was locked from the inside, but that was no problem at all for the powerful giant. Monkey broke down the door and leaped into the bedroom. By that time, however, the intruder had already throttled Tamayo to the point where she was losing consciousness. Monkey immediately jumped on the culprit, who let Tamayo go and turned to come at him. Normally, Monkey would have found the intruder easy meat, but after a few exchanges, the intruder's muffler slid off. Monkey froze at the sight of his face, and Tamayo, who had been drifting into semi-consciousness, screamed. It was Kiyo.

Monkey was paralyzed with shock. Kiyo dashed out of the bedroom just as Toranosuke and Kokichi came running. They, too, stood dumbfounded when they saw Kiyo's face, allowing him to escape into the snow.

"It was about one o'clock when this news reached me, and we got busy, setting up a cordon and so forth. Then I returned to the Inugami villa. Tamayo, the poor girl, had an awful bruise on her neck and was crying hysterically."

"Tamayo was crying?" Kindaichi asked in surprise.

"Of course she was crying. She'd nearly been strangled to death. She may seem strong, but after all, she's a woman."

"And Matsuko?"

"Yes, Matsuko. I have trouble with that woman. She looked like a witch, with those glittering eyes, and she wouldn't say a word. It'll take some doing to make that one talk."

"Still, I wonder why Kiyo went to such lengths to try to kill Tamayo. And where has he been hiding all this time?"

"Well, we'll just have to catch him to find out." Chief Tachibana was in a good mood because he was starting to see the light at the end of the tunnel. Kindaichi, in contrast, fell silent, deep in concentration.

The cars had already reached the road leading up the Yukigamine Mountains. As they climbed, houses disappeared beyond Hazama Shinden and Hazama Village, but since quite a few skiers had already gone up the same route, the snow had been trodden down considerably and the cars had much less trouble advancing than expected.

"Chief, I think we'll make it to the eighth level."

"Great."

At Sasa-no-umi, a plain-clothes detective on skis was waiting by the roadside. "Chief, he's gone this way for sure. We're chasing him down right now."

"Good."

The cars climbed on, snow squeaking under the tires. In the clear, blue expanse of sky, the sun sparkled, and the brightness of the snow covering the mountains and ravines stung the eyes, while occasionally, from beside the road, snow would fall from the branches with a thud. When they reached Jizozaka at the eighth level—as far as the cars could safely go—everyone got out and began putting on skis.

"Mr. Kindaichi, will you be alright?"

"I'll be fine, but I have to warn you, I'll look pretty ridiculous."

Indeed, Kindaichi was a sight to behold. He took off the Inverness and half-coat that he was wearing over his kimono, and then removed his hakama trousers, pulled up the hem of his kimono, tucked it into his sash, and put on socks and ski boots over his long, knit underdrawers.

"Mr. Kindaichi, you look—" Chief Tachibana burst out laughing.

"Don't laugh, Chief. Just watch how good I am."

True to his word, Kindaichi was the most expert on skies of anyone in the group. With a ski pole on each shoulder, he scampered lightly up the mountain, while Chief Tachibana lagged behind, out of breath, lugging his potbelly up the slopes.

Soon the group had passed the ninth station and was approaching the peak at Numa-no-daira when they met a plain-clothesman skiing down from above.

"Hurry, Chief. We've found him, and we're chasing him right now. The bastard's got a gun."

They quickened their pace up the mountain. Suddenly they heard an exchange of gunfire from above.

"Damn, they've started shooting." Kindaichi hopped up the steep path like a jackrabbit, soon reaching the summit at Numa-no-daira. But when he got there, he could not help but stop and cry out, "How beautiful!" despite the pressing situation. The rolling hills of snow extended far and wide before him, and beyond that, the rugged mountains of Yatsugatake, also covered in white, looked close enough to touch. The deep blue sky, the ridges of snow with their light purplish glow…

Kindaichi's ecstasy, however, did not last long, for he again heard gunshots from down the slope that was now before him. Far below he could see three plain-clothesmen encircling and gradually closing in on a man who was dressed like a repatriated soldier. The policemen who had climbed up with Kindaichi immediately swooped down the slope like a flock of swallows to join the others, while Kindaichi followed, his kimono tucked up in his sash.

The repatriated soldier was now surrounded on all sides, with no possibility of escape. Having thrown away his ski poles, he was standing defiantly on his skis, face ghastly. His eyes were red, and blood trickled from the corner of his mouth. He fired another couple of shots. The police answered in kind. Kindaichi sped toward the group, yelling, "Don't kill him! He's not the killer!"

Startled by those words, the repatriated soldier turned back toward Kindaichi, and for just a moment, his eyes blazed fiercely, like those of a wounded boar. He turned the hand that held the gun and raised it to his temple.

"Stop him!" Kindaichi shouted. That same instant, someone must have managed to shoot the soldier in the hand, for the man dropped his gun and lay kneeling in the snow. Several plain-clothesmen immediately pounced on him and handcuffed him.

Chief Tachibana and Furudate drew closer. "Well, Mr. Furudate, do you recognize this man?"

Furudate studied the man's face with bated breath but soon averted his eyes grimly. "Yes, there's no mistake. This man is Kiyo Inugami."

Chief Tachibana rubbed his hands together gleefully, but soon he turned toward Kindaichi with a frown. "Mr. Kindaichi, you said something strange just now, that this man isn't the murderer. What did you mean?"

Kindaichi abruptly began scratching his head with great enthusiasm and said, beaming, "J-just like I said, Chief. Th-this man's not the murderer, although he'll probably insist that he is."

At those words, Kiyo, who had been glaring at Kindaichi with fierce eyes, shook his handcuffed hands in utter despair and collapsed sideways onto the snow.

# Confession

December 15. Although the sunny weather that had continued from the previous day had melted much of the snow that had been burying the shores of Lake Nasu, the people of the town and its surroundings were gripped by an icy tension. They all knew that the prime suspect in the case of the Inugami clan, the series of grisly murders that had terrified the region, had been captured the day before in the snowy Yukigamine Mountains; that the suspect was none other than Kiyo Inugami; and that the showdown between Kiyo and the others concerned in the case was about to take place today in the large room deep inside the Inugami villa. They were aware, too, that this case, which had begun last October 18 with the death of Toyoichiro Wakabayashi, was finally drawing to a close. What no one could say, however, was whether Kiyo Inugami was indeed the murderer, though that, too, would be made clear. Therefore, the people who lived around Lake Nasu watched the Inugami villa with bated breath.

That same tatami-mat room deep in the villa was now filled with tense faces—all tense, except for that of Matsuko, who, with her usual obstinate expression, sat calmly smoking shredded tobacco in her long, Japanese pipe, a tobacco tray by her side. What could this woman be thinking? Surely she, too, had heard that the real Kiyo had been captured yesterday in the Yukigamine Mountains. With that piece of news—no, even before that, in fact, the moment the

results of the hand print comparisons were announced—
she would know that the body found sticking feet up
out of the lake was not her son's. And yet, not a trace of
emotion showed in her attitude or expression. Meeting
the looks of suspicion and hatred from her sisters with
seeming total indifference, she sat in detestable calmness,
smoking her thin, red, bamboo-stemmed pipe. Even the
fingertips that kneaded the shredded tobacco leaves were
perfectly steady.

At a little distance from Matsuko sat four people huddled together—Takeko and her husband, Toranosuke, and
Umeko and her husband, Kokichi. In contrast to Matsuko's
composure, this group was stricken with suspicion, terror,
and anxiety. Takeko's abundant double chin shook constantly, no doubt from the overwhelming tension.

Further apart was the solitary figure of Tamayo, sitting
and waiting. While as lovely as ever, she was not herself: her
eyes, staring abstractedly, showed signs of a painful sorrow.
Tamayo, who had always remained so prim, proper, and
elegant, no matter what anyone said to her, no matter how
hatefully anyone glared at her, today seemed shaken. The
strong sense of self that had always supported her seemed
to have snapped in two, and strong shivers would occasionally run through her body.

Sitting at a little distance from Tamayo was the koto teacher
Kokin Miyakawa. Apparently she was still unaware of why
she had been summoned to this event. She sat nervously in
the presence of the three dreaded half-sisters.

A bit further from Kokin sat Kindaichi and Furudate, the
family lawyer. Having lost all composure, Furudate incessantly coughed, rubbed his forehead, and shook his leg.

Even Kindaichi seemed excited, for he continued to scratch his head as he glanced at the others in the room.

It was exactly 2 p.m. when the doorbell sounded in the distance. Everyone tensed, and soon, close upon the clamor of approaching footsteps from the other side of the veranda, there appeared Chief Tachibana, followed by Kiyo Inugami, staggering forward with his arms restrained on either side by a police detective and his handcuffed right hand wrapped pitifully in a white bandage. Reaching the sliding door, Kiyo stopped and looked around nervously at the assembled faces, but the instant his gaze reached Matsuko, he swung his face away. As he did, however, his eyes locked solidly with Tamayo's, and for a while, the two remained immobile, like a tableau vivant. Soon, though, Kiyo made an anguished sound deep in his throat and averted his face. Tamayo slumped, head hanging, as if she had been released from a spell.

It was Matsuko whom Kindaichi observed with the most interest during Kiyo's entrance. The sight of her son's face affected even her, for her cheeks instantly flushed and the hand holding the pipe trembled. She immediately reverted, however, to her usual ornery expression and resumed kneading her tobacco quietly and calmly. Kindaichi marveled at her strength of will.

"Bring him in here." At Chief Tachibana's command, one of the detectives pushed the shoulder of the handcuffed Kiyo. He staggered into the room and seated himself before Kindaichi, as indicated by Tachibana. Two detectives sat behind him so they would be able to restrain him if necessary. Chief Tachibana sat next to Kindaichi.

"So?" After a short silence, Kindaichi turned to the chief and asked, "Were you able to find out anything new?"

His lips drawn tight in a frown, Chief Tachibana sullenly took a wrinkled brown envelope from his pocket. "Read it," he said.

Kindaichi took it from him. On the front was written "Confession" and on the back "Kiyo Inugami" in cursive style with a thick fountain pen. Inside was a piece of cheap stationery, with a statement written in the same handwriting as on the envelope:

I, Kiyo Inugami, committed all the murders that have occurred in the Inugami clan. No one else is involved. I confess to these murders before taking my own life.

KIYO INUGAMI

Kindaichi showed little interest in this confession. Without a word, he put the piece of stationery back inside the envelope and returned it to Chief Tachibana.

"Did he have this on him?"

"Yes, in one of his pockets."

"But if he intended to kill himself, why didn't he just go ahead and do it? Why did he see the need to resist the police in that way?"

Chief Tachibana knitted his eyebrows. "What do you mean, Mr. Kindaichi? Are you saying that Kiyo had no intention of killing himself? But—you were there yesterday, so you should know—if one of my men hadn't managed to shoot him in the hand, Kiyo would have killed himself for sure."

"That's not what I meant, Chief. Yes, Kiyo did in fact intend to kill himself, but he wanted to do it spectacularly and dramatically, and draw as much attention to himself as possible. Doing so would enhance the effect of his confession."

Chief Tachibana seemed unconvinced, but Kindaichi ignored the expression on his face. "Actually, what I said just now is wrong. I asked why Kiyo had seen the need to resist the police, but that's wrong. Kiyo wasn't resisting at all. He was just pretending to. He never pointed his gun at any policeman but always at the snow. You saw that too, didn't you, Chief?"

"Now that you mention it, I thought it a bit strange myself."

Kindaichi happily scratched his head. "Please remember that well, Chief. It'll serve as evidence in his favor when his sentence is determined."

Although Chief Tachibana again screwed up his face in dissatisfaction, Kindaichi paid that no heed and continued, "By the way, did Kiyo say anything specific about this confession—exactly how he killed the victims, for example?"

"Well, actually," said Chief Tachibana with a scowl, "he refuses to say anything at all. He just keeps insisting that he is guilty of all the murders and that no one else is involved. He won't say anything else."

"Just as I thought. But Mr. Kiyo—" Kindaichi turned his affable smile toward Kiyo, who all this time had remained with his head hung in silence. His face indeed looked identical to that rubber mask his imposter had been wearing. But while the mask lacked all life and expression, the face in front of them now was most human and racked with a heartbreaking look of agony. Though the tan the sun of Southeast Asia had given him still remained, his face was haggard and drawn. Despite that, he was not unkempt. He was clean shaven and his hair—although of course disheveled—was neatly cut, as if he had recently been to a barber.

Kindaichi, for some reason, gazed gleefully at Kiyo's neatly trimmed hair. "But Mr. Kiyo," he said again, "it's simply not possible for you to have committed all those murders. In the case of Toyoichiro Wakabayashi, for example, it was October 18 when he was killed, but it wasn't until November 12 that you returned to Hakata from Burma using the name Sanpei Yamada. You've probably already heard from the chief, but the night Mr. Také was killed, the night of November 15, a man who appeared to be a repatriated soldier calling himself Sanpei Yamada spent a night at the Kashiwaya Inn in Lower Nasu. Moreover, after he left the inn, they found in his room a bloody towel printed with the words 'Hakata Friends of Returning Veterans.' So, when the police made inquiries to Hakata, they found that there had been a man calling himself Sanpei Yamada among the shipload of repatriates who arrived in Hakata on November 12. Moreover, this man gave as his final destination the address 3-21 Kojimachi, Tokyo, the same address we have from the Kashiwaya Inn and the address of your house in Tokyo. In other words, you returned to Japan using an assumed name, but when asked for an address you couldn't think of an appropriate one, and so you gave that of your house in Tokyo."

Kiyo remained sitting in silence. It seemed that the others were listening more attentively to Kindaichi's monologue than he was.

"Now the Sanpei Yamada who arrived in Hakata on November 12 departed the following day for Tokyo. Since it would have been possible for him to make it to the Kashiwaya Inn in Lower Nasu on the night of the 15th, it follows that the Sanpei Yamada who appeared at the Kashiwaya Inn on the night of the 15th and the repatriated soldier called

Sanpei Yamada who landed in Hakata on the 12th are one and the same, that is, that they both are you. Mr. Kiyo, do you understand what I'm trying to say? In other words, how is it possible for you, who arrived in Hakata only on November 12, to have been the one who committed the murder of Toyoichiro Wakabayashi on October 18?"

As everyone watched Kiyo with bated breath, he nervously raised his face for the first time.

"I... I..." he said, lips trembling. "I don't know anything about the Wakabayashi murder. I'm just talking about the three people from this house who were killed. The Wakabayashi murder has nothing to do with this case."

At that, Kindaichi suddenly began scratching his head with its tangled mess of hair so furiously that Kiyo, who was not familiar with Kindaichi's habit, grew wide-eyed in surprise.

"Ch-Chief, did you hear him just now? Mr. Kiyo tacitly admitted that he is the Sanpei Yamada who returned to Hakata on November 12 and the Sanpei Yamada who appeared at the Kashiwaya Inn on November 15."

Recognizing that he had been had, Kiyo glared, a fierce gleam flashing in his eyes. Then, as resignation overtook him, his shoulders slumped and his head drooped forward.

Beaming, Kindaichi said, "I didn't mean to trick you, Mr. Kiyo, but I did want to confirm that. We've saved ourselves a lot of trouble now. By the way, it hasn't been clearly proven yet that the Wakabayashi murder is connected with the Inugami murders, but common sense would indicate that the same person was responsible. Let's leave that aside for now, though, and turn to the last murder, the murder of the fake Kiyo Inugami. He was killed sometime between ten and eleven on the night of the 12th, but the autopsy report stated that it was about an hour after that when the body was plunged head-first into the lake. Mr. Kiyo, were you here, that is, in Nasu, at that time?"

Kiyo remained silent, now determined never to open his mouth again. Kindaichi smiled broadly and rang for the maid. When she appeared, he said, "Could you bring in the people who are waiting in the other room, please?"

The maid left and returned immediately with two men, both young, one wearing a black jacket with a stand-up collar and the other wearing the khaki uniform worn by repatriated soldiers. Chief Tachibana frowned in puzzlement.

"Chief, let me introduce these gentlemen to you. This is Mr. Keikichi Ueda, who works at the Upper Nasu train station. He was on duty taking tickets at the exit gate when the train from Tokyo arrived in Upper Nasu at 9:05 on the night of the 13th. The other gentleman is Mr. Ryuta Oguchi, a pedicab driver, who was waiting to pick up fares in front of the station around the same time. Now, Mr. Ueda, Mr. Oguchi, do you recognize this man?"

As Kindaichi pointed to Kiyo, the two men nodded immediately.

"That man," began the station employee, who must have already prepared what he was going to say, "is one of the passengers who got off the train from Tokyo that arrived at Upper Nasu Station at 9:05 p.m. on the night of the 13th. I remember well, because that was the night it was snowing so hard and he was acting rather strangely. His ticket had been issued at Shinjuku Station in Tokyo."

The pedicab driver added, "I remember him, too. When the 9:05 train from Tokyo arrived on the night of the 13th,

I was waiting to pick up fares outside the station, but only a few people got off that train. I asked this man if he wanted a ride, but he didn't say a word, kind of turned his face away, and walked quickly away in the snow. I'm positive. The night of the big snowfall."

"I see. You might be summoned by the police again sometime, but that's all for now. Thank you very much."

When the two witnesses had left, Kindaichi turned to Chief Tachibana. "This morning, I took Mr. Kiyo's photograph and made inquiries at Upper Nasu Station. His hair—it bothered me, because it looks like it's only been three or four days since it was last cut. But Mr. Kiyo would never get a haircut around here, for he would not be able to hide his face at the barbershop, and even if the barber himself did not know Mr. Kiyo, he couldn't be certain someone who knew him wouldn't walk in. If Mr. Kiyo had gotten a haircut, therefore, it had to be somewhere else, so I went to the station to find out when he had arrived in Nasu. If he had been hiding his face, the photograph wouldn't have done any good, but I assumed that he probably wasn't doing that anymore. After all, he is, as you see, dressed in the manner of a repatriated soldier, but around Nasu these days, everybody is on the look-out for a man dressed like a repatriated soldier who is hiding his face. So, while doing his best to avoid attracting attention, Mr. Kiyo could not hide his face, and he ended up being seen and remembered by those two witnesses."

Kindaichi then turned to Kokin Miyakawa. "Mrs. Miyakawa, you also arrived by train at Upper Nasu Station at 9:05 p.m. on the 13th, didn't you?"

"Yes, I did." Kokin's voice was so soft as to be barely audible.

"You had read about Kiyo's murder in the evening paper in Tokyo and had rushed here in shock?"

"Yes."

Kindaichi looked at Chief Tachibana with a smile. "Chief, do you see? Mrs. Miyakawa learned about the murder in the evening paper and rushed here from Tokyo. That means that Mr. Kiyo, who arrived from Tokyo on the same train, could also have read the evening paper in Tokyo. At least that's a possibility. In other words, Mr. Kiyo, too, could have read about the murder of his imposter in the evening paper and hastened to Nasu in dismay."

"But what for?"

"To pretend to kill Miss Tamayo."

"Pretend? Did you say pretend?" Tamayo's face jerked up. Color rose to her face, and as she looked at Kindaichi, her eyes filled with a strange ardor and shine.

Kindaichi answered in a comforting tone. "That's right, pretend. Mr. Kiyo had no intention whatsoever of really killing you. He just pretended to try to kill you so his confession would be more effective."

Suddenly, emotion consumed Tamayo's body. Shaking violently, she stared back at Kindaichi, eyes wide with feeling, but then her eyes suddenly grew misty, the tears began to flow, and soon she was sobbing uncontrollably, choking on her tears.

# Shizuma and Kiyo

Tamayo's outburst surprised even Kindaichi, and he remained dumbfounded for a while, staring at her. Kindaichi had always thought Tamayo a strong woman—which she indeed was. He had thought, however, that her strength unfortunately often made her unfeminine. The Tamayo weeping in front of him now, however, was a pitiful creature, sending forth a painful message of solitude with every sob. He thought he was seeing her soul for the first time.

Kindaichi cleared his throat and said, "Miss Tamayo, was what happened the other day… was Mr. Kiyo's attempt on your life such a shock to you?"

"I… I…" Tamayo continued weeping audibly, her hands pressed to her face. "I just couldn't believe Kiyo was guilty of those murders. So… so… when he tried to kill me, I thought maybe he had done so because he suspected me of being the murderer. I couldn't bear that. It was so painful. I don't care what anybody else thinks. I don't care at all. But I just couldn't bear for Kiyo to think me a murderer. No, no, I couldn't bear that." Tamayo began weeping passionately again, shoulders shaking.

Kindaichi turned to Kiyo. "Mr. Kiyo, did you hear what she said? In your attempt to protect someone, you nearly killed Miss Tamayo's soul. You should think more carefully before you act. Miss Tamayo, don't cry any more. Why did an intelligent woman like yourself not realize that the attack on you the other day was just a charade? After all, Mr. Kiyo had a gun, so if he had really wanted to kill you, he could have done so with a single bullet. If he were planning to kill you and then to escape unscathed, that would be one thing, but he was prepared to kill himself from the first. It's not that he tried to kill you, failed, was chased down by the police, and then tried to commit suicide when there was no way out—that's just not a plausible scenario, since he already had a signed confession in his pocket. No doubt he had it with him even before he left Tokyo, because I can't believe he would stop to buy stationery and an envelope while he was running from the police after his attack on you. No, he was determined to take his own life even before he left Tokyo. A man who is prepared to die would not be concerned about a gunshot being heard. So, on the night of the 13th, if Mr. Kiyo had really wanted to kill you, he could have shot you dead and then killed himself as well, there and then. Following that line of reasoning, you can see that the attack of that night was a charade."

"I understand," Tamayo answered quietly. She was no longer crying, and as she gazed at Kindaichi, her eyes were filled with indescribable gentleness and gratitude. "You have saved me from the agony of hell. How can I ever thank you?"

They were the first tender words he had heard from her. Kindaichi, totally abashed, stammered, "Oh, i-i-it's nothing, n-n-nothing at all," and briskly scratched his head all around. Soon, however, he swallowed hard and continued. "Now. So we know that Mr. Kiyo came here from Tokyo on the night of the 13th and that he pretended to attack Miss Tamayo. We still cannot state positively, however, that he is unconnected with the murder of the fake Kiyo on the night of the 12th, because it would have been possible for him to kill his imposter that night, leave for Tokyo on the last train or one early the next morning, and still be back in Nasu at 9:05 on the night of the 13th. That is not impossible, although any way you look at it, it is quite illogical, for after all, why go to so much trouble, when he could have just gone ahead and attacked Miss Tamayo also on the night of the 12th and then killed himself? Moreover, there's also the issue of Mr. Kiyo's hair."

Kindaichi smiled at Kiyo's head. "I'm positive Mr. Kiyo's hair was cut quite recently. So if we distribute his photograph to all the barbers in Tokyo and call their attention to it, we'd no doubt be able to find out where he got his haircut. Even if locating the barber turns out to be inadequate to establish his alibi, we should be able to trace his movements from there and find out where he was on the night of the 12th. Mr. Kiyo, how about it? Do you think we'd be able to establish an alibi for you?"

Kiyo remained sitting with his head hung, his shoulders shaking violently and his forehead covered with oily sweat. It was obvious that Kindaichi's words had found their mark.

Chief Tachibana edged forward. "Are you saying that Kiyo came to Nasu on the night of the 13th to play the role of the murderer in order to protect someone?"

"Exactly. The murder of the fake Kiyo must have come unexpectedly for Mr. Kiyo, too, and when he learned about it in the evening paper of the 13th, it was a devastating shock. Also, whereas before, in the cases of Také and Tomo, it had always been contrived to make it seem the culprit had come from or been outside the estate, no such measure had been taken this time, so he felt if he did not act, the real murderer would be found out. So, Mr. Kiyo made up his mind to sacrifice himself to protect the real murderer."

"Who, then—who's the murderer?"

Chief Tachibana's voice sounded like he had something stuck in the back of his throat, but Kindaichi's reply was quite nonchalant. "I think it should be quite obvious by now—Mrs. Matsuko, of course."

Silence filled the room. No one was particularly surprised. Everyone had realized the truth midway through Kindaichi's explanation. So the looks that were turned in unison toward Matsuko the moment Kindaichi said her name were loaded with disgust and hatred but not with surprise. Even surrounded by these malicious eyes, however, Matsuko remained perfectly composed, and as she sat quietly working her tobacco, a faint, wry smile appeared on her lips.

Kindaichi edged forward. "Mrs. Matsuko, you will tell us everything, won't you? Yes, I'm certain you will, for everything you did was for Mr. Kiyo's sake, wasn't it? If Mr. Kiyo manages to play the role of the murderer successfully, then all your efforts will have been for nothing."

Matsuko, however, neither heard nor saw Kindaichi, but gazed intently at her son. "Kiyo, welcome home. If I had known that you would return safe and sound like this, I would never have acted so foolishly. Nor would I have needed to, since Tamayo would surely choose you."

Her words and tone were filled with a gentleness hitherto unimaginable from the usual Matsuko. Tamayo blushed, while Kiyo sat with downcast eyes, his shoulders trembling.

"Kiyo, dear," Matsuko continued, "when did you return to Japan? Oh, that's right. Mr. Kindaichi just said that you landed in Hakata on November 12. Then why didn't you wire

283

me from there? Why didn't you come home right away? Then I wouldn't have had to kill those people."

"I… I…" Kiyo began speaking as if groaning in pain, but then, with a shudder, he abruptly raised his face in determination. "No, Mother, you know nothing about any of this. This is all my doing. I killed the three of them."

"Be quiet, Kiyo!" Matsuko's words lashed out like a whip. She immediately softened her tone again, however, and continued, "Kiyo, dear, your attitude is torturing me. I know you're doing this for me, but your actions are torturing me. If you understand what I'm saying, then tell me everything honestly. Just what was it that you did? Was it you who cut off Také's head and carried Tomo's corpse to Toyohata Village? I never wanted you to do anything like that."

Kindaichi began furiously scratching his head. "J-just as I thought. So, you weren't accomplices in the usual sense of the word. Mr. Kiyo was secretly cleaning up after Mrs. Matsuko without even telling her."

Matsuko turned to Kindaichi for the first time. "Mr. Kindaichi, I'm not a woman who would try to enlist someone—especially my own son—to help me with something like this. Besides, if I'd known that Kiyo had returned unharmed, I wouldn't have needed to kill anyone."

"I understand. I imagined that was probably what had happened. But since that would involve figuring in so many chance occurrences…"

"Yes, chance. Horrible chance occurrences. Horrible chance occurrences happening again and again."

It was Kiyo who spoke with a groan. Kindaichi looked compassionately at his haggard profile. "Ah, Mr. Kiyo, you admit it, too. Yes, it's for the best. As your mother says, it's best you tell us everything honestly. Will you tell us? Or shall I speak in your place?"

Kiyo looked at Kindaichi's face in surprise, but when he saw the detective's confident look, he immediately slumped dejectedly and said, "Please, you tell them. I can't do it."

"Mrs. Matsuko, is it alright with you?"

"Please, go ahead," Matsuko answered with a voice that was perfectly composed, smoking her pipe as calmly as ever.

"Alright, then, I will speak on your behalf. Mrs. Matsuko, Mr. Kiyo, please don't hesitate to correct me whenever I'm wrong." Kindaichi paused briefly and then continued. "As I said before, Mr. Kiyo returned to Japan on November 12 under the assumed name of Sanpei Yamada. I have no idea why he was using such a name, although I'm sure he will eventually tell us. Anyway, the first thing he did upon returning to Japan—having once been a repatriated soldier myself, I speak from experience when I say this—he read a newspaper. All repatriates are starving for news about what is happening back home, and to answer that need, all the repatriate reception centers have back issues of newspapers bound together for them to read. Mr. Kiyo, too, no doubt reached eagerly for these back issues as soon as he had landed in Hakata. And what he discovered there…"

Kindaichi looked around at the faces in the room. "As you know, it was November 1 when Mr. Inugami's will was read in front of the fake Kiyo. This became nationwide news and was written up extensively in the newspapers of November 2. Mr. Kiyo must have read one of those articles in Hakata and received a terrible shock, for he learned that someone had entered his home pretending to be him."

"Kiyo!" interrupted Matsuko shrilly. "Why didn't you wire me immediately? Why didn't you tell me he was an imposter? If you had... if you had... all this wouldn't have happened."

Kiyo tried to say something but immediately hung his head as if he had lost his nerve. Kindaichi answered for him. "That's right, Mrs. Matsuko. It's just as you say. If he had, all this wouldn't have happened. But Mr. Kiyo had some ideas of his own. No doubt he had some suspicions about who this imposter was—someone whom he could not despise, someone for whom he perhaps even felt some compassion. So, instead of exposing him directly, he tried to conduct matters in secret—something that turned out to be a mistake."

"Just who was this imposter?" Chief Tachibana asked. Kindaichi hesitated, for it was a name that it pained him to say, yet it was not something that could remain unsaid. "I can't be sure unless I ask Mr. Kiyo," he mumbled, "but if I may be allowed to exercise my imagination, I think... I think... it might have been Shizuma."

"Ah, I knew it!" Kokin Miyakawa cried out. Making sweeping motions in front of her with her hands, she shuffled once, twice, forward on her knees. "Oh, God, so that really was Shizuma. I had that feeling, ever since you asked me if Shizuma and Mr. Kiyo resembled each other. Oh, God, then when he took my hand that day, he knew he was holding his mother's hand." Suddenly, tears began to stream from Kokin's nearly blind eyes. "But it's so cruel. How can God be so cruel? Yes, Shizuma was wrong to return to Japan pretending to be someone else, but how can God be so cruel as to kill him before he could reveal his identity to his own mother, who had been waiting for him so anxiously?"

Kokin's lament was understandable. What unfortunate people they were. No one would ever know why Shizuma had decided to pretend to be the heir apparent to the Inugami throne, but his impersonation had prevented him from revealing his identity to his own mother, even though she was right before his eyes. What was more, his pretense had led to his murder. If the true facts of this case had not been brought to light, he would have been forever buried as Kiyo Inugami, and Kokin would have forever waited in vain for her son.

Kiyo sighed gloomily, while Takeko and Umeko drew up their shoulders in fear. Only Matsuko remained calm and composed, playing with her long pipe.

Waiting for Kokin's outburst to subside, Kindaichi turned to Kiyo. "Mr. Kiyo, were you together with Shizuma in Burma?"

"We were both in Burma, but in different units," Kiyo replied softly. "But because we looked so much alike, our resemblance became a topic of conversation in both units, and one day Shizuma came to meet me. He knew my name, and when he introduced himself and told me about his background, I recognized what he was talking about. My mother and aunts would never talk about it, but Grandfather had told me what had happened. You forget old grudges when you are fighting on the front lines, and Shizuma, too, let bygones be bygones and shook my hand in friendship. For a while after that, we would come and go and enjoy talking about each other's past, but then, the fighting gradually intensified, and we were separated. According to what Shizuma told me later, he had heard that my unit had been wiped out, and had assumed that I had been killed as well.

Then, when he was wounded in the face like that and ended up being separated from those who knew him, he decided to take my place. Everything was so crazy on the Burmese front, you could get away with a far-fetched plan like that without anyone becoming suspicious." At that point, Kiyo sighed deeply again.

# A Series of Coincidences

"I see. So you could not bring yourself to turn Shizuma over to the police, and hoping to carry things out in secret, you returned to Nasu hiding your face and found lodgings for the time being at the Kashiwaya Inn."

"But Mr. Kindaichi, why did Kiyo need to hide his face?" asked Chief Tachibana.

"Chief, that's obvious. The masked Kiyo was already ensconced in the Inugami villa. If the real Mr. Kiyo were recognized by any of the townsfolk, there would be talk of two Kiyos and all his efforts would have gone for naught."

"Oh, I see."

"But the fact that Mr. Kiyo had hidden his face turned out to be very useful later on, although, of course, that was not a consideration at the time. Anyway, having settled into the Kashiwaya Inn, Mr. Kiyo left at about ten that night, stole onto the grounds of the Inugami villa, and secretly called to the masked Kiyo, that is, Shizuma, to meet him. Mr. Kiyo, where did you two meet and talk?"

With a nervous expression, Kiyo glanced around uneasily. "Inside the boathouse," he gasped.

"The b-boathouse!" Wide-eyed at the revelation, Kindaichi gleefully scratched his head. "That's right below the scene of the crime. By the way, Mr. Kiyo, just what were you intending to do with Shizuma?"

"I... I..." Kiyo's voice reverberated with profound sorrow, as if he was cursing the world and reproaching the human

289

race. "I had miscalculated badly. The newspaper I read had said nothing about the fake Kiyo having been wounded in the face and wearing a rubber mask. So, I had thought I could simply change places with Shizuma without any problems. Of course, I intended to give him a fair portion of the estate, but with Shizuma looking the way he did—something I had not expected—there was no possibility of our changing places unnoticed. As we were discussing what to do…"

"Mr. Také came to the observation deck above the boathouse, followed soon thereafter by Miss Tamayo, correct?"

Kiyo nodded grimly. Everyone in the room tensed, for they knew they were finally reaching the crux of the story.

"Také and Tamayo must have talked for about five minutes or so, when we were startled by the sound of confused footsteps, as if there was a struggle going on. Then, Monkey came running and dashed up to the observation deck, and soon we heard a loud thud, as if someone had fallen on his behind, followed by footsteps scampering down the stairs. Peeking out the boathouse window, we saw Monkey and Tamayo hurrying toward the house like they were running from something. Monkey was supporting Tamayo in his arms. Just then, someone suddenly emerged out of the shadows of the boathouse. It was… it was…"

"It was your mother, wasn't it?"

Kiyo clasped his hands to his face. Everyone looked at Matsuko breathlessly, but she continued to play languidly with her long pipe, her usual stubborn expression on her face. Takeko gave her a savage look.

Kindaichi raised his voice. "Mr. Kiyo, get a hold of yourself. This is the most important part. Your mother went up to the observation deck, didn't she?"

Kiyo nodded weakly. "It seemed that Také had already started down, because we heard voices from the middle of the stairs, but then they both went back up to the observation deck. Immediately we heard a low groan and the thud of someone falling and saw Mother come rushing headlong down the stairs. Shizuma and I were sitting there staring at each other in astonishment, but wait as we did, we neither saw Také come down nor heard him make a sound. So we crept up the stairs and saw…"

Kiyo again covered his face with his hands. Who could blame him for the bitter, mortifying, torturous anguish he felt, for he had seen Také's dead body, murdered by his own mother. Could there be a more horrifying experience? Everyone in the room felt their clenched palms grow clammy with sweat, and despite what he had said, Kindaichi could not find it in himself to make Kiyo describe the scene any further. "Then you and Shizuma performed the grand magic act of trading places by making use of the mask and muffler. I suppose it was Shizuma who thought of that."

Kiyo nodded weakly. "After that, the tables were turned. Until then, I had reproached Shizuma. He had been shaken and nervous, unsure of what to do. Now our roles were reversed. Shizuma was not an evil man, but his bitterness toward my mother and aunts was intense. He insisted that I back off and permanently cede the position of Kiyo Inugami to him. He said that he would marry Tamayo and inherit the Inugami estate. 'If you refuse,' he said, 'I'll tell the police your mother's a murderer.'"

It was an unthinkable dilemma. If Kiyo tried to claim his proper place, he would have to see his mother accused of murder. Yet if he wished to protect her, he would have to give his rightful place, position, fortune—and even his beloved—to another and live for the rest of his life hiding in the shadows. Had anyone ever faced a more torturous choice?

"And did you agree to his terms?"

Kiyo nodded weakly again. "Yes, I did. It was the only thing I could do. Just then, however, Shizuma remembered the incident with the hand print that had taken place that night. Mother had refused adamantly, so he had been saved from having to give them his hand print, but now that a murder had been committed they would no doubt insist the next day, and he would be exposed as an imposter. Thus also faced with a dilemma, Shizuma thought of the rubber mask. He told me to put it on and play the role of Kiyo for just one day."

What a bizarre turn of events, for it was Matsuko who had thought of putting the rubber mask on the fake Kiyo. How could she have even dreamed then that it would eventually serve such a purpose?

Kiyo inhaled as if with a sob. "I agreed to everything and anything. I felt like I was drunk with cheap liquor and could only do as I was commanded. Then, Shizuma descended from the observation deck and returned with a Japanese sword he had found somewhere. Astounded, I asked him what he intended to do, and he said, 'This is all to save your old lady. The more brutal the crime, the less likely they'll be to suspect a woman.'"

Kiyo could not bring himself to describe the subsequent scene, and Kindaichi did not make him. Kokin Miyakawa sat with her thin shoulders trembling, thinking of her son's horrible deed.

Sighing deeply, Kiyo continued, "In retrospect, though, Shizuma must have acted not only to save my mother but to fulfill his own mother's curses as well. Anyway, after he had cut off Také's head, we exchanged clothes, and I put on that eerie rubber mask. Shizuma asked me where I had come from, so I told him about the Kashiwaya Inn and how, worried about gossip, I had never let anyone see my face. He clapped his hands together and laughed. 'Great,' he said. 'So tomorrow, you stay here and take my place, and I'll go to the Kashiwaya Inn and take yours.'"

Kindaichi looked at Chief Tachibana. "Chief, do you see? The fact that Mr. Kiyo had hidden his face with a muffler became useful. On November 15 and 16, there was a double impersonation, the two of them playing each other's roles at this house and at the Kashiwaya Inn. With just the eyes showing, there was no danger of anyone at the inn noticing that horrible damage to Shizuma's face."

How remarkable it all was. Everything hinged on coincidence, an accumulation of chance incidents. Yet it took an extraordinary intelligence to take those coincidences and weave them into such a plot—an intelligence that Shizuma possessed and that enabled him to arrange this most monstrous camouflage.

"Having changed into my clothes and hidden his face with my muffler, Shizuma descended the stairs and rowed out of the boathouse. I dropped Také's headless corpse and the sword into the boat from the edge of the observation deck. He immediately rowed out toward the middle of the lake. As Shizuma had commanded, I put Také's head in place of the head of the chrysanthemum doll and then sneaked back into the room he had indicated."

Kiyo's face showed increasing signs of fatigue. His eyes glazed, his upper body began to weave, and the lapses in his voice became more frequent. Seeing this, Kindaichi took over for him and continued. "So those were the events of the night of the 15th. The next day, the comparison of the hand prints took place—something that indeed became a fatal blind spot for me. Because there is no more certain proof of identity than a hand print or fingerprints and I never dreamed that such a daring act was being played out, I fell into the trap of believing that the Kiyo with the ravaged face was in fact the real Kiyo Inugami. And that belief became a major stumbling block for my deductive reasoning. But Miss Tamayo, you were aware of the switch, weren't you?"

Tamayo stared at Kindaichi's face in surprise.

"When the results of the comparison were announced and we found out that the Kiyo in the mask was unmistakably the real Kiyo Inugami, twice you began to say something. What was it you were going to say?"

"Oh, that…" said Tamayo, the color draining from her cheeks. "I… knew. No, that's not right. I didn't know, but I sensed it. I sensed with my whole being that the man who was hiding his ravaged face with that mask was not Kiyo. I guess you could call it a woman's intuition."

"Or the intuition of a woman in love?"

At Kindaichi's interjected comment, Tamayo exclaimed lightly and flushed, but she immediately calmed herself and continued, "Perhaps that's so. No, I'm sure that's so. In any case, I was so certain that man was not Kiyo, that when I heard that the hand prints were identical, I was stunned. Just for a moment, I wondered if the man in front of me was really the man with the ravaged face, so…"

"So?"

"So I wanted to say, 'Take off your mask. Take off your mask and let me see your face.'"

A sharp groan escaped Kindaichi's lips. "If only you had done so, the other murders at least would not have occurred."

Tamayo hung her head disconsolately.

Kindaichi was flustered. "No, no, I'm not blaming you. I'm blaming my own incompetence. Anyway, to go on, that night, Mr. Kiyo, you changed places with Shizuma again, didn't you?"

Gloomily, Kiyo nodded without a word.

"You met with Shizuma below the observation deck. Quickly changing clothes, you knocked him out with an uppercut, as instructed, and escaped. The reason Shizuma removed his mask and exposed his face on purpose was to show everyone that he was not using a stand-in, that he was indeed the man with the ravaged face."

Kiyo nodded weakly again, but just then, Tamayo interjected, "But Mr. Kindaichi, who was it that sneaked into my room that night?"

"It was Shizuma, of course. He arrived at this house earlier than the appointed hour. Since everyone was still gathered in this room for Mr. Také's wake, he crept into your room."

"But why?"

"Now that Shizuma is dead, we can only guess, but I think he wanted to retrieve that watch—the pocket watch with his fingerprint."

"Ah!" Tamayo exclaimed, covering her mouth with her hands. Everything had fallen into place for her, too.

"Shizuma never dreamed that Kiyo's hand print could be found lying around in a place like Nasu Shrine. But with the argument about the hand print on the night of the 15th, he first became aware of your scheme, that perhaps you had intended to get his fingerprint on that watch. Shizuma used Mr. Kiyo to give the family a hand print, supposing that once they had it they would never insist on taking fingerprints again. If, however, you brought out that watch and compared the fingerprint on it with the one on the hand print of the real Mr. Kiyo from Nasu Shrine, his plans would fall through. So he wanted to find the watch. This shows that Shizuma was not in this house on the 16th, because if he had been, he would have known from your statement of that morning that you had given the watch to Také the previous night and that its whereabouts thereafter were unknown. But, you know, I still wonder where that watch could be."

"I have it." It was Matsuko who answered coolly. Opening a little drawer in her tobacco tray packed with shredded tobacco, she dug out a gold pocket watch buried among the leaves, placed it on the tatami, and passed it with a shove toward Kindaichi. Seeing the gold object whirling and sliding on the tatami floor, all those in the room felt their hair stand on end, for here indeed was the strongest proof of guilt: the one who had that watch had to be Také's murderer.

Matsuko smiled wryly. "I don't know anything about fingerprints. But when I stabbed Také from behind, this watch slid out of his pocket as he staggered forward and fell. Picking it up, I realized it was the watch Kiyo... the fake Kiyo... had refused to repair for Tamayo. I had no idea why Také had it on him, but since it made me uncomfortable I decided to take it with me and hide it."

Again chance had been at work, for Matsuko had not been aware of the true significance of the pocket watch when she had decided to hide it. A series of coincidences, as so often is the case in life. Thus, much of the mystery in the case of the Inugami clan had been elucidated, but there still remained a great deal more to be told.

# The Inconsolable Wanderer

"Thank you very much, Mrs. Matsuko. Now that we have the watch, everything falls into place." Kindaichi cleared his throat awkwardly and turned to Kiyo. "Mr. Kiyo, I think we now know what happened with the first murder, so let's move on to the second. You look very tired, so I'll proceed by asking you questions, and you answer to the best of your ability. Alright?"

Kiyo nodded weakly.

"Now, I don't know where you hid after you left this villa on the night of November 16, but on November 25, the day the second murder took place, you were in the abandoned house in Toyohata Village. There you saw Mr. Tomo carry Miss Tamayo into the house and try to take advantage of her, so you jumped out from your hiding place and fought, eventually managing to tie him to a chair. Then you phoned Monkey, correct?"

Nodding with spiritless eyes, Kiyo said, "Yes, that way, I thought when Monkey came to rescue Tamayo, he would untie Tomo as well."

"I see. But Monkey ignored Mr. Tomo's plight and simply took Miss Tamayo home, so it was only after much effort and much time—probably about seven or eight that night—that Mr. Tomo managed to untie the ropes. Having finally freed himself, he pulled on his undershirt, shirt, jacket and so forth and hastened outside, and since Monkey had taken his motorboat, he rowed back to the villa in the rowboat Monkey had come in."

"What! You mean Tomo came back to this villa that night?" Chief Tachibana cried out in surprise.

"Yes, Chief. You saw those rope burns all over his skin. The rope must have been quite loose to have caused so many abrasions, but when we found Mr. Tomo, bound and gagged, it was biting into his skin without any slack at all. That proved that someone had retied him. Also, the button from his shirt—Miss Sayoko was found holding it in her hand, but since she has not stepped outside the estate at all since that day, she must have found it here somewhere, either inside the villa or on the grounds. So, I deduced that Mr. Tomo must have returned that night and been murdered here."

Chief Tachibana groaned in comprehension. "Then Kiyo carried the body back again to the abandoned house in Toyohata Village?"

"I think so. Mr. Kiyo, I'd like to hear about that from your own lips. Why did you come to this house that night?"

Kiyo's shoulders trembled violently again, and staring at the tatami with glazed eyes, he began to speak softly. "It was a coincidence. Everything was an accursed coincidence. Having left the abandoned house in Toyohata Village, I knew I couldn't go back there. I had made absolutely certain Tomo never got a look at my face, but the police would certainly soon find out that the repatriated soldier had been there and step up their efforts to track him down. Until then, I had been hiding here and there, not wanting for some reason to leave this area, but now, I thought, I had no choice but to go elsewhere, perhaps to Tokyo. For that, though, I needed a fair sum of money. So, hoping to discuss it with Shizuma, I sneaked onto the estate again and whistled to him to come out. I had gotten money from him once before in the same way, and that night, too, Shizuma came out immediately and we met as always inside the boathouse. When I related what had happened that day and told him I wanted to go to Tokyo, he was elated, for he had long been wanting to drive me away from this region. As we were talking, however, someone rowed up to the sluice gate from the lake and, finding that it would not open, climbed over the fence onto the grounds. Surprised, we peeked out cautiously from the boathouse window and saw that it was Tomo."

Kiyo paused, but continued immediately. "I was astounded, for I had thought that Monkey would surely have untied him and that Tomo would have been home a long time ago. He looked exhausted and disheveled, and passing in front of the boathouse, he staggered toward the house. We were just sitting there watching him from the back, when all of a sudden, two arms shot out of the dark from behind him and wound something like a rope around his neck."

Pausing, Kiyo shuddered violently and wiped the sweat from his forehead with his bandaged right hand. A dreadful silence pierced the room, and black flames of hatred flashed from Umeko's and Kokichi's eyes.

"The struggle was over in an instant, and Tomo collapsed to the ground. The person who had strangled Tomo came out of the shadows for the first time and stood stooping over him, but eventually straightened and glanced around. And I... I..."

"Saw who it was?"

Kiyo nodded weakly and shuddered again. What a horrible trick of fate, for Kiyo had witnessed another of his mother's monstrous deeds. It was the cruelest of fates anyone could experience.

"That night…" So began Matsuko, completely ignoring the fierce looks directed at her from the others in the room and speaking in a flat tone, as if reciting from memory. "I was in the middle of a koto lesson when I needed to go to Kiyo's room for some reason. I don't know if you're aware of this, but the round window in that room looks out on a portion of the lake. It was open when I entered the room, so I happened to glance outside and saw someone approaching the grounds in a rowboat. The boat soon disappeared behind the boathouse, but I realized it might be Tomo, for Umeko had been fussing since early evening about him being missing. So, creeping out of the annex, I waited in the shadows and saw it was indeed Tomo walking toward the house. I removed the belt from my kimono sash and slipped it around his neck from behind. He must have been terribly weak because he hardly resisted at all."

A ghastly smile appeared on Matsuko's lips. Umeko burst into hysterical tears, but Kindaichi ignored her and asked, "You injured your right forefinger on Mr. Tomo's shirt button, did you not? And the button was torn off at that time?"

"I suppose so. I didn't notice it at the time. Only after I returned to the annex did I realize I had hurt my finger. Fortunately, the bleeding stopped immediately, and I continued playing the koto despite the pain. Mrs. Kokin, though, seems to have seen right through me." Once again, the corners of Matsuko's mouth rose in a horrible smile—the smile, no doubt, of a cold-blooded killer.

Kindaichi turned once more to Kiyo. "Mr. Kiyo, please continue with your account."

Kiyo glared at Kindaichi, angry, but continued his accursed tale. "When we could no longer see Mother, we

301

both ran out to Tomo. Shizuma and I carried him back inside the boathouse and tried to revive him somehow with mouth-to-mouth resuscitation, but it didn't work. Shizuma, worried that he might draw suspicion if he stayed away too long, returned to the villa, but I desperately continued trying to revive Tomo. In about half an hour, Shizuma returned and asked if I had had any luck, but when I answered in the negative, he told me that we couldn't leave the body on the estate. 'Take him back to Toyohata Village,' he said. 'Take off his shirt again and tie him onto the chair, just like he was before, and they'll think he was killed there.' He said that and gave me money to go to Tokyo and some koto string, along with instructions on how to use it."

Kiyo's voice faltered and became barely audible. Even so, gathering the last of his strength, he spoke in gasps. "What else could I have done? I had no choice but to follow Shizuma's command. When Shizuma opened the sluice gate, we found the rowboat Tomo had come in floating just outside. We placed his body in the boat, and I started rowing toward Toyohata Village, Shizuma closing the sluice gate after me. When I arrived at the abandoned house in Toyohata Village, I arranged Tomo's body as Shizuma had told me to, walked to Upper Nasu, and immediately left for Tokyo. Then, until I saw the evening paper two days ago, I just wandered around Tokyo, aimlessly, hopelessly, laden with the darkest sorrow and anguish." Suddenly, tears began streaming from Kiyo's eyes.

# Shizuma's Dilemma

The afternoon shadows must have grown longer, for the splattering of melting snow that had sounded noisily until just a while ago had died down, and a chill gradually invaded the corners of the large room. Kindaichi drew up his shoulders, not so much from physical cold, but because he felt chilled to the depths of his soul by Matsuko's demonic deeds and by the cruel fate and wretched circumstances Kiyo had been forced to endure.

This, however, was no time to wallow in emotion. He turned again toward Matsuko. "Mrs. Matsuko, it's your turn at last. I hope you will tell us everything."

Matsuko pierced Kindaichi with her vulture-like eyes but quickly smiled wryly and said, "Yes, of course, I'll tell you everything. After all, the more I talk, the less my dear son will be accused of."

"Then, please, if you'll start with the Wakabayashi murder."

"Wakabayashi?" Matsuko stared in surprise, but immediately chuckled and said, "Yes, of course, that one. I'd forgotten all about it since it happened while I was gone from Nasu. Yes, I was the one who had Wakabayashi make a copy of the will. He stubbornly refused at first, of course, but I threatened him, cajoled him, and finally, since he was indebted to me for a previous favor, he couldn't refuse. He gave in. Now, you can imagine how infuriated I was when I read the will. The anger and hatred I felt toward Tamayo, who had been treated so generously in the will just because she was descended from Father's benefactor—I could have torn her to pieces and still not have been satisfied. It was then that I made up my mind: Tamayo had to die. I'm a very strong-willed woman, once I make up my mind. I tried all sorts of little maneuvers—throwing a viper into her bedroom, tampering with the brakes on her car, boring a hole in her boat—but each time, I was foiled by that Monkey."

She sucked on her pipe. "After a while, though, I found I had a problem, because Wakabayashi had become aware of what I was doing. He must have been in love with Tamayo, and when he saw her being exposed to danger time and again, he began to suspect me. I knew this was bad. No matter what happened in the future, I couldn't let it be known that I had secretly read the will, so before I left to meet Kiyo in Hakata, I gave Wakabayashi a pack of cigarettes that included one that was poisoned. I never thought they would do their work with such exquisite timing, though." Matsuko let out a ghastly, scornful laugh.

"How did I get the poison? I'm sorry, but that is the one thing I won't tell you, because I don't want to get anyone else in trouble. Anyway, after that, I went to meet Kiyo, but as I studied the will carefully on the way, I changed my mind about killing Tamayo. I realized that if Tamayo died, Kiyo would indeed get control of all the Inugami businesses, but the estate would be divided into equal fifths, with Kiyo receiving only one-fifth and Kikuno Aonuma's brat receiving twice that."

Her wrath undiminished even now, Matsuko ground her molars audibly. "And, when I examined the will even more closely, I realized that Kikuno's brat would get his hands on a part of the estate only if one of two things happened:

if Tamayo died or if she refused to marry any of the three grandsons and thus forfeited her right of inheritance. For the first time, I marveled at how thoroughly Father had planned things. Father knew us well. He knew that we might try to harm Tamayo, and he used the incident with Kikuno Aonuma to prevent that. Understanding thoroughly just how much we hated Kikuno and her son, he arranged it so the only way we could prevent that wretched Kikuno's brat from getting a piece of the estate was to keep Tamayo alive. How ingenious he was!"

Kindaichi had realized that as well. For that very reason, when he had heard that Tamayo had been faced with danger time and again yet had always managed to escape unharmed, he had been unable for a while to rid himself of the suspicion that perhaps all those attempts on her life were a sham, an act played out by Tamayo herself, and that it was she who had seduced Wakabayashi and secretly read the will.

"So, if Tamayo had to be kept alive," Matsuko continued, "then it was imperative that she marry Kiyo. I was sure she would, though, because I knew she was fond of Kiyo—no, in fact, I knew clearly that she was more than fond of Kiyo. So I went off to meet Kiyo in Hakata absolutely confident that things would go well, but the minute I laid eyes on his face, that confidence was smashed to pieces. Imagine my shock, my despair when I saw that face."

She sighed passionately. Kindaichi edged forward and said, "Sorry to interrupt you, but… didn't you realize at all that the man with the ravaged face was an imposter?"

Matsuko stared at Kindaichi with a dreadful glint in her eye. "Mr. Kindaichi, I may be an obstinate woman, but surely I wouldn't bring home someone who I knew was an imposter or do such horrible things for him. No, I didn't see through him at all. There were, of course, incidents I found strange, but he told me that the blow to the head he had received when he was wounded in the face made him forget everything about the past, and I believed him. Oh, yes, the time I was really puzzled was the night they insisted on taking his hand print. I lost my temper, became stubborn, and refused to bend, but I was secretly waiting for Kiyo to speak up and agree to their demands. Instead, though, he took advantage of my protests and got by without giving his hand print. That time, I must admit, I felt something sinister. The thought crossed my mind that maybe Také and Tomo were right and he was an imposter, but I expelled that suspicion from my mind. The next day, when Kiyo volunteered to give them a new hand print, I was thrilled, and when the hand prints were found to be identical, I was ecstatic—so much so I thought I would faint—and I regretted ever having doubted him, even for a second. So I didn't even dream of doubting him again until much later."

After a pause, she continued. "Anyway, going back to my story, when I saw how hideously ravaged his face was, I knew I couldn't possibly take him back home like that, because Tamayo would surely feel an aversion to him. So, after considering various options, I had that rubber mask made for him in Tokyo. I had it made exactly as Kiyo's face used to be, so it might help Tamayo remember the old days, even if only a little, and feel love for him."

Matsuko sighed. "But all those efforts were in vain. Even to a mother's eyes, it was more than obvious that Tamayo disliked him. I understand now that she had sensed he was an imposter and that was the reason for her feelings, but how was I to know that? I knew it would be difficult to make Tamayo choose Kiyo unless Také and Tomo were both dead."

"And so you carried out your plans, step by step."

A terrible smile rose to Matsuko's lips. "Yes. Like I said just now, I'm a very strong-willed woman when I make up my mind. But let me say here and now that in Také's case and in Tomo's, I didn't care very much at all about concealing my crime. All I wanted to do was to kill the two of them, and it didn't matter to me whether I was arrested or even executed. I just wanted to remove those who were in my son's way. I had no concern for my own life." No doubt that was the truth, the true motive behind the actions of this extraordinary, demonic killer.

"Then it must have come as a great surprise to you when you realized that despite how you felt, someone was going around after you, skillfully hiding traces of the crime that would point to you."

"Of course I was surprised, but I must admit, I really didn't care much. I became worried, though, because the masked Kiyo seemed to be involved in these little tricks in some way. I felt concern, but at the same time, I also felt something sinister. We never said a word about it to each other, but the way he could camouflage things so easily sometimes made him seem like a horrific monster."

Kindaichi turned to Chief Tachibana. "Chief, do you see? The actual murderer in this case was not contriving to hide her crimes at all. It was two accessories after the fact who were cleaning up after her and trying to redirect suspicion. That's what made this case so interesting and so difficult."

Chief Tachibana nodded and leaned forward toward Matsuko. "Then, Mrs. Matsuko, let's finally turn to Shizuma's murder. That, surely, was your doing alone."

Matsuko nodded.

"Why on earth did you decide to kill him? Did you discover his identity?"

Matsuko nodded again. "Yes, I learned who he was. However, let me first of all tell you how I found out. With Také and Tomo gone, we had won, so I nagged and nagged the masked Kiyo to propose to Tamayo. But for some reason, he refused to do so."

Chief Tachibana frowned. "I wonder why. According to what Kiyo just told us, Shizuma had said he intended to take Kiyo's place and marry Tamayo."

At that moment, Kindaichi, scratching his head with furious abandon, started stuttering terribly. "Th-that's what Sh-Sh-Shizuma intended to d-do until November 26, when Tomo's b-b-body was found." Kindaichi finally realized how he sounded and, gulping hard, regained his composure. "But after Tomo's body was found, Mr. Oyama, the priest of Nasu Shrine, threw an explosive piece of information our way—the secret hidden inside the Chinese chest. We found out that Miss Tamayo was not the granddaughter of Mr. Inugami's benefactor, but was in fact Mr. Inugami's real granddaughter. That meant that Shizuma could not marry Tamayo."

"Why not?"

Chief Tachibana still did not seem to understand, but Kindaichi said with a smile, "Chief, don't you see? Shizuma was Mr. Inugami's son, so if Miss Tamayo was Mr. Inugami's granddaughter, that would make them uncle and niece."

A cry escaped Chief Tachibana's lips. "I see, I see. Of course. So Shizuma didn't know what to do." He rubbed his fat neck with a big handkerchief.

Kindaichi heaved an emotional sigh. "Yes. Thinking back, Mr. Oyama's explosive revelation of that horrible secret was the climax of this case. Shizuma was thus faced with a dilemma. Legally, both Shizuma and Miss Tamayo were not listed in the family register as being related to Mr. Inugami, so they would not have been prevented from marrying. But when Shizuma thought about their blood relationship, he couldn't go ahead with the marriage, either. According to Mr. Kiyo, too, Shizuma was not particularly evil but was just consumed by the desire for revenge, so he was no doubt constrained by the same compunctions as we would be."

Sighing deeply again, Kindaichi turned to Matsuko. "By the way, Mrs. Matsuko, when exactly did you discover Shizuma's identity?"

"About half past ten on the night of the 12th." Matsuko smiled somewhat bitterly. "That night, too, we were arguing back and forth about proposing to Tamayo, but gradually our words became more heated, until finally he couldn't restrain himself any longer and divulged exactly why he couldn't marry her. In retrospect, I suppose he thought that even if he told me, I wouldn't be able to do anything since he knew my secret. You can imagine, though, how surprised and angered I was. I felt like the room was spinning. I continued asking him to clear up various points, but then he must have noticed the murderous expression on my face, for he suddenly rose and tried to flee. That made me snap. When I came to my senses again, he was slumped dead, and I was clutching in my hand the belt from my kimono, the belt that I had wound around his neck."

Kokin screamed and lunged forward onto the tatami. "How horrible, horrible. You're a fiend, a devil from hell. How could you do such a horrible thing?"

Kokin choked on her tears, her shoulders quivering, but Matsuko did not so much as bat an eye. "I didn't regret killing him one bit," she said. "I thought it was bound to happen sooner or later anyway, and I had just done what I should have done thirty years ago. But on reflection, that boy certainly was born under an unlucky star, wasn't he? What a time I had disposing of his body, though. Chief, Mr. Kindaichi, isn't life ironical? When I killed Také and Tomo, I didn't care a bit about concealing what I had done, and I thought, let them catch me if they want. But those times, someone always cleverly covered up my crime for me. This time, though, when I didn't want to be captured just yet and wanted desperately to stay alive for a while, there was no longer anyone there to help me."

"Excuse me," interrupted Kindaichi. "Why didn't you want to be captured this time?"

"Because of Kiyo, of course. Since the hand prints had been a perfect match, the Kiyo of that day had to be the real Kiyo. Shizuma admitted it, too. I was so infuriated at the time, I forgot to ask Shizuma what had happened to Kiyo. I had to find out."

"So you made the corpse do that acrobatic stunt."

"Yes, it took me over an hour to think of that, for after all, I'm not a very smart woman. But by setting up that riddle, I could make people think that body was Kiyo's, and as long as people believed that was Kiyo, I figured that I, Kiyo's mother, would be above suspicion."

Thus, the curse of the ax, zither, and chrysanthemum,

which Shizuma had tried to stage, had been fulfilled magnificently—ultimately with Shizuma's own body.

"As soon as I had thought of the riddle, I carried his body to the boathouse, placed it in a boat, and rowed out of the sluice gate. I rowed near where the water seemed shallowest and plunged his body upside down into the mud. The ice was still not that thick then, but as the night wore on, it thickened and produced that ridiculous scene."

# The Final Chapter

Matsuko's story had come to an end, and all the mysteries surrounding the murders in the case of the Inugami clan had been solved, but no one felt their hearts grow any lighter. Instead, their stomachs grew as heavy as lead with the all-too dark and gloomy truth. The falling twilight suffused the hushed stillness of the room with an even more bitter chill. The sky seemed to have grown overcast again.

"Kiyo." Matsuko's shrill voice pierced the silence like the cry of some sinister bird deep in the mountains. Kiyo raised his face with a start. "Why did you return to Japan using an assumed name? Have you done something you are ashamed of?"

"Mother!" Kiyo cried hotly and then glanced around at the others in the room, his face aglow with indignation. "Mother, I have done nothing to be ashamed of, not in the way that you mean. If I had known that people had changed so much back in this country, I would never have used an assumed name. But I didn't know. I thought the Japanese people would be just as they were when they saw me off to war, proudly waving the flag and confident of victory. I made a grave mistake on the battlefield. As commanding officer, I made a wrong decision that caused my entire unit to be killed. After that fiasco, one of my men and I, the only ones in the unit to survive, wandered around the hinterlands of Burma. How many times I considered killing myself to take responsibility for my mistake. How, I thought, could I ever have the gall to even set foot in Japan again? Eventually, even my lone surviving comrade died, and I was captured by the enemy. I used an assumed name on the spur of the moment, because I felt I was disgracing the Inugami name by becoming a prisoner of war. But… but… when I returned to this country, I found…"

Kiyo's voice trembled, and he gulped down his fiery emotions. So that was the reason why Kiyo had returned to Japan using an assumed name. True, that might have been a rather unusual thing to do, but pride and sense of responsibility had supposedly been ingrained in all Japanese people before the war, and the fact that Kiyo had continued to possess those traits even after his country's defeat was no doubt evidence of his purity of heart. At the same time, it was this very quality that unfortunately had kept him from preventing this atrocious series of tragedies.

"Kiyo, are you telling me the truth? Is that the only reason why you were using an alias?"

"Mother, I swear it. I have nothing to be ashamed of besides that," said Kiyo hotly.

Matsuko smiled and said, "That puts my mind at rest… Chief?"

"Yes?"

"I suppose Kiyo will have to stand trial."

"I'm afraid that's unavoidable," Chief Tachibana said awkwardly. "No matter what the reason, there's the matter of being an accessory… an accessory after the fact. And there's also the illegal possession of a firearm."

"How severe will the punishment be?"

"I can't say."

"He won't receive the death penalty, will he?"

"No, of course not. And besides, I think there are considerable mitigating circumstances."

"Tamayo."

Tamayo's shoulders jerked as she was abruptly addressed thus by Matsuko. "Yes?"

"You will wait for Kiyo until he is released from prison, won't you?"

Tamayo paled, but soon color rose to her cheeks and tears glistened in her eyes. With a voice full of determination, she stated clearly, without hesitation, "Yes, I'll wait. Whether it takes ten years or twenty… if Kiyo wants me to."

"Tamayo…" With a jangle of his handcuffs, Kiyo clasped his knees with both hands and hung his head.

Just then, Kindaichi whispered something to Furudate, the family lawyer, who nodded firmly and drew towards him a large cloth-wrapped bundle that he had placed behind him. As all eyes were drawn to the bundle in wonder, Furudate unwrapped it, and there appeared three rectangular, paulownia wood boxes, each about thirty centimeters long. Lifting the three boxes, Furudate strode up to Tamayo with slow, stately steps, sat down on the tatami, and reverently placed them before her. Tamayo stared wide-eyed in amazement, her lips trembling in an attempt to speak. As Furudate removed the lids from the boxes one by one and placed their contents on top of the boxes, cries of emotion rose from all those present, and murmurs like the sound of reeds swaying in the wind filled the room, for here were the three heirlooms of the Inugami clan—the golden ax, zither, and chrysanthemum.

"Miss Tamayo," said Furudate, his voice quivering with emotion, "in keeping with the will of the late Sahei Inugami,

I present these heirlooms to you. Will you please present them to the man you have chosen?"

An embarrassed flush colored Tamayo's cheeks. Her eyes swept around the faces in the room hesitantly, but when they met Kindaichi's, they stopped, transfixed on his, for she saw him nodding lightly to her with a beaming face. Tamayo drew a deep breath, and then, in a barely audible voice, said, "Kiyo, please accept these... if you'll have me."

"Tamayo... thank you." Kiyo rubbed his eyes with his bandaged hand.

Thus was decided the heir to the vast fortune and businesses of the Inugami clan, a man who, however, was fated to languish in a dark prison cell for several years.

Matsuko, who had been watching the scene before her with an air of satisfaction, took another pinch of shredded tobacco and filled her long-stemmed pipe. If Kindaichi had been more attentive then, he would have noticed that she had taken the tobacco not from the box containing the leaves she had been smoking until then, but from the drawer of her tobacco tray, from which she had removed the pocket watch a while ago.

"Tamayo," said Matsuko as she quietly smoked her pipe. "Yes?"

"I have one more favor to ask of you."

"What can I do for you?"

Matsuko refilled her pipe with another pinch of tobacco from the drawer. "It's about Sayoko."

"Yes?"

Startled at the mention of Sayoko's name, Takeko and Umeko looked at Matsuko's face, but the latter still sat calmly smoking her pipe, repeatedly emptying and refilling

315

it with new pinches of tobacco. "Sayoko will be having her baby soon. Since the father is Tomo, it will be both Takeko's and Umeko's grandchild. Tamayo, do you understand what I mean?"

"Yes, I do. And?"

"The favor I am asking is this. When that child grows up, I'd like you to give him or her half of the Inugami fortune."

Takeko and Umeko looked at each other in surprise, but Tamayo answered decisively, without hesitation, "Mrs. Matsuko... Mother, I understand completely. I promise to do as you wish."

"You will? Thank you. Kiyo, you remember, too. Mr. Furudate, you're a witness. And if the child turns out to be a capable boy, let him participate in the family business, too. That's the least I can do for Takeko and Umeko to make up for... what... I've..."

"No!" Kindaichi ran up to Matsuko, treading on the hem of his hakama trousers in his panic. But the long-stemmed pipe had already plopped from her hand, and she had slumped forward onto the tatami.

"No! No! No! It's the tobacco. The same poison that killed Wakabayashi. I didn't notice. I didn't notice. A doctor... somebody call a doctor!"

By the time the doctor had rushed to the scene, however, Matsuko Inugami—that most demonic woman, that extraordinary killer who had shocked the nation—lay dead, a trickle of blood seeping out from the corner of her mouth. It was a twilight so cold even the snow lay frozen over Lake Nasu.

# TRANSLATOR'S ACKNOWLEDGMENTS

I wish to thank Mr. Ryoichi Yokomizo for graciously giving me the opportunity to translate his father's book; Miiko Kataoka and the late Lynn Wakabayashi for making it all possible; Monica Borden, Aika Imai, Phil Ouellet, Ana Reed, Anne Torige, Masa Uno, and Vio Yamawaki for their excellent advice; and last but not least, my parents and especially my husband for their endless patience and support.

YUMIKO YAMAZAKI

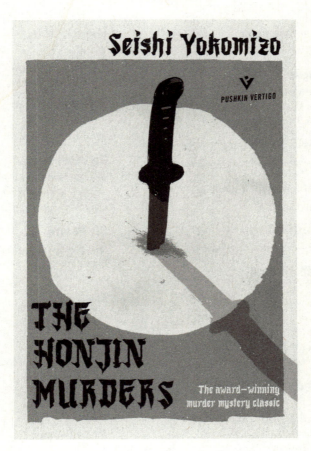

# AVAILABLE AND COMING SOON
# FROM PUSHKIN VERTIGO

**Jonathan Ames**
*You Were Never Really Here*

**Augusto De Angelis**
*The Murdered Banker*
*The Mystery of the Three Orchids*
*The Hotel of the Three Roses*

**Olivier Barde-Cabuçon**
*Casanova and the Faceless Woman*

**María Angélica Bosco**
*Death Going Down*

**Piero Chiara**
*The Disappearance of Signora Giulia*

**Frédéric Dard**
*Bird in a Cage*
*The Wicked Go to Hell*
*Crush*
*The Executioner Weeps*
*The King of Fools*
*The Gravediggers' Bread*

**Friedrich Dürrenmatt**
*The Pledge*
*The Execution of Justice*
*Suspicion*
*The Judge and His Hangman*

**Martin Holmén**
*Clinch*
*Down for the Count*
*Slugger*

**Alexander Lernet-Holenia**
*I Was Jack Mortimer*

**Margaret Millar**
*Vanish in an Instant*
*A Stranger in My Grave*
*The Listening Walls*

**Boileau-Narcejac**
*Vertigo*
*She Who Was No More*

**Baroness Orczy**
*The Old Man in the Corner*
*The Case of Miss Elliott*
*Unravelled Knots*

**Leo Perutz**
*Master of the Day of Judgment*
*Little Apple*
*St Peter's Snow*

**Edgar Allan Poe**
*The Paris Mysteries*

**Soji Shimada**
*The Tokyo Zodiac Murders*
*Murder in the Crooked House*

**Masako Togawa**
*The Master Key*
*The Lady Killer*

**Emma Viskic**
*Resurrection Bay*
*And Fire Came Down*
*Darkness for Light*

**Seishi Yokomizo**
*The Honjin Murders*
*The Inugami Curse*